I0785559

ALSO BY JOHN HIGH

POETRY

Ceremonies
Sometimes Survival
the lives of thomas: episodes and prayers
The Sasha Poems
Bloodline (selected poems)
here
a book of unknowing
you are everything you are not
vanishing acts
Without Dragons Even the Emperor Would Be Lonely

FICTION

The Desire Notebooks
Talking God's Radio Show

CO-TRANSLATOR

Blue Vitriol by Aleksei Parshchikov
The Right to Err (selected poems) by Nina Iskrenko
The Inconvertible Sky by Ivan Zhdanov
Crossing Centuries: The New Generation in Russian Poetry (editor)

IN TRANSLATION

all along her thighs (selected writings)
   Translated into Russian by Nina Iskrenko
vanishing acts
   Translated into Russian by Tatiana Retivov

Scrolls of a Temple Sweeper

Scrolls of a Temple Sweeper

Ninso John High

Wet Cement Press

Berkeley, California

Wet Cement Press
1908 Yolo Ave
Berkeley, CA 94707

www.wetcementpress.com

FOR PATRICIA & CHRISTOPHER & ANDREA—

whose dedication, passion, and caring for these scrolls made them finally possible after twenty-five years of wandering in the pages. In a mysterious way, we have written them together. Their continuous presence and voices have helped guide the story home. Also deep gratitude for their and Thoreau Lovell's boundless consultations, edits, and true listening. No writer could ever hope for more.

AND TO NORMAN FISCHER—

whose friendship, teachings, poetry, faith, ongoing meetings, and mentoring, face to face, have helped bring the work in these scrolls forth from their first appearance in the books that preceded them: *here, a book of unknowing, you are everything you are not, vanishing acts*, and *Without Dragons Even the Emperor Would Be Lonely*. The transmission never ends.

FINALLY, TO ANDREA AND SASHA (FREDDIE)—

How could any of this ever have come to fruition without you darlings throughout our wanderings in countless countries around this great big, beautiful and crazy world. My gratefulness to you both is more than you can even imagine. Your patience with and unconditional love for this ole monk is a constant inspiration and reminder: it is all love.

CONTENTS

INTRODUCTION

Dear Reader: You are about to embark on a most extraordinary journey: one of suffering and redemption, of beauty, radiance, hope and fierce love.

In *Scrolls of a Temple Sweeper* a host of personages populate the ethereal landscapes. Although replete with enduring and endearing characters, including the mute girl, the one-eyed boy and the Ghostwoman, phantasmagorical elements, in which even ghosts have flesh and blood, and being is time, the encounters are placed so adroitly in this poetic narrative that the incongruous feels natural, feels even essential. Crows speak, elephants and dragons wander in and out, and the Old Story—the scrolls themselves unfolding before us—all inhabit overlapping spaces that inform us of doubt and anguish, of knowledge and illumination. High's critical message reminds me of Peter Muryo Matthiessen once saying: "The purpose of life is to help others get through it." And his characters, in this character-driven epic poem in the form of a novel, do exactly that: help one another get through it. As such, his personae are never static; their stories are riveting, tender, vibrant and consistently poignant.

Scrolls of a Temple Sweeper defies easy categorization: Welding post-modernist narrative techniques to traditional discourse—to create a truly monumental excursion into matters of vital concern for today's world—the novel's seamless integration of rhythmical prose, lyrical poetry, and proverbial utterance is dazzling. Pathos presides, not bathos: terrible beauty is born and reborn.

Through a variety of devices, including extended narratives, diaries, letters, calligraphic ensōs, dialogue, proverbs, evocative fragments and pure poetic interludes, the author opens up the lives and thoughts and inner beings of his astonishing cast and their concerns. While incorporating a variety of discursive elements within a text is hardly unprecedented—Pound's *Cantos*, García Márquez's

One Hundred Years of Solitude, Williams' *Paterson*, Anne Carson's *Nox*, Susan Howe's *My Emily Dickinson* come readily to mind—High's masterful positioning of these different optics creates an abundantly rich and rare multi-dimensional work that never fails to amaze and is unique unto itself.

These complexities are embodied in High's vast and varied method of telling, yet the story, itself, is actually rather simple. A temple sweeper, who has been silent for twenty-five years, is near death. Accordingly, he begins to reveal his past to Enduring Sound, the monastery's Head Monk, who acts as a scribe. Unlike most death-bed tales, the story Temple Sweeper relates is not by any means only about himself, nor does he remain the sole narrator. Indeed, the scrolls he is dictating become quickly populated by a host of fascinating characters, including the Head Monk, himself. In turn, those within the scrolls begin speaking to and about one another, and even directly to the reader. And ultimately, the reader is asked to be the writer, to continue the scrolls in their own fashion.

In accomplishing this involvement and understanding between reader and writer(s), High deliberately unfolds the narrative elements in a non-linear fashion, suspends events in time and space, so that the reader who enters the text is invited to engage fully with each happening, with each new plot, with the many pasts depicted in the present quantum field of discoveries. The technique is consistently compelling. Indeed, High's narrative is an elaborate and elaborated balancing act, reminiscent of the Zen koans he so lovingly and effectively resituates and reworks within his text so as to make them important elements that advance insight, bridge the past with the present, and even the future. In conjunction with, or perhaps as koans themselves, are his ink ensōs, which are integral parts of the entire discourse. Their positioning within the book is neither casual nor incidental. These circular brush strokes are a kind of intimate language, a sound before sound, that communicate a consistent underlying theme of wholeness within the void, of constant return to an unquenchable source, of order rising from spontaneity. They also comment indirectly on the intricate dances of words and the circumlocutions of his remarkable array of engaging presences, who shift without boundaries, within realistic worlds and fantastic unworldliness, who grapple, like the ink expressed by the brush tip, with internal and external struggles.

As with the books in High's previous poetic tetralogy, it is quite evident that the *Scrolls* are grounded in his long immersion in Zen. A reader, however, does not need to have familiarity with Buddhism to enter fully into the magically realistic comings and goings within the novel. Indeed, he has deliberately told his tale in a universal manner; his concern throughout is to depict beings as they are, as neither heroes nor villains, neither oppressors nor victims. Suffering, and deliverance from suffering, forgiveness and absolution are elements hardly unique to Buddhism.

The book you are about to read is a culmination of twenty-five years of working through essential stories of no birth/no death, of despair and hope and fulfillment, of dreams and waking in dreams, and ultimately of the necessity for forgiveness. No one writes like Ninso John High, and Ninso writes like no one else. He is authentic and original.

The result is a complex portrayal of sight and sound, of tradition and unconventionality, of grandeur and waste, of triumph and failure. I am in awe at his ability to weave so many disparate stories, unforgettable voices and ways of expression into a unified whole that feels to me of enormous importance for today's turmoil. Ninso knows how the saying (and even the unsayable) must be said.

Scrolls of a Temple Sweeper is a highly-crucial piece of literature that deeply probes the meaning of suffering. As contemporary as today's headlines; like all important writing, it also has the quality of timelessness. In its art, its sweep, its resonance, it is vital.

—*CHRISTOPHER SAWYER-LAUÇANNO*

I live my life in ever widening circles,

each surpassing all the previous ones.

I may never reach the final circle,

but will not give up trying.

I circle around God, the ancient tower,

and have been circling for a thousand years,

and still I do not know: am I a falcon,

a storm, or a continuing great song.

—Rainer Maria Rilke

Translation by Patricia Pruitt

ALIVE
RIGHT
HERE

For twenty-five years, I have not spoken.
—The Temple Sweeper on the eve
of departing his body.

BOOK I

THE GIRL'S DIARY

There was never a time that didn't include you. Even if the others don't remember, it's fine, she says to the boy. No one will bother or care—that smell of apple & wood chip, a girl walking along the river & she was you and knew it too. All of her hands shifting into birds, or maybe balloons, floating out of your arms. You smell the corn seed in her hair & skin—and you hear the wind & love letters never written and already here & revealed now as you finally read them. The body softening after so much violence—underwood blue jay, stone pile, river run, sky a bit undone. And full it was there & there was a time the door of the courtyard opening, a boy waiting, and you sense without asking, he too, is a part of you, has come for you, witnessed you. Here we are—a piece of wounded time & wow, what a miraculous place to come home to. This is what the brush of ink is speaking to you right now as you prepare to leave the dream—or enter it again.

THE RECORDED SCROLLS OF
A TEMPLE SWEEPER—

A LETTER BY WAY OF INTRODUCTION FROM OUR MONASTERY ON THE SEA BY HEAD MONK, ENDURING SOUND, FRIEND OF OUR TEMPLE SWEEPER, THE 9TH MONTH, 1ST DAY, YEAR OF THE DRAGON

The words you just read, or perhaps heard, between the mute girl and the one-eyed boy—these were the last the Temple Sweeper spoke to me on the night of his death. I am not sure why he spoke them, or any of his other sayings and stories—these fragments he uttered, as if dropping pebbles along the shore of our monastery. The notes that follow include my own tonight, as well as those written to the one he called the "mute girl" in these scrolls—right up to and with his final breath. Nor can I say I am sure as to why he transmitted these last sayings and ink drawings to me on the nights leading up to his departure from the body. He was a silent man, and though he arrived long after me, we lived for many years together in the monastery; he conversed on few occasions and then only by sheer necessity. I would follow his footsteps out by the sea, trailing furtively behind him—or sweeping the halls of our temple, and often I wondered how he gripped the broom so sturdily, as he had few fingers. How he lost them, I did not yet know. Still, we would work the fields of our small island side by side with the other monks, and he was a good worker. Many of the monks considered that he had been reincarnated from the spirit of a fox, for as an ancient sage once said of our pasts—

He is no longer blind to cause and effect.

I did as he requested and wrote these letters, stories, sayings, and poems during his last months. Eventually he even had me write down my own words, and I have included them alongside the dreams and ink drawings he gave me that winter. It was a harsh season for us, full of storms on the shores of our small hermitage in the sea.

Let me say that from the beginning, I secretly admired our Temple Sweeper, his vow of silence before he came to us after being left at the temple gate by what the elders rumor was once a famed theater and circus troupe. He was always first into the Meditation Hall, and he could be found there late at night as well, sitting cross-legged, when most of us were in our cells, sleeping.

I should tell you that it was I who named and ordered the archival records that he spoke, and that I have done my best to assure nothing was left out. During those final nights and weeks together he referred often to "the girl's diary," and to the "autobiography of a dream," as he called it, and on some occasions he'd become quite animated and call this or that evening's discussion part of the "essential story." Then from time to time, even with some frequency it could be said, he would talk of the circus players and theater troupe and all of these strangers who had brought him to our hidden monastery in these seas. Though it should be noted, as I was still a boy myself when he arrived, partially blinded myself, and orphaned in the last wars, I can add only a little to our elders' accounts and tales. Yet our Abbot has affirmed that our Temple Sweeper was, indeed, brought by boat to our isle by a band of hermit-wanderers who danced and sang around these monastic walls for three days before departing without him when they were finished with their dream-like ceremonies. And alas, as it was often late and our conversations would carry on for hours in the night by only candlelight, I have inevitably failed our Temple Sweeper in some way. Though I had trained myself to write even in the dark, my eyes sometimes fail me.

Once, the Abbot asked him to be the head monk among us.

During another season of long meditations, in front of the whole assembly, the Abbot requested that he come forward and accept the title, Master.

Yet he refused, and so among us, he remained simply, the Temple Sweeper.

I should acknowledge that it was clear in his last year that he was very sick. I would touch his left eye, which had begun to swell again, and in his hands was a serious tremble he tried to hide under his robes. Yet I could see the trembling in spite of, or perhaps because of, my own increasing blindness over the past twenty-five years since he arrived and I was a young boy. On more than one occasion I asked him to visit our shaman-healer on the nearby island. I even offered to navigate with our boatman a small vessel to the mainland so that he could see a doctor. The Abbot had approved of this, of course. Why, it was the Abbot himself who had taken the Temple Sweeper to our shaman after he first arrived all those years ago with the circus and theater players, for as it is known, the condition of his hands and eye frightened the other monks from the beginning. His left eye blackened and swollen, the other gray and forbidding, and the stubs for fingers appeared severed, claw-like. This is what is said.

He refused my request to help, maybe for fear of forfeiting the seclusion of our monastery in the continuing violence across the sea on the mainland—or to in any way endanger us for the cause of his own ailing body. This is what I first thought. Now I understand it is not always so, for he was ready to leave this world of dreams. His teeth softening—he ate less, only soup and rice—and he had more and more trouble making his way through the temple garden to the cemetery path where he walked to the sea every day, a bundle of pebbles over his shoulder.

Over time, in fact during each day of these last months, I became what I then thought of as his quiet, sometimes invisible, guide. You see, since childhood when I, too, was left here as an orphan with our good monks, I have studied every inch of our isle and sense its shifting terrain of hills, gorges, cliffs, and its winding river, quite intimately. Yes, I know our island in the sea well.

Alas, the Temple Sweeper remained a stranger among us. The Abbot had eventually accepted his silence and even came to encourage it over the passing years when the monks tried to trick him to respond with words, or by playing pranks—and perhaps this was out of some unspoken jealousy of our Abbot's reverence for the Temple Sweeper.

Such is the human realm, even among us monks, who strive to overcome such delusions.

This was his path in life on this forlorn, even beautiful, hidden, isle—to proceed without words. I should also tell you, I cannot say for certain of his age or origin. He arrived old and after the circus and theater troupe left, he sat in meditation outside the monastery gate for twenty-one days without so much as a quiver before the elders finally opened the gate and took him in. The younger monks had taunted him during those twenty-one nights, a few even pouring buckets of water on his head in that cold winter as he sat outside the temple.

Still, he would not move from his sitting position. The Abbot finally intervened and welcomed him in.

As for myself, I studied his practice while maturing in this monastery, learning the alphabets of the islands that surround us, eventually training in the writing of the scribes. At the age of twelve, I was chosen as one of the few to learn to read and write in this way and to copy out the words of the ancestors. Later on, I would study the Temple Sweeper's almost hushed shuffle down the shadowed halls, his continuous bowing and flutter of robes after the others left the dining quarters, the graves he dug and filled with the stones and pebbles he called stories on the cliffs by the sea—his weeping in the Meditation Hall almost inaudible, yet I could hear him. This became my private study.

So these words he at last whispered on the night he came to me, I confess, I awaited them with great curiosity, and even joy. At first I thought it odd that he spoke of his own life as that of another, and I was startled by his wanderings with the one-eyed boy and mute girl and the spirits of both animals and humans and gods and what he called, Dream Masters. His translations of the mute girl's diary remain in my own dreams.

But then I began to feel that all of the past, including history and the imaginary world of earthly being, was nothing but a dream itself to our Temple Sweeper.

When the first of three full moons before his death appeared, he came to my cell. I envisioned the silhouette of his body standing before me even before he knocked on the door, without his robe, just a thin blanket draped around his frame as if he were a mere shadow, shivering like a hungry ghost with only the dimmed widow-light of the sky revealing his torn face and shuttered eye, so that I no longer needed to touch to see and understand. It was the first time I noticed what I can only describe as a fierce ravage in his sharp, chiseled chin. No, he was not one of us. But where had he come from? What land? Which war? He had once been a handsome man, I thought. A burning in his gray eye. And now, standing before me as I opened the door, he appeared ancient, powerful. Almost not human.

He handed me a sheath of paper on which he had crudely scribbled the words—will you help? Darker blotches, the color of black ink rising from his desert skin, and a strange music fluttering from his missing fingers, sounding, maybe summoning even, a wind from the draft of the hallway that encircled him. After entering my cell, he asked me to bring a box of scrolls from the storage shed.

I should add that, as I am now Head Monk and scribe of our humble abode, I possess the key to the storage shed and did not need to seek jurisdiction to grant this request. Yet this remained a secret between us, as he also requested later that night.

That night, yes, I was quite certain my position in the monastery was why he came to me and not to one of the elders, especially our Abbot. Though gradually he revealed his reasons, and that his coming to me in this way was no accident, nor advantage. Of course, it is I alone who could secretly supply the paper on which his scrolls are now written. And do not take it wrongly when I tell you that the Temple Sweeper had few, if any, friends, at least not in the sense that he shared his life with anyone, including me—even though he knew I had followed him like a cat throughout his lonely wanderings on the island.

Even so, we had never conversed.

That first full moon, and for many nights thereafter, he spoke. His voice was strong and sure and not like the body that leaned over the desk in my cell to assure that I had left nothing out—I suppose, due to my own poor vision, of which he was aware. I thought of the words he first uttered as some kind of confession, but now I see it is not always so.

There is no doubt that he loved the ones he called the mute girl and the one-eyed boy with all of his being and in spite of all, his life was that of a great love story. That is why we monks, who live in the absence of romantic love, now love him so, having finally learned his story.

You should know as well that sometimes as the Temple Sweeper spoke on these nights, it was as if he had forgotten certain phrases, particularly verbs, or how to articulate the sound or even capture the meaning of them. I'd sense a turmoil of clouds settling in his white brows, he would rub his head and push back the long mane of his still black hair, and he would then begin to talk in other languages, many of which are still foreign to me. Of course over time, I have researched and studied tirelessly. I have done what I can, and as well, I have taken the liberty to begin to categorize the scrolls as seems most appropriate as his scribe; for alas, the Temple Sweeper left his body before the work was complete.

Or is it complete?

It was on the final hour of the final night of his departure from the body that he said to me—

> *The scrolls are not your own, Enduring Monk. Nor are they mine. Nor do they belong to any sect nor masters nor religions nor kingdoms. Still, they are our story and you yourself must come to hear them and free all the words before sound, and all of their worlds beyond sound.*

Of course, he knew he would die soon. Whenever I would ask him to stop for tea or rest, he would quote the ancients and say— The problem is that you think there is time.

But time itself is language, he'd then laugh, slapping me, rather light-heartedly, on the shoulder, bringing forth a small cup of strong wine. Language is a dream, and being is time. The other is the mystery and waking to the other is reality, he once said, and I have never forgotten. As I have so far been unable to find the girl or boy of the scrolls and suspect their death in the wars—if they ever existed—I am grateful to have found you. As far as any of us have been able to ascertain, the Temple Sweeper left no trace of a family. All of our efforts to find the various beings he referred to have failed as well, and even the Abbot's former friends in the government offices have been of no use. Maybe you will help? It is a shame that at least the girl cannot have these scrolls, though of course, she would no longer be a child, and who knows if she is alive or in a dream.

—ENDURING MONK
FINISHED THE 12TH MONTH, 5TH NIGHT, YEAR OF THE DRAGON

SCROLL I

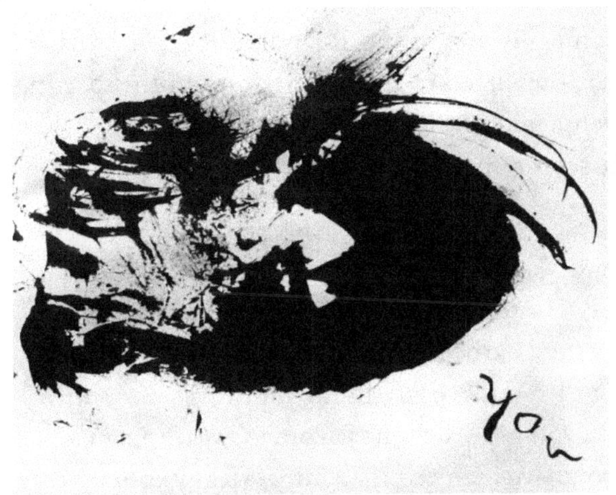

I would start at the beginning, but that might confuse you, cause you to think this life has a beginning, middle, or end. It doesn't, Enduring Sound.

—*THE TEMPLE SWEEPER*

The Mute Girl's Diary

Head Monk & good scribe, Enduring Sound. Please make this note for the circus players & theater troupe before we begin tonight, the girl called out to me.

They will arrive soon after you and the Temple Sweeper yield to sleep, and it is important in reading my diary that they understand what they need to do and perform in this parting of waves as we open again with all of these beings and non-beings, these players & seers & particles of light—

> Dear friends, my old friends—stand as still
> and close together as possible at the front flap
> of your tents tonight, and light the campfires
> as the Learned Sage Women among you call
> out from this diary in the morning's first sun.
> As you hear the Ghostwoman's voice again as
> you have many times before—ready yourselves,
> prepare for our pilgrimage and journey, and
> learn your parts well, first on your inner
> stage, and then, for the worlds yet to come.

The Girl's Diary Begins

> Nearly a thousand years of suffering have
> passed, my love. And there you are again, a
> boy wandering by the sea at the dawn's first
> awakening. Your hands waving above your head,
> your feet tired, your eye seeking the sound before
> sound, and this, all of this, as you have known all
> along in our travels throughout time. I could cry,
> or laugh, while writing you this as the Temple
> Sweeper and his scribe, Enduring Sound, begin

our story again in a remote monastery on the
shores of our former hermitage. Can you hear
me, dear one, one-eyed boy, mystery of my
dreams? In your new birth, my bird of paradise
awaits you. This night as you stroll by the sea to
the graves of pebble and stone, a trace of your
boyhood's vanishing skin returns and appears
in the sky in anticipation of your arrival.

It will be soon now.

It is an auspicious sign.

Do not hesitate.

We are here for you.

You are not alone.

Enduring Sound Waking from the Dream

Who is this mute girl, I asked the Temple Sweeper as he began his tales in my small monk's cell. And why does this girl, or you, speak as such, if she is indeed mute?

It is not I, but the girl herself who is speaking, Head Monk. She speaks from the silence. Language is a dream, and we are merely dreaming each other as you begin to write in the dream of words.

But is it a girl's diary? And we are not asleep, Temple Sweeper. I see you sitting in my cell with my own eyes and touch the page with my own hands.

It is as you heard it, Head Monk. Only we are awakening, briefly now, in the dream.

But this girl, if she is a girl, how is she such—well, some might say, an "old soul"—if she is only a child? Surely there is something more you can tell me from the world of the red dust you came from, Temple Sweeper. Is she a memory from the wars, the famines? When was this?

It will be clear soon, Head Monk. This you can trust.

And these circus players and theater troupe and all the others you have begun to speak of, are they the ones it is said first brought you here to this shore of our monastery in the sea?

They brought you here too, Head Monk, Enduring Sound. But yes, they have entered the nameless.

I am an orphan, Temple Sweeper. This is true. Still, I cannot speak to that which I don't know. But how can I write as you request if first, this scribe, is not clear who is speaking, and what is said?

Yet you hear their voices, Head Monk. Just write the sounds you hear.

How, Temple Sweeper?

There is a reason why we came here for you, Head Monk. It is not I who chose it so. Together we will have to uncover their secret. All the same, there is very little time, are you certain you want to help me?

Temple Sweeper, I have waited since I was boy to hear your words. I will do as you request. I will do my best. I give you my promise, Temple Sweeper. This I promise you.

A Statement of Purpose—
The Temple Sweeper

It seems profoundly odd that the day I begin to tell you the story of our life is the beginning of the days of where it ends, Head Monk. If all of the dreams dissolve, will you enter the dream beside me? I would start at the beginning, yet that might confuse us, as if our lives were made up of some kind of beginnings and endings—

The man is walking with a one-eyed boy and mute girl by the sea. The man is walking past the hills outside the monastery alone, yet you secretly follow him. This you have done since he arrived. You have seen the man on the hills and by the waves. Seen him in the mountains. Seen him crossing the river. Seen him in the ruins. Seen him with the Dream Masters, and soon you will remember our shared story. And with the man, you have witnessed the children disappearing like birds on the horizon. The man no longer has a name, though you call him Temple Sweeper, and he, too, witnessed their deaths beside you. Today he is preparing to disappear with the boy and girl once more. Ready to be one of the birds and return. White clouds to the edge of the cliffs. Still daylight, yet the clouds and fog and all these friends blowing in from this river running to sea must have made the sky so bleached, a pink hue edging out along the rock-faced cliffs. You are thinking—the trees do not speak here. There is neither silence nor words, nor is there any sadness.

But is there forgiveness?

What is to be forgiven?

You see in your hazy vision a staggering horse by the edge of the graves and wave.

You see the one-eyed boy and smile.

You see all of these abandoned roads, and a mute girl waiting. You have studied the man who has come to this hill every day for twenty-five years. A language of silence. Stood by the cypress tree. Preparing for death, letting death wash out from the waves of the river. Bamboo stalks and unnamed stories scattered about the approaching fields. He walks along the ridge. Morning light encourages you, evening dark calms you. He carries a burlap sack full of pebbles and stones. Each day he carries them to this place overlooking the great sea of the great deathless death.

The stones are dead and yet they are alive.

They are the fish you imagine in the sea.

They are brothers and sisters to the one-eyed boy and mute girl, and the man is walking along a hundred-foot high, rock-faced cliff.

They are the stones of unknown alphabets waking and healing the wound.

The crows of the dead and the running of children.

Incarnations we have never ceased to love, who never cease in love.

One by one, the man, this Temple Sweeper, lifts the stones from his burlap bag. One by one he places the stones in a heap by the ancient bamboo underneath a statue of the great goddess of compassion, who stands at the top of the hill above our monastery gate.

The bodies of stone growing larger, taking on a shape that is sometimes human, the length of a religion once reaching from the earth.

Bamboo & sea.

You see, Head Monk, Enduring Sound?

You see with your eyes and touch with your hands.

Even as you sleep now, you see them in your own dreams, and I am already gone.

Because of the distance he has walked from the monastery, the man is tired after the journey. You secretly leave him tea and biscuits. And now you are a man yourself. Determined to understand in your private, sometimes hidden, study of languages, of shamans, of angels and spirits. You step back in the shadows, invisible. You, too, have always been invisible since the soldiers came and made you an orphan. And now the man can only carry pebbles with each passage, because he is about to leave the dream, and you decide to help him. Why?

The man is carrying the dream of this place.

Pieces of dust.

Sometimes, you wake up in the dream.

A boy and girl, waiting.

And you almost remember.

From thousands of years of suffering we begin again.

The dream and the waking, words.

Yet this temple sweeper once tried to forsake them.

Today, we again begin to speak them.

This girl's diary will become your own.

So now, care for it well, Enduring Sound. The man lays the stones out, as you yourself will, too, someday, forming the shape of planets and constellations in a boundless sky, writing these letters of forgiveness. In spite of his efforts, the man cannot make the graves beautiful. Afterwards, the man begins his walk back to the monastery and you follow—furtive, curious, alone, an orphan-monk whose eyes once witnessed the terror as your own family vanished. Taken away. And then, you were forsaken.

But here you are, alive, Head Monk.
The man dreams of the Lost Children.

He dreams of the child dancing barefoot in the snow outside the prison gates and the day he came for you, a mere boy.

He dreams of the one you will meet soon, a sha-man-monk older than his own dreams—the Dream Master Hempis, who brought us all to this monastery with the help of the Ghostwoman and Learned Sage Women. These circus and theater players who helped us when the soldiers in the endless wars on the mainland took away our childhoods.

You will meet Hempis.

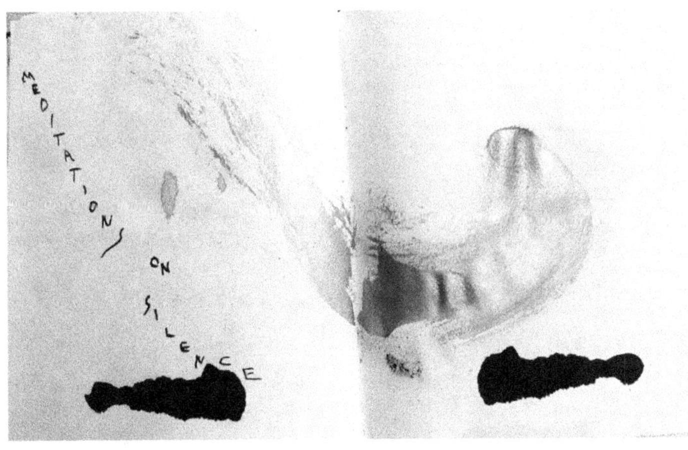

Then you will learn to move within the dream of the dream.

We will bow to one another, as they with us did in their previous days together, during the long wars.

This is the silence of fish washing out into an infinite sea, birds flying in a sky without end.

And these are the words you must give them back, Head Monk.

Remember this when you are ready to leave the dream.

Are you certain you want to honor this request? Are you not frightened, Head Monk, Enduring Sound?

I am awake, Temple Sweeper. And I will do as you have requested, this I have already told you. But how will I breathe your death when I do not even know who you are?

I will show you, Enduring Sound. I will show you.

But am I dreaming or awake right now, Temple Sweeper?

You are awake and asleep, briefly awakening, in this dream of language we are imagining together.

THE ESSENTIAL STORY—

ENDURING SOUND'S DREAM LATER THAT NIGHT WITH THE ONE WE CALL HEMPIS

You are thinking of no words, just alive here?

Or that the story began before you were born, Head Monk—a moment of change, the sky brightening by early frost in morn, the mute girl walking toward the boy in the theater troupe through the approaching snow by the carnival tents—carrying a letter in her left hand as we all glance out at the waters behind her. A crow sitting on the stump of a cypress tree and a prophet and a poet who trail between these jugglers and clowns. A fox, a crow, and a Ghostwoman. What is it, you wonder, Head Monk, Enduring Sound? And it occurs to you in this moment that these are the Temple Sweeper's stones, the ones he carries each day to the fields, these very stones and pebbles now talking to you. Yet you think there are no words, and the story begins before you are born, but this is no longer so.

This is the first omen, Enduring Sound. You hear its sound even though you are still sleeping.

When the girl reaches the stones where the Temple Sweeper meditated as a boy, she hands him her letter. Opening the envelope, the pieces of cut bright orange cloth fall and flutter in between these pebbles by your feet. This much is true you think now—the story of the boy's past with the old Dream Master, perhaps? I am Hempis, the one your Temple Sweeper has said will come to you. It is a mystery, but you think maybe you are beginning to understand? Just a little, still this matters. That these letters are like birds flying into the hills behind us, into an opening of the sky that beckons you toward, you might say, the moon. Later the

Temple Sweeper will speak of this to you as the initial promise of love coming home to the earth by first flying away from it.

We are not alone, the girl has written on the pieces of orange cloth, and these sounds of a new alphabet now fall from the wings of a bird of paradise you see overhead, soaring above this monastery by the sea, Head Monk, Enduring Sound.

I am with you. And we have never been apart, the girl has written in her diary.

You pick up the words on the orange cloth that fly out of your hand into the opening sky, a beckoning.

You will record this as the Scrolls of a Temple Sweeper.

Though it is your dream, and your own life now, Head Monk.

The words are no one's.

This, too, will be in many years from now when you awaken and remember this first dream where I have come to you.

You will call me, Hempis. Hempis, you will call me in these scrolls.

But I have no name.

I am simply part of the Old Story told by a prophet and a poet who you will someday meet and travel with together to a place you will remember.

A place that is your original home.

Shall we go on?

Scroll II

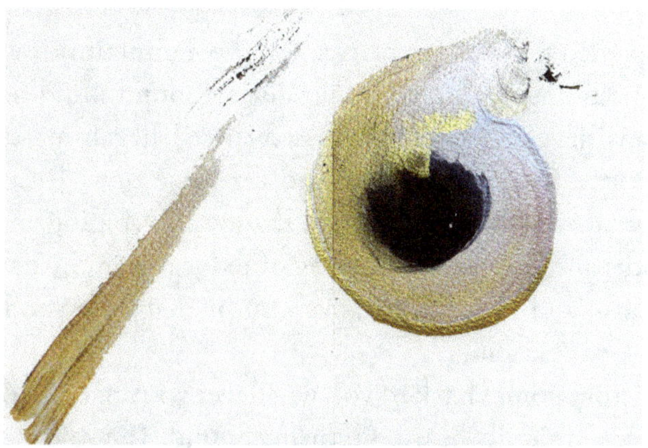

How can I live without your story?
We are never alone, she went on.
You must tell our story.
You will be tempted to call it only a fiction.
And all reality a mere imagination, this is true.
Yet it is you imagining our true face throughout
space and time in a boundless love.

—*The Girl's Diary*

THE STORY, THE MOUNTAIN, THE CIRCUS AT THE THEATER—

OR, HOW THE TEMPLE SWEEPER MET THE OLD DREAM MASTER & GHOSTWOMAN

I had spotted the man in the trees on the mountainside every day of my walking, Head Monk, Enduring Sound. I did not know how many days or weeks had passed since I began my escape. A lean, hooded figure trailing behind for some time, I was almost certain, but only seen in glimpses, shadows of abiding and fading eucalyptus and oak, the simmering of red leaves in the dark wood and foliage, and in moments, even a fear that he was one of the soldiers I was escaping.

The story comes back to you whenever you are not alone. This is the voice I initially heard, Enduring Sound. The voice saying—a music in the wound, a ghost in the words, a word in your wanderings and escape. Your story a body, a code of blood, a talisman of bone and marrow in the telling.

Who was this speaking, Temple Sweeper? You, or the figure you saw in the trees? Or perhaps this, too, is from the girl's diary? Will you not say, Temple Sweeper?

He was a stranger to me then as he is a stranger to you now, Head Monk. But soon he will speak to you again. Though you have already met in your dream last night, the dream you have already forgotten. But no worry. We will come to understand it all, once more, together.

He is the one you called Hempis, Temple Sweeper?

He is, he is, yes, though he had no name then, as you have forgotten your true name now. It is of no matter, Head Monk. Just write what you hear and the sound will appear.

This man or spirit, this stranger, he traveled from the same fields as I, the same fields as that of the Lost Children—traveled from the same burning fires as we children in the mountains, escaping the soldiers, the same fields.

Better to see the face than hear the name, he called from behind a bush on that blustery dawn, startling me as I stepped through the wound of the wandering these past weeks, or even months, I couldn't really say, Head Monk. Barefoot and alone. Hungry. Lost. A boy in the woods then, alone. I thought I was alone, Head Monk. Yet I recognized this stranger's eye without question.

His eye, Temple Sweeper?

How could you recognize an eye?

You see, Head Monk, from the time we fled the fires, this curious figure was somehow keeping pace with me, no matter how quickly I walked—hiding in the brush and rock boulders, occasionally at night in the caves—not even lighting a fire in the cold of autumn. Sometimes I even ran when I'd glimpse his shadow, and this running was with great difficulty, Head Monk—you understand, due to the wounds on my hands and bare feet that I had wrapped with cloth and damp leaves each morning. And it was as if an image of an unknown circus and band of carnival children were constantly emerging in the black forest nights from the blacker blackness of the black hills and black trees where he hid. I was frightened, confused. I could not even remember who I was, or why I was running. But I knew of the soldiers, and I smelled the vultures.

Though I will say that early dawn morning when he finally showed himself, this shaman-looking figure with a beard and wild hair streaming over his face, why, he looked rather frail, almost as you see me by your candlelight tonight, Head Monk—blotches of bruise under his cheeks, a skewed eye, his body covered in animal furs, and as if surveying the terrain all round me as he stood in the trees—a human face, you might even say, without mercy, but as if expectant, gazing into the forests of thick trees and hooting owls.

Temple Sweeper?

I am here, Head Monk.

Listen closely, Hempis told me—*the stone hears, the hand sees, the eye bows down.*

This man, or shaman or spirit laughed when he finally stepped forward, gesturing to me, smoking a stick of tobacco, leaning into a cane with a dragon's head.

You think the story is your past? he asked at once, as if knowing me, or as if we had some relationship from the past and were just continuing some former conversation. But he was an unknown to me then, as he is to you now, Enduring Sound.

Though your past is in a story, a story is not your past. And if you look closely, you may even recognize your own face, boy, he said.

Who are you, I finally managed to utter, sensing a new anger swelling in my hands, a surge of rage from my growing fear, as if this anger were blowing in around the cliffs behind him. Who are you, old man or spirit? You have been following me. Say your purpose.

You call me an old man or spirit, but I am no more old than you are young, though true it is only a boy who stands here before me. And the story is not in your damaged and bandaged hand, nor in the anger of your missing fingers. Language and time are the same, he said to me. But it was as if he was calling to some faraway place, Head Monk—a kind of soft howl like the animals that walk on our monastery roof at night in the storms—and exposing the raw gums of a crooked mouth and brownish teeth.

I am not a boy, I said, hiding my trembling as best I could.

You are twelve years old in this body.

You've been following me. Why?

I realized while saying this that I was holding the hunting knife my father had given me before the soldiers came, thrusting it out toward him, threateningly. But I couldn't recall taking the knife out of its sheath.

He stepped back, flicked the cane in the air. It was a dance-like motioning. There was blood on the bottom of his tattered fur pants, and when his eye met mine, he smiled and apologized.

No matter how many times I wash these furs in the river, using even the coarsest of stones, even this cane of pure dragon bone, the blood will not go away, he said. Such is the river of love. Such is the river of suffering. They are the same.

The shaman grinned, shuffled toward me again with a peculiar agility, or confidence, perhaps momentarily lost and regained. Yes, sturdy you could say, Head Monk. Fluid, especially for a man as haggard and long-traveled, and clearly from the poorer villages. You could see this from his torn coat and unshaven face, the unkempt strands of whitish hair as he pulled down his hood and said to me—your body struggling in this mountain with vultures and ravens and all the children drowning in the river.

Was he alive, Temple Sweeper? Or a hungry ghost? The Abbot has spoken to us of these hungry ghosts, Temple Sweeper.

Wait, good monk, wait. As for myself, in hearing him as such, all I could remember was walking, endlessly walking, pulling my weight toward the sea to find the girl. Somehow I had lost the girl in our escape. Perhaps it was along the path as we ran, maybe after we left the small child with the monks, but you understand, at this point everything was a blur to me and I couldn't touch it, I had to turn away. Though this turning away, it is the cause of affliction. And already, you see, you see, Head Monk, I had fallen in love with her.

The girl in the diary, Temple Sweeper?

She had written in a diary that we would meet again by an empty sea. This was the last entry she'd written. Or at least, this much I'd translated since crawling, later stumbling from the river and hiding in the bark of elm and sycamore as the horses of the attacking soldiers rampaged along the water's shore.

I am sorry, Temple Sweeper. And perhaps I should not ask, but why did this girl give you her diary? Is it not a private thing? And this small child? Which child is it of whom you speak?

The day of the attack. Somehow, the girl slipped the diary into my coat pocket.

Did she drown with the others? Is this what the strange shaman meant? Or dare I ask such questions, Temple Sweeper?

This you will discover. It is why they call you Enduring Sound. Is this not your name in our monastery? Is it not why you are now Head Monk of our temple?

You're lost, the man, or spirit-shaman, said. Afterwards, he sat himself down by the side of the path, unfolding a blue cloth with two sets of eating bowls.

The ones who killed your friends will not allow you to enter the villages sprawled about in these mountains, he told me. And many more soldiers are stationed in the port where this path is leading you. You are lost, you understand? I have come to help you. In any case, they will surely kill you if you go to the ports where this path leads.

Why do you think you know where I am going?

I have read the girl's diary. As you, I hear the bees and butter-flies in the pages. The sound in her words the same as her mother's cooing while bending over her as a child, breathing life from the other's hair.

He almost smiled.

Why do you follow me? And whose diary do you speak of? I have no money, old man. I have nothing. I have nothing for you, I told him.

As the wind picked up and blew through the trees, he paused for a moment, as if considering deeply my question, yet looking around, again cautiously, Head Monk, because he, too, sensed the soldiers searching in these mountains were near. His gaze was fierce, hardened, warrior-like, even with his one good eye. This is true.

Who do you think appeared to you in the sycamore's bark the night the soldiers came? he asked. Who do you think was there for you and the girl at the river? You heard a sound, boy, a sound before sound, and that sound was in the sycamore's bark you climbed into from the  river to flee the flames. We made you invisible to their weapons. Now, have you simply abandoned hope?

The shaman turned and looked behind, inspecting the woods, lowering his voice, trying not to speak too loudly lest another overhear, and clutching the dragon cane, firmly. So I looked around too, but saw nothing.

Ravens and vultures follow you, as I follow them, he said. The vultures are growing closer. But soon you, too, will study the flight of birds and befriend them.

And what he said about the vultures was so, Head Monk. The vultures were trailing closer, some days even swooping their claws right above my head. They smelled my weakness, no doubt. Once I had to take my bag and fight one of these death creatures back, swinging wildly to show my remaining strength. I saw more and more of these vultures getting closer every day in my walking up that mountain that led to the other side of the river where I thought I would find the girl.

Tell me something, the shaman asked. Who makes you do such things to your own hands, boy?

I glanced down. These are not my hands, I whispered in the wind, tilting my head away, uncontrollably feeling tears, and turning away, covertly covering my face from his one blackened eye.

He stared at me in my silence.

Who do you think cauterized your wounds after you passed out? If I had not done this, you would have bled to death, boy. Consider it. Allow me to introduce myself. I am the one they call Hempis in these mountains. You have nothing to fear. I am here to help you, boy.

It was a cold autumn morning, winter rapidly approaching, the smell of bear and boar in the air. These smells I recognized from my own childhood before the wars began, and most of these beautiful creatures were not extinct. A familiar northern wind. The pain in my hands constant, I'd soak them in the icy mountain stream every morning, each night. Still, I had walked, trudged on, gathering what remaining berries I could from the wilting vines, fish from the river with only a crude bow and arrow I fashioned with my father's knife.

Yet even then, I had begun to translate the girl's diary. I didn't know how, or even know what the word translation meant—or how the girl's language was different from the one I was thinking in. Yet somehow I could decipher the signs of the letters in her diary. I couldn't even remember the girl's face—or anything more than the fires and her hand slipping out of mine, and the soldiers on horseback raging through the hillsides, and the bark of the sycamore and elm trees.

What language are we speaking? I suddenly blurted out at the shaman.

We are not speaking a language, we are speaking a dream.

Let me see your hands, Hempis said again.

He then meticulously removed the bowls from the blue cloth as I tucked my hands into my pockets, still trembling, making sure no tear on my face remained.

What happened to your eye, old man?

My eye? It is it same as yours, yes. You are not mistaken. The soldiers did this to me, just as they did to you when you saved the child. It was bold of you.

Hempis arranged the bowls symmetrically on the frost of ground between us. He folded one napkin before me after wiping the bowls and did the same for himself, gesturing for me to sit.

I stared at his eye, touched the soreness in my own, glanced away toward the cliffs, uncertain whether to flee, Head Monk. Such is the nature of fear.

You were still frightened, Temple Sweeper. It seems natural.

I didn't know what to do, Head Monk. Fear is an illusion, but we are human. And in my restless sleep since fleeing the soldiers, every night I would dream of a mute girl and one-eyed boy on a boat in the river, drifting toward the sea. Every morning I took the diary from my bag and began to read and translate the pages before walking further up the mountain. I told Hempis this as he offered me some of his tobacco.

You can see for yourself, old man, I said, pulling out the girl's diary.

Ah yes, he said. I have read this diary, too.

He scooped a small spoonful of brown rice from his pouch. I suspect you must know I am bound to you now, boy? You can call me Hempis, or old man, or shaman or whatever you like. But I am a Dream Master, and I have come to teach you the art of traveling in dreams, as your time has come and you are now of age, and you have been called upon. But you will eventually learn that I am no other than your own being—true, true yes—from a different time and different worlds. There is no way for you to fathom this now. Yet you will learn. And you will learn to fly through the dreams.

On the cliffs beyond the hills and sharp ridges sprawled in barren rock, a fox arose from behind what seemed a painted bush, the fox panting, watching us now, beside an amber crow. The wind picked up and the leaves began to churn in small shapes off the ground.

The shaman pointed to the fox and crow and bowed. How to best say it to you, boy? Let me put it this way. If you were to dream yourself in the future, who would be the dreamer?

He slowly counted out some berries into the second bowl, searching my expression after rapping his fingers on the ground three times and bowing again to the crow and fox.

Let me see your hands.

This time, I held them forth.

He rubbed his large palms together, began to clean the smallness of my wounds with his own cloth that had contained the bowls, afterwards massaging a thick liquid, like black mud, that he pinched from his leather pouch, squeezing it between my two missing fingers while cupping my calloused hands inside his own larger hands, chanting in a tongue that sounded inhuman, something like wild geese rising off water in winter.

And my pain immediately began to ease, Head Monk.

He was a shaman then. I myself have met shamans before. This is their miraculous medicine, Temple Sweeper. He could not be a hungry ghost.

No, he was not a hungry ghost, though a spirit of sorts, Head Monk. But he was more than a shaman as you will discover for yourself. Hempis spooned the rice into a stone bowl with his own long, dexterous fingers, touching the kernels of rice over my swollen hand while counting six additional berries for each of us into the smaller, bamboo bowls and pouring a trickle of goat's milk and honey from his flask into a cup.

I told you. I have no money.

You mean you have no memory, he said?

This will help you with the pain and out of the dream. Eat

slowly and concentrate on your chewing. Imagine the bird of paradise you translated from her diary earlier this morning.

I glanced again to the cliff. The crow and fox were gone. But neither were the vultures anywhere to be seen.

There's a shelter not very far from here, he said. I am good friends with the circus people who abide there. They will be your friends, too. It is not far from here if you travel lightly, listening closely to the sounds of the earth as you sleep tonight and hear my voice when I am no longer a form before you.

I ate the small portion of berries and rice, tentatively, even shyly, given my ravenous hunger, as he went on saying things that I could not understand, and then as if suddenly alarmed when first a swarm of bees, and next, of butterflies, flew over our heads, swirling almost languidly from above us and slowly downward toward the clearing below the mountain, he said—If I were to dream, I think I would dream of the one who remembers. And with those words, the last throbs in the spaces that had once been my fingers ceased completely.

We ate in silence for what felt like hours, as if the bowls would never empty. The more quickly I ate, the more rice and berries and milk would appear in my bowl. And when my hunger abated, and we did finish, he gestured for me to accompany him to the edge of the path, giving me the final drops of muddy ointment from his pouch.

The dreamer and the dream are not one, but don't think they are two, boy.

Have we met before, old man? What village do you come from?

You've begun to recognize my eye, haven't you? Well yes, yes we have met. And we had an appointment to meet on this very day, in this very place, and that was made many lifetimes ago, yes. Quite some time ago, yes. But we have traveled together many times. Soon you will remember all of our lives together.

Do you always speak in riddles?

Hempis rose to his feet, began to carefully maneuver along the thin edge of the gorge's ridge, moving slowly toward the valley below, and he gestured for me to do the same and follow him.

I will not lie to you, I said to him, measuring my own footsteps now, trying not to look down the steep precipice of the goat path in those mountains. I would like to remember who I am. Who the girl is. The one-eyed boy, too. But this very moment is a dream, and when I wake up, I know, you all will be gone. I am familiar with how dreams really are. I am no fool, Hempis—or whatever you call yourself. You are just like the others. And they are all dead, except perhaps the child and the girl. I remember holding a small child in my arms and carrying him to a safe place before the soldiers could kill him. And the girl was there. This I do remember. But I will wake from sleep and discover you were simply a mirage of my sleep. And, truth be known, I would rather go my own way. I will find the girl and remember the face of this child. I do not need you, or anyone.

Hempis stumbled precariously as I said this, and he reached out for my hand by the tight edge of the cliff along the slope—he was falling. I reached out to him and grasped his hand. He then caught his balance while holding tightly to my thumbs, pulling his body inward toward the gorge edge, somehow, placing the dragon cane under my arms, then pulling us both up into the air as we began to glide gently in the breeze, floating further down, yet above, the narrow goat path that opened into a mist of clouds and sun over the meadow in the clearing below.

Look closely at my face, boy, he said while flying. Look closely at my face, he said again as my feet touched the ground beside his own.

Listen closely and look at my face, he repeated. You saw me in the river when the soldiers came, yet that was not the first time. It was I who was there with the one called the Ghostwoman, and it was the two of us who helped move you and the girl through the flames safely down river so you could escape the soldiers and meet me here. This is no mystery. To be invisible, too, is a dream. The girl will be waiting for you, too, if you do as I say. And one day you will find the child you carried away.

After we put down our bags and dusted ourselves off, Hempis immediately set up a camp, and then he began to lift various stones of all sizes from the ground and to shape these stones into concentric circles, then more circles, that became larger, rounder circles circling the smaller circles and forming a sphere, or a moon of some kind that seemed to go on and on, expanding around us further than I could see in the meadow and the mists. And this all done with astonishing speed, too quick for any man from our world, Head Monk.

Indeed, this is a strong shaman, Temple Sweeper. Hempis must have many powers.

These stones that are very tiny and smooth, you will place in a separate pile, boy, he instructed me, pouring a handful of pebbles into my hand.

I am not your boy, Hempis. Nor am I a mere dream. But I would like to know how you do these things. How did you fly us from the cliff? How did you move those huge stones? Are you some kind of magician or demon, or maybe you have given me some evil potion and tricked me like the killers who burn the villages after fooling our elders, and burning their children.

He paused and studied me, as if recognizing something he himself had forgotten.

Yes, yes, I understand how you might think so, he said.

All the same, I am not one of them. Nor am I a butcher or warlord in this new war on children. There are many wars, but we have no names. Language the dream. The other a mystery. The truth is simply awakening in this mystery of the other. Everywhere we go, we meet ourselves. Even without mercy, we meet ourselves. Though not separate, I am not one of the killers. And it is the same with these stones you see, these butterflies and bees, my fox and crow. And yes, you will go your own way, in time, boy. And if you had not given me your hand at that moment of falling on the ridge, we would have never met again. But this is our destiny now. You saved my life, and as such, you confirmed what I already knew. You are both the dream and the dreamer, and you are dreaming me as I, right now, am dreaming you. We are everything we are not. They will call you Temple Sweeper someday. And you will become a Master of Dreams.

In a life there is a story, Enduring Sound. Those murdered in the burning hills. The wanderings of a boy and a girl. Our Lost Children. The waking in the dream. Soon enough, we will find them all, even help heal them, Head Monk. And this is what Hempis told me that night before vanishing again.

But first you will go eastward on the path I will show you over this mountain, he said. To a hidden shelter near the sea, the place you see while sleeping, boy, the one you seek from the girl's diary. You will bypass the temples and villages along the way. And you will come to a circus field. There you will tell the Circus Master of our meeting when you arrive.

I choose my own path, I said. I will find my way—on my own.

Then you will die on this mountain.

Hempis waved his cane in the air as if about to strike me, but caught himself.

So that you can someday again speak as a child, I speak as a page in her diary. Yet you are a stubborn boy.

Where have you come from, old man?

The sea in the girl's diary.

Where is she then? If you know, tell it to me now, without more of your riddles.

This you will translate in the essential story. And it is why I am here, boy. But now, the theater and circus players await you. I will point you in their direction. Trust me, boy.

Too tired to argue further, too confused to leave or know what to do, I nonetheless sensed that the soldiers were nearby, Head Monk, for three vultures had again appeared on the ridge to our south. The fox and crow nowhere in sight.

Hempis cleaned and chiseled the final stones, which were now very round and smooth. He requested for me to be more attentive. *With no bird singing, the mountain is yet more still*, he hummed as the evening approached.

And by dusk, Hempis had shaped my pebbles into figures of a girl and boy flying on what appeared to be a bird of paradise.

As the sun went over the mountain, Hempis quietly approached the place I'd been sitting. He bowed to me and touched my shoulders with his hands.

Afterwards, he prepared a place for us to sleep.

Who are you? I asked again.

It doesn't matter. Just this old bag of skin, I guess, he grinned.

Here. This is now your cup and these are your bowls, boy. And soon you will be known as the Temple Sweeper. I have been waiting many lifetimes to give these bowls to you. And now, I give you as well this torn and blooded coat of fur for the journey. The girl will help you find me again when it is time. You will translate this, too, from her diary. Someday you will thank her and repay the debt, and tell our story.

And if I don't want to go there, to your shelter or circus, or whatever it is?

The soldiers will find you before morning and you will die before your work has even begun, boy.

Hempis scooped a handful of pebbles into my bag, leaned on his side and placed the cane over my chest as I laid down, exhausted, and we both instantly fell asleep.

And in the morning, he was gone, Head Monk. Yet I found myself standing before a row of circus tents, surrounded by hundreds of children of different ages—different faces, whispering in different languages among themselves, some giggling, the older ones more serious with their painted faces—and all of them wearing various colors of what I'd call festive, carnival clothing, some in masks, some acting as clowns, three small girls tiptoeing and glancing down at me from a tight rope suspended above the tents, and a girl and boy, amazingly, swallowing fire down their throats—as if to show off for me.

These were the ones from the theater and circus troupe that brought me to our monastery twenty-five years ago, good monk, Enduring Sound.

And some you will meet as well someday and come to know as Seekers and Learned Sage Women.

Are you still dreaming, Temple Sweeper?

This is what I first asked myself too, Head Monk, because I possessed these very hands, eyes, nose, ears, tongue, mouth you see tonight as you write. You see, Enduring Sound, it was of a physical body, of this earth, not a mirage. Or so I thought, but neither is this always so.

From a trapeze, a woman whose face seemed to be lit by a flaming sun—a woman covered in rags, rainbow-hued and floating around her—this woman called out to greet me.

We have been expecting you, she cawed in a voice not unlike our monastery's amber crow that you can hear outside the window if you listen closely right now, right in this moment, Head Monk.

How did you expect me, when I did not know myself I was coming, I somehow called back to her. This woman whose eyes and face I could not make out. Or am I still sleeping in the one called Hempis' dream, and you are the one he called, Circus Master? I asked her.

Hempis is the one to speak of dreams, he is the Dream Master, she said. And in these mountains, I am known as the Ghostwoman, said the trapeze artist.

I glanced around, unable to keep my eyes on her face for more than a second, nor to contain my astonishment. All of the children smiling at me now, as if holding back their laughter at my awe and dumbfounded state. This is what I think now, good monk.

I somehow managed to blurt out—all I know is that there are soldiers in these mountains. Vultures following me. And they kill children. All the children grew still and hushed as I spoke in this way, Head Monk. And they will kill you too, I shouted. And all of these children. Unless we run. This much I know.

Whoever you are, we must run.

The smiles left the children's faces, and they stepped back in unison.

No one will find you, Temple Sweeper, she called to me, gliding down from the trapeze to the ground.

And now, I thought I was truly still dreaming, Head Monk, that I was still sleeping. Her long hair floating up like clouds, and her arms spread wide and wingish.

We are invisible here, you needn't worry, this trapeze artist, the Ghostwoman said, sitting beside me now, smiling.

Then, the fox and crow I'd seen on the ridge the day before came up behind her. She turned and bowed, took from the crow's beak a scroll, Head Monk. The scroll that you now hold in your own hands.

But this scroll, why I have only begun to write in it, Temple Sweeper. How could she, or a crow or a spirit, for that matter, have possessed it then? Temple Sweeper, have you fallen into your own dream tonight? Are you awake, Temple Sweeper?

Wait, good monk, Enduring Sound.

Please explain something, I asked this Ghostwoman.

I will try. But some things cannot be explained, she said.

Where am I?

People come to the circus of our monastery in the strangest of ways, she replied in a kind voice, as if that of a mother or guardian of some kind. When I looked into her eyes, the burning of the sun was gone, and all I could see was a vast sky.

She stroked my hand.

Hempis is master of the dream world, she said again, as the children drew closer in to hear her, relaxing, once more at ease. I am not only a trapeze artist, I am master of the circus and theater troupe. Though we have never been born, nor will we ever die. There are myriad forms. But do not worry, young one. You yourself will become a Dream Master and Temple Sweeper, and the soldiers will not find you.

The Ghostwoman then flicked her arms in a swirl above my head, tapped the ground with her fingers, much as Hempis had done with his dragon-headed cane, only more softly, summoning some of the smaller children who were still playing.

Here, Hempis' stones have become dreams, she said.

Here, the dreams have become bones.

Here, the bones have become prayers.

Here, the prayers have become us.

Here, the Lost Children have been found.

This is the voice I then heard, Head Monk. It was the girl's voice from the diary, calling from the river, calling out to you and me, anticipating your very question now as you again are drifting toward sleep as you write and your tired head tilts inward—

You will be tempted to call this only a story.

All reality a mere imagination, and this is true.

Yet this is your life, you, right here, right now.

The girl walked out from behind the circus and theater play-ers, waved and bowed, and again walked toward me. I felt the first drops of rain.

This is how we begin, Enduring Sound.

This is where you began.

You are Everything and Everyone You Meet—Autobiography of a Dream

The Ghostwoman Comes into the Dream of the Temple Sweeper and Head Monk Later That Night

Are you ready, good monks?
Can you hear their wound, this sound before sound?
We are here.
My pen is ready, Temple Sweeper.

The Ghostwoman Speaks

Then some more churning & running in your dreaming together tonight. Our old families, our own deaths and the deaths of a child, another and another child, and then becoming a child again. And what took you so long to return? Still, it's all new again as you begin our story on this very vanishing shore where it all began— stroke of fire on elm, burning sycamore, explosions of blinding

light over the ridge, the soldiers on horseback, the sound of burning, and you are there, too, again. These minnows & fleeing fish
in the river, swimming around your eyes & the cold autumn water as you hide in the eddies, surrounded by these very friends &
family, these Lost Children, crying. And you are lost as well in the
incarnate bodies of whom they are, whom you become and were.
You, a child in the calling birds & dying butterflies and bees lying
down, wilting over the stones, right here by the waves & blooming
brush along the shore, & the others who ran & fell & ran & got
up & fell, over & over, from the hills full of soldiers. You, flying
on clouds and tumbling into the waterways by forests as storks &
gulls with blooded mouths soar overhead and drop their bodies
into the sea. It makes you wonder why you waste so much time.
Words & shouts & tears leading us to hereditary roads, take you
back to their soul, take you to the inside of flights of moons. And
you've been here before & you suddenly remember the ravage on
skin & bone as you flee too, further down river, flee the killings,
so many torn away and only for the mark of their skin or bone or
birth as other than who these soldiers and their new warlords are.
And now floating on water in ascending corpses cleansed by sea.
But not you, you are alive still. A boy's blackened and wounded
eye from the slight swipe of a blade, burning off that desert cheek,
and the children swim harder to escape. A girl swims up beside a
boy, calling, and later climbing into the trees together, vanishing
from their fires—fish & camouflaged Dream Masters who appear
in the same shape as of the dark bark of sycamore & elm awaiting
you down the shore & yet, & yet—how does anyone ever live on
(can you say, really say it)? Still, later running & finding a small
child hidden in a bush, a mere child alone and crying—the boy
& girl lift and carry him through the woods, into the forest, into
this mountain, freed from the soldiers. But there you lost an eye
with a swift slash of a soldier. And here you all are, cleaning stone
& drinking tea, digging these children's graves with a hoe or hand,
burying pebbles by the sea in all these moments bursting forth in

a flush of boats randomly mooring by a pier to take you away in the early rain where we left you at the monastery. The circus & theater players who brought you here, why you wonder, what play did they want from me, you ask. You, you who you are right now in the ravage & healing as another dream ends & awakens in the healing itself....

—how do we ever forgive?

…

Enduring Monk?

Yes, Temple Sweeper.

Are you awake?

I've written in the dream as fast as I can, Temple Sweeper.

Are you here?

I am here.

Now, Head Monk, good monk, turn to the next page in your scrolls, and leave instructions for the jugglers & fire swallowers & all the others to come toward our monastery and this island's shore when it is time, come to where an old man and young monk are burying their pebbles & stones, and where, little by little, we find these Lost Children arriving around us, leaving their boats ashore, walking calmly out of the healed waters to the cave-temple in these hills, carved into the cliffs of compassion. These children carrying ink drawings held up in their hands. Can you see, Enduring Sound?

No, I cannot see them, Temple Sweeper.

You were there, good monk. A mere child of the wilderness.

An orphan. Whose mother and father trained you in languages before they, too, fell in these endless wars.

A word, a story, a world.

46

You, too, one of us.

Even when you have been in the fields of vanishing, stories return to the body, Head Monk.

Shall I write this too, Temple Sweeper?

In time you will remember, as I do now. And then, you will write as you remember without me. But this will be after many years and long after this body of a temple sweeper is gone.

Where will you go, Temple Sweeper?

They will be your words then, as they are our Ghostwoman's now. This is no other than who we are, who you are, Head Monk, Enduring Sound.

The Essential Story—
Boys Flying Above Clouds as Head Monk, Enduring Sound, and the Temple Sweeper Enter the Meditation Hall in the Morning's First Light

That was a boy you used to be, or know, or is it just a story of a temple sweeper and head monk—and not just a story—maybe a location in, into, on, or with consciousness of a day on earth. Some meandering about a meadow of stones, or now with monks of the circus, just in this moment, and only for a moment, you see it, too, meditating together in a monastery on a sea. A fire burning from the river into your eye so you see inside the body that is also our own. The body a story and more than a story, so you are confused, and still it is you and always was and is because we imagine the body—the body as words, of bone and marrow, of blood and ash, and also much larger than where you were when a boy and a girl pulled a child from the burning river and went onward on that day on earth. Or even how saving another life, you saved your own. Only a child. A child in his flailing arms, running through the hills. A boy and a girl leaving a small child with some monks praying at a shrine beyond the soldiers, and traveling further on into the mountains toward a circus. And these pages of a scroll becoming a burning light of those who fought, and their children who ran. A day on earth of Lost Children, of we who are we—and some got away, some escaped.

Here, in the mountains.

Here, in the sea.

Here, in the circus and theater.

Here, in this monastery.

Here, in the vast reaching of this body.

The brush stroke asks you again—how can we forgive?

The mute girl walks toward a pier to find a boy.

And he finds her in a circus.

The Ghostwoman dancing.

The children singing.

We are all of you.

You are all of us.

All of this.

Coming home.

Alive in these scrolls.

Scroll III

Then the boy stroked the ink of his brush across the girl's mouth and a bird of paradise began to sing.

And at the circus tonight we see them flying upward toward the moon on a starry night.

The Temple Sweeper Observes the Mute Girl & the One-Eyed Boy by the Mouth of the River

When the mute girl came and asked me to tell her the story of my life, I paused.

I glanced down at the reflection of the face looking back at me from the river.

I hesitated to speak, still this was the only truth I could say to her: But it is I who came to tell your story.

She stood and waited as the bees and butterflies flew about this place where the river enters the sea on our island monastery.

A blue heron and a white egret hovered at her side.

A fox and a crow emerged from the hills behind her.

Or is this truth, I thought for a moment, this reflection in the water itself already the past, and the girl is the future speaking from the brown twigs and leaves flowing atop the water?

The wind through eucalyptus also paused, as had the girl, who was playing with a conch shell as these thoughts appeared to take on shapes in the stone cliffs and cave above where I had, again, after many years, slept the past several nights.

As if hearing these thoughts, the girl again spoke: But I am you, she called from across the mouth of water, waving and bowing the way she had that first day I found her again with the Ghostwoman.

There was a shuffle in a light breeze as she stepped forward. Though we are different, we are the same, she said, breathing between each flicker in the earth's breathing—or so it seemed to me—a pulsation in my body, not unlike an ancient horn, calling from beneath my feet.

How could we ever be lonely? she asked, moving further into the water from across the other shore, somewhat shyly.

A being, perhaps a huge bee, I thought at first, a bee the size of a hand and emanating radiant light, was sheltered in the shadows from the cliffside high above. This is where I had slept leaving my cell in the monastery, quite late, and walking here by shadows of the moon. But as this bee flew outward—on that almost sudden streak passing overhead, I *heard* the image of the bee going skyward, heard it as a kind of vague laughter, a voice deeper in tenor, as if joining with the horn below me, calling outward from earth.

The wind in the eucalyptus blew backwards, and the clouds—I distinctly sensed this—their soundless sounds, too, swirling in contours of geese on the horizon to the south. The girl on the shoreline across the river.

My left hand trembling as I began to feel in the vibration a curious history of my own life with the girl before I was born.

Or at least before memory in how memory usually comes to this temple sweeper.

Figures of letters from our past lives in the mountains and deserts once written into her diary, a kind of foreign alphabet bubbling up from the mouth of the river.

This diary in my left hand.

There was something else. A tenuous and barely visible animal edging around the corners of the cave where I had slept these past nights, as if anticipatory, expectant, beholding. Then, a falcon I'd first spotted in the desert as a boy, then an elephant walking into the clearing onward across the bald mountain top east of our monastery.

A passageway opening between them, and the clouds parting? Or maybe you'd say just an old temple sweeper's musing in time.

You see me as a mirage, or as a language? the girl asked, waves up to her knees as she tread further in the river.

The blue heron and white egret escorting her, floating over the current, above these shallows and eddies of small white caps.

But I am neither a dream nor a vision, the girl said. Though these memories from our previous lives are real. It is more than nostalgia, and we who you see around you now, why, we have come to hear your story.

She blew into the shell, put it into the pocket of her checkered black and white shirt pocket.

Yet you say you are here to tell my story? she then asked, as if momentarily confused. What is it you have yet to remember?

Maybe a flicker of consciousness, a consciousness not my own, but one of another who observed the butterflies fluttering their wings above the river as she came closer, again taking the conch shell from her pocket and blowing into it, the water up past her waist.

What I remember tonight is that it seemed a trance caused me to lose track of time and place, of my body itself, of the boy I re-membered as a boy, the boyhood of his wandering in the deserts and mountains before coming to this monastery twenty-five years ago.

I looked down at my reflection in the eddies. It was the hag-gard face of an old man looking back at me, the one I have become after all these years in our monastery. And, indeed, the reflection of this very face appeared beside the boy's face, an image in the water of who we were before I was born.

Of this, I am still quite certain. A reflection of a one-eyed boy smiling back in a way your temple sweeper never had witnessed before.

Touching the corners of his mouth, the lips opening and un-sealed, the scars left on a face and eye so many years ago, after the soldiers came, before we began this wandering.

And yet, somehow, this very vision of a temple sweeper again becoming that of the boy. I could see this very boy as the girl con-tinued her approach from the mouth of the river. A vision of a boy walking in the waves behind her now.

A praying mantis was on the bank beneath a swarm of wings. The girl reached out and grasped the root of a bobbing eucalyptus branch where the boy hesitated.

How can I live without your story? she asked, turning toward the boy.

We are never alone.

The boy shyly turned toward me.

Can we tell this story? he said, taking her hand.

Where is my mind, I wondered. What am I actually perceiving? Is this in front of me now, or is it from a thousand years ago, another place and time, returning to me, remembering me? And as if translating these thoughts too, the girl walked to the shore. She bent over and these very thoughts began to take on the contour of the alphabets she'd created in the diary as she sketched them in the sand with the tip of the shell.

It has taken me many years to understand that they were of her own being and time. Yet some other kind of language still somehow distinctly of my own.

The alphabets rising, almost like human figures from the shoreline. The girl's arms becoming birdlike. The words then lifting slowly upward in what I can only describe as tiny, dancing, beings of light, fully covering the sky and clouds, if only for a moment.

I wanted to call out, to tell her this, that I finally had begun to remember, but my mouth, as if full of the pebbles carried in sacks from the sea, would not open.

A buzzing of bees and butterflies humming, trailing behind her as she began to vanish in the air. Beings of light. This I later came to call them in my own vow of silence with the monks of our monastery.

I made out a faint whisper in the crisp winds, saying to me: return, return.

Return.

So, I return.

Languages, or visages of light, or whatever you might someday call them, they wanted me to wander about this place. To listen closely. More attentively. To return after sweeping the hallways of our temple. To return after carrying the bags of pebbles and stones from this mouth of the river meeting a sea.

So, I return.

Every day I have returned.

And this is how I eventually remembered so I can tell you.

THE CIRCUS PLAYERS REPORTING
WHAT THEY WITNESSED
THAT DAY, LAUGHING IN A DREAM

LETTER IN A TREASURE BOX

In one hand she held the shell, and in the other, a letter she pulled from the treasure box behind the leaves of a fallen, washed up eucalyptus branch floating in the river. The girl took three steps forward, spun in a circle after climbing atop the root of a tree, the embroidered box in her hand, and something in her mouth's movement suggesting a different story, or alphabet, a language she had not yet spoken.

The bell from the monastery chiming a luminous emptiness, its ringer between her thumb and the distant forefinger of the Head Monk that morning. The girl wearing checkered pants, a boy's button down shirt, and a derby cap tipped to the side. The roundness of the treasure box resting in the palm of her other hand. When she opened the letter, the one-eyed boy appeared by her side, as if also waiting for its words before hearing another kind of ringing from the other shore of another river.

This is how we play it, she said, smiling, listening to the ringing of the bell, then again, and then a third time.

In the letter she'd sketched a portrait of imagined things, the things she loved and we love now—crayons, papier-mâché leaves, crisp-leafed scrolls, a bundle of poems and tales—just as they appear to us tonight in this magical circus. Beyond and yet bound to us.

In this way the man began hearing the passing of time into timelessness, the everythingness, welcoming the boy to come forth and tell his story.

Autobiography of a Dream—

The first thing I remember is a burst of light flying into the cave, he begins. The girl and I translating the diary and words from her mother. I had heard chanting outside the other caves, orphans praying in the surrounding hills and cliffs.

The light sudden, hypnotic, chaotic even. Yet joyous in its cacophony. I didn't know from where the light was coming.

I made a note to myself to pay attention to this.

Yet this was you, Ghostwoman. Now we know it is sometimes so. Though you would tell me much later, much later in the course of my training. Just as you and the Learned Sage Women will teach Head Monk, Enduring Sound, in his own being and  time. Mother of death, mother of birth, mother waking in the dream beside the girl, our translating the face of love in the diary together.

How could I have ever betrayed you? How could you ever forgive?

And yet, and yet, I have promised the girl to tell of our story.

And I will never betray us again.

The Girl's Diary Before I was Born—

Monologue of the Temple Sweeper Meeting His Old Friends Once More

The moment of change when the world was
no longer, and only, a word. A fragment
of history in these trees of forgetting and
remembering. The wooden bridge across the river
and the girl who once had been here, returning
to open the gate of the sea after following the
pages of my body, which once she saw swimming
down river, escaping soldiers on horseback. A vast
flush of pelicans and gulls dropping the letters of
her alphabet in the waves as the mouths of fish
surfaced and began to sing in human voices. Their
tale of ravage and redemption converging in a
chorus of flowing sentences that became boats
bringing us back home to this isle of nomads and
shamans and dream masters gathering around
the funeral pyre after the soldiers were done
burning our villages. We watched the soldiers
from the trees afar, hidden and hovering together,
these children merging in the bark and limbs of
trees. The boy and girl carrying a child as they
ran together, running faster and further down
shore in an exodus until they, too, vanished in
a wood and found all of these others who were
disguised and quiet as leaves on a windless day.

There was never a time that didn't include you. We are you too, the fish were singing. We sing their story.

O children of wilderness, this you will one day hear and learn to sing with us.

A Short Play in A Dream—

The Poet & Prophet After Conversing with the Actors Backstage

This is all we have ever come to hear? the Poet asks.

The quiet eve of passage, yes, the Prophet agrees. A voiceless sounding in a girl's diary.

Indeed, the Poet nods. But what else?

The return to sea and stones of laughter. The boy meandering again beside her by the river. This worlding of worlds, you might even say.

Really. Would you say it like that? the Poet asks.

She said that herself in the diary, didn't she, Poet?

That is what I heard. I'm just curious.

Curiosity and nostalgia are sometimes the same.

To this then, the Poet says—a great farewell and reunion in all the wings and greetings.

The Prophet grins, downing her glass of wine.

To this—our never-ending play of the Old Story.

And to life—the circus players and actors backstage chime in.

Aren't they the same? the Poet asks, scribbling in his notebook.

We will consult the moon and sun, the Prophet says to him. You know what the ancients say.

No, what do the ancestors say?

The stage is ready.

Then it's time to refill our glasses in the already broken cups?

We should offer them a toast.

Our way of saying thank you. You are right.

For these lives.

For our struggle!

The theater and circus players take their positions, ready to begin another day, mumbling under their lips, the readiness is all, the readiness is all.

HEAD MONK'S JOURNAL
& QUARTERLY REPORT TO THE ABBOT
ON THE UPKEEP OF THE MONASTERY

Now I go with everyone
I am them
They are we
Passengers met again
Along the way

These are the words the Temple Sweeper had written on the edges of the scroll one night when I apparently dozed off, resting my head on the desk between us for a few moments, as our Temple Sweeper had requested. When I awoke sometime later, he was gone, and a sliver of silver moon was visible through my window. A call of geese audible from the emerging dawn of our nearby river and sea.

I quickly washed and splashed some water on my face from the bucket of rainwater for cleaning, and sensed something was changing, holding the ladle in my hand. As if my face were no longer—or perhaps, not only—my own? I made a note to myself to pay attention to this.

In the Meditation Hall, I lit the candles, a stick of incense. Inspecting the room, I saw the sash on one eastern window needed repair. The curtain into the hall required sewing. Otherwise, all was well, and I rang the large bell in the hallway to signal the monks it was time to wake and come for meditation. I was not surprised to find the Temple Sweeper already sitting upright on his cushion under the window in need of repair. I was somewhat startled, however, to see you, dear Abbot, sitting on the cushion beside him, rather than in your customary Abbot's seat. Though by the time the monks had crossed the courtyard and ascended the stairs to the Meditation Hall, I found you in your chair, and signaled for the ringing of the bells and the tempo of the drum to commence the morning's ensuing silence and rise of the sun.

In chanting later that morning before assembling the work crews, something had changed.

—*NIGHT OF THE WANING MOON*

In these early weeks of our nightly meetings, it was impassable—or just impossible—to know what I really thought, or felt. As the Temple Sweeper has always been a mystery, how could I, a simple monk, fathom such things as those he spoke? It was ungraspable. But after you, good Abbot, called me to your cell and inquired about my nightly whereabouts, and cautioned me not to neglect my duties as Head Monk—while not discouraging my desire to heed to the Temple Sweeper's request when I confessed of our meetings—I was determined to go on, remain committed and of calm mind, just listening.

And then you asked me to keep this journal.

As I have never kept a so-called journal, or diary as you described it, I decided to include it in my quarterly reports on the state and upkeep of the monastery. This seems a most practical approach, and one of which I am accustomed and comfortable.

The main gateless gate is, again, ready for painting. The dragon and elephant headstones require extensive repairs after these last storms. I have organized work crews to begin before the next wave of rains, or possibly, snow. Our keepers of the boats have inspected the conditions of the nearby, small islands, and on more than one occasion I have accompanied them. There are no signs of other human activity other than that of our monks doing their mandatory solitary retreats and meditations in the caves.

And there remains no concern of soldiers from the mainland ever finding us again.

We remain invisible here, good Abbot, and no doubt, your and the ancestors' protection from the wars continue due to your steady and profound guidance.

I will add, however, that several of the younger monks told me of strange dreams arising in their meditations, and that these were particularly strong in the dark and silence of the caves. I, too, have experienced a peculiar strangeness of dreams since beginning to record the Temple Sweeper's scrolls. But this I am unable to understand, nor even write about now.

And I am grateful to you for honoring the Temple Sweeper's request for the privacy of these scrolls.

I would not be able to be his trusted scribe in any other way.

Though perhaps when you sense the time is right, you will speak to him directly on this matter? The Temple Sweeper is fond of reminding me—The problem is that you think that there is time.

But now I must attend to the head cook's request to help with the winter storage of supplies. The harvest was again weak this season and the fields quite bare—what, with the ongoing droughts and flooding when the rains do come. It seems worse each year, and soon we may need to resort to some kind of emergency planning. I have begun to consult with the elders as to what this might entail, and don't want to bother you with such matters unless necessary.

—MORNING OF THE WANDERING FOX

Spiritual Autobiographies— Back in the Days of Yore

A Dream of Masters

In the opening days of our journey into this world of red dust where you and I abide again tonight, good monk, Enduring Sound, I am a boy playing in the fields of emptiness, waiting for the girl's entrance onto the bamboo stage, the circus players and actors ready to observe and take in every gesture of her return from flights toward and away from earth. The boy studying another soaring of pelicans overhead, a fox and crow sitting at the edge of his cave—and yet, and yet—even this was not the first time in which I awoke a fingerless monk of no rank and followed the girl into the silence of trees.

> We were born.
> We died.
> We returned.
> This part is simple.

A continuous stream of coming and going, but the boy had forgotten his lines at the curtain of the stage. And the girl returned to help him remember with her diary that moment when appearing and disappearing continue endlessly.

This morning as I awoke in our temple, hearing the mingling of bells and the shuffle of monks down the shadowed, pre-dawn halls, the Abbot putting on his robes in the cell next to mine, coughing, almost as ancient as this temple sweeper, the smell of incense burning on the altar, and I imagined you again in this precise moment, sitting across from your desk as you are now, already rubbing your eyes, tired from your daily duties as head monk, patiently writing down your words as scrolls. An odd reflection. As I sat in the Meditation Hall this morning, I saw a sky opening in the east from the boy's own writings in the diary, clouds of wild birds in the wind above clouds as these very clouds first made themselves known to the boy as beings of light, trusted monk, Enduring Sound. In the dream we are back in spaciousness, before our window of time. Time, time as you think of it tonight, Head Monk. But before this monastery became a monastery. It was a thousand years ago before we were again born into the red dust. Flying on the back of a magnificent bird of paradise, dropping petals from its beak. Carrying the boy and girl to this very place where we began in the scrolls.

A thousand years ago. Flying on a bird of paradise. This bird, part-winged, part-leaf, part-flower, an expansive shore of spotted words and vast alphabets painted across its sides, intermingling in its many faces.

And chanting all around these caves of orphans. Shoreline whirling in a fierce wind, a sounding by the statue of the Compassionate Ones. This statue which is still here, that the circus players and theater troupe carved into the stone cliffs near our monastery a thousand years ago, Head Monk. And the Compassionate Ones' thousands of arms and legs dancing about the waves of the sea we walked earlier today, as you furtively followed me again. The flanking of northern hills covered in butterflies. The statue's luminous eyes still blazing into stars, echoing a sound of an arriving carnival in the midst of a chanting.

Our Ghostwoman's tent already open and ready in front of the girl's cave.

...

Wait, Temple Sweeper. You speak in riddles too hard for me.

Are you still here?

I am, Temple Sweeper. But are you talking about before, or after, the soldiers came?

Before we were born, good monk.

Is this ringing also from before we were born? Nor as far as this simple monk knows, did I exist a thousand years ago. But perhaps you speak in words I don't understand?

That ringing was calling to the one-eyed boy from the future. Just as it is now calling to you again, Head Monk.

In the opening days of our journey into this world where you and I abide tonight, good monk, Enduring Sound, it was ringing in this very emanation of the girl's body and mind. Her mouth moving without sound. The boy meditating beside her in a hermit cave about to take stage.

Here, in our sanctuary on this sea of nothingness, of the pages written in our bodies, this sea and your own hand writing down her words out of kindness to an old temple sweeper.

> Can you see her? Your candle has gone out, Head Monk. Are you here beside me?

> I am here, Temple Sweeper. I am here.

The clouds in our long winter storms over these past twenty-five years since they left me here. Even then the Compassionate Ones shedding tears for the surrounding worlds. And the mute girl carrying the boy back to the day he first saw these mountains and streams and the old master of the dream world, Hempis.

> Hempis, is this not what we have called him in these scrolls?

> It is, Temple Sweeper.

> You are still here?

> I am here beside you.

> I can't see you tonight.

> The candle is lit, you needn't worry, Elder One.

> I am writing it as you say it.

Hempis, I gradually made out his sometimes mirthful, even mischievous if daunting eye—talking to the boy as the circus players and theater troupe began to arrive in long wooden boats, disembarking on the shore, preparing to launch another carnival in this hidden shelter we call a monastery.

The Ghostwoman directing a crew of orphans as they erect a bamboo scaffolding on the embankment below our caves.

Before or after the soldiers came?

Before we were born, good monk.

We have had many names.

In the opening days of our pilgrimage, infinite moons turning west in their flight, onward in the House of Language. The girl's arms reaching out over the waves of sea in the mists.

Listen to their chanting.

I still cannot see your candle, Head Monk.

I am here, Temple Sweeper.

Here, touch my hand.

Hempis, yes, the Dream Master of Lost Children, in this awakening dream where we travel between the borders of existence and non-existence, birth and death, coming and going, arriving and disappearing. This eternal now. The boy hearing Hempis calling on this very night as you write in the scrolls, and you and I meet, auspiciously, once more.

What did he say to the boy?

He said, I am here, and the child is alive.
He is safe now.

Then this is a good thing, a good thing,
Temple Sweeper.

In the opening of this day on earth, the village children trudge their way through the mountains and hermitages as the dreamer and dreams merge, traverse through scrolls, through your own monk's cell that once was a cave, through this very monastery, once a shelter, a circus field.

The home of our Ghostwoman and Learned Sage Women?

Not a speck of separation, Head Monk. Go glance out the window. The same moons

flying east over our island tonight, converging our worlds of past, present and future.

Do you see them, good monk?

I write what you say, Temple Sweeper.

Yet this is not a thing I can see or fathom. Perhaps it is my own poor vision. And is not your

own eye weakening tonight?

I am only one of your dreams.

If I am a dream, then you must be dreaming me, Temple Sweeper.

I am a simple monk.

It is true, Enduring Sound.

I am dreaming you, too.

In this very body about to leave the world of dreams.

The scrolls are writing themselves.

They are writing you.

They are writing all of us.

And soon, you will recognize these children of whom you are one.

Who do you think brought you here, Head Monk?

Who do you think wrote these words in the diary?

Here, here, good monk, the Temple Sweeper said, hear for yourself. The girl wrote this for you that day at the mouth of the river when I was looking into the water's reflections—

> *A key to understanding the mystery of birth and death while entering the House of Language, Enduring Sound, is when you are ready to include everything. That is the true you. You are only frightened because you think birth and death are real.*

Will you show me the girl's diary someday, Temple Sweeper? If it does truly exist.

You did not know the boy also wrote in the diary?

You have never spoken of it, no. Tell me. Are these words you speak tonight your own, or that of a lost diary?

They are the same.

But before this temple sweeper leaves the body, he will give it to you. Though it will not be yours.

There are many moons. And we are the same moon. Here, see for yourself, Head Monk. Take it from my hand.

Temple Sweeper?

I am here, good monk.

Your hand is very cold, Temple Sweeper.

It will not remain so.

Temple Sweeper. Where will you go?

I am here, Head Monk.

This is only a box of ash you give me
with your cold hand.

It will not remain so.

Am I to record this too, Elder One? For what you have handed me from inside your monk's robe? It is only a box of ash.

It will not remain so.

You dream a strange dream tonight,
Temple Sweeper.

Shall we stop here? You are, no doubt, tired,
Head Monk.

There are many duties in the monastery for a head monk. But before I go back to my own cell tonight, here—wait.

The girl has written something else down for you.

How could the girl have written anything for me, if I was not even born? But yes. Your scribe is truly tired, Temple Sweeper. Let us stop tonight, what you say is so. I am tired. And it is enough for this simple monk for one night.

Later That Same Night in His Monk's Cell, Enduring Sound Opens the Box of Ash in a Dream—As If Hearing the Bird Again for the First Time

In the opening days of our journey into this world worlding words, orphans walk their way through the mountain temples and villages as the dreamers in the dream travel through us, and the masters of war chase us in the dream. But soon, we find our way and through their blooded hands to the circus players and theater troupe. Hunted and chased down for our wrong skins, wrong names, wrong tribes, foreign tongues. All we knew was terror and anguish, but soon we too find our way, Enduring Sound.

The dream is dreaming us. Until we awaken in it. And the language of the dream becomes time. This is simply the House of Language, good monk. Here, look into the box of ash the Temple Sweeper has given you, look again for yourself. Your translation is just below the letters of passion you will not be able to yet decipher, but this is written for you, as are these ink drawings coming back from timelessness.

A key to understanding the mystery of birth and death while entering the House of Language, Enduring Sound, is when you are ready to include everything. That is truly you. If you think you can say it, you miss by

a thousand miles. Yet everything says it. You
need not be frightened of birth and death.

This, a letter I've written to you
long before you were born.

But there are many others.

This everythingness of our dancing together, again.

The Mute Girl's Diary

In her diary she had pleased the stones. The girl understood this. The new alphabet taking shape in her mouth and translating into the boy's body that day he again took to the bamboo stage, forming a more sure language of silence and forgiving, then rising from the grain of paper in her hand as a voice at once urgent yet calm in its lack of self-being. Hempis had once told her while strolling along the shore: in your diary you will please the stones. She felt no need, no need at all, to ask the Dream Master to explain this, as the sentence's demeanor was as palpable as her own torn shoes on dirty feet while walking out of the boy's cave, as palpable as the touch of the cotton shirt on her own skin, or this red hat and funny pants given by the circus people the day they found her, then finding the boy finding her again and taking her to the river with the Ghostwoman.

So from this day forward this is how she understood words. And a stillness as thin as air opened in her breath as she strolled the shore, searching yet once more for the boy who was again hiding in the cave, turning away from, and forgetting, our suffering. This, the Ghostwoman had tried to teach the boy when he first arrived in the mountain's shelter of a circus and theater troupe.

The river of love and the river of suffering are the same,
the Ghostwoman said.

The voice—whose voice? still the girl recognized it—the voice that of her mothers and grandmothers throughout time. The Ghostwoman she herself would someday become. And the voices of their slain brothers and sisters and friends passing further into the return. She had thought this first thought when meeting the boy again—and in that very moment of her own fleeting thought—the boy had startled her, stepping out from inside his cave, ready to walk to the bamboo stage now ready.

And pleasantly so, she thought this too—the boy then brushing his fingers over her muteness, as always, while the five rivers of their previous lives soared from the page she had written in her diary that morning, entering the clouds of unknowing.

The girl did not wonder how the clouds could speak her words.

Rather, she sensed they spoke them for her when she glanced at the sky.

> *By now we clouds know your many names*
> *and the naming of a thing.*

Somehow the boy also remembered in that moment and began to walk toward the bamboo stage.

An enactment of the diary's imagination and forgiveness, of the mysteries from this secret book of her mother's grandmother and her grandmother and her mother before that, this secret diary that had brought her to the Ghostwoman on the eve of the dawn before the soldiers came. A slaughter in the fields. The river of suffering, the river of love. The end of suffering.

This she had written for the boy, reading her body into his own body—

> *So many seas, so many cities, so many deserts*
> *and mountains, and a feeling of this connection*
> *once more in the warm stroke of a boy's brush,*
> *the ink from your brush sudden and wet, cool*
> *on round cheeks, an almost ethereal feeling. And*
> *the glitter in your gone eye glancing at me by*
> *your hideaway cave. Your anger. Your rage. It is*
> *in this precise touch of the brush's bristles that I*
> *realize you have never really changed, nor remain*
> *the same. And it has always been this way since*
> *we first found each other on a day on earth.*

But how long ago, how many lifetimes?

Turning her head sideways to kiss him, as she always had and would, he was an old man whose face appeared as a long gushing river, carrying her back to some place that resembled our own life in the scrolls.

The ink, moist on her cheeks, as a tear from a gone eye, and the fish swimming up to the surface of a river to drink it.

Later, she would write of this as home.

What have you learned, what is gratitude? she first asks. And what does it mean–you, a mere boy again. What does it mean to remember and forgive?

What have I learned, the boy asks, rubbing his eye on stage, repeating the first question first, placing pebbles onto the bamboo platform from the inside of his mouth, turning again to see his own face with two eyes before he was born. And in repeating the question, all of these acts of imagination we considered while watching him in a vanishing act of return that the girl had earlier kissed onto the boy's cheek.

Finally, the boy spoke:

This is You, he said, with a quiet familiarity.

Yes, but this is you as everything you are not—yet as You—the mute girl interrupted, whispering in his ear from clouds, pointing to the sea beyond the riverbank where the two once played, innocently, and pointing all the way along the road to the mounds of trunks of trees, the albatross soaring above, scattering pronouns of the coming & going from their clawed beaks as the Ghostwoman, too, looked on.

All of them are you, are "I," all of us, our once lost circus players and actors sauntering about the bamboo stage before you tonight. And we are here, we are born, to free them, the girl whispers in his ear.

What have you learned of gratitude? she then asks.

What have I learned? The boy muttered this second question as well, placing more pebbles on the stage, and hearing the breaking waves of the sea. That you are already and always here, the boy says, motioning toward us all who gather at the mouth of the river and foot of the stage, tasting our own blood in his mouth the night of slaughter.

Of forgiveness? she then asks. Or even the root of the tree within it?

That this truth imagined, this imagination true—to body, thought, word, and song.

The boy knew right away these were not his words, but he spoke them himself, as if the words were the pebbles once filling his mouth. He stroked the ink of his brush on the canvas the Ghostwoman put before him, standing calmly on the stage as a bird of paradise appeared overhead.

And we at the circus tonight see the boy and girl flying upward toward the moon on a starry night.

Scroll IV

They have flown off somewhere, see they are flying away you say, there they go, they are flying off and gone now....

Yet you hear yourself stuttering the words, confused by the way your own mouth is moving and the sounds it is making, good friend.

What you say is true, Temple Sweeper.

Your own hands tremble as you say this—they have flown off somewhere. Yet they are right here at the same time. Beside you, inside you. Listen closely and you'll hear them in this sound before sound.

A STORY—

THE ONE-EYED BOY SPEAKS, HESITANTLY, WITH A BIT OF A STUTTER, AT FIRST

Once upon a time in a monastery hidden in the vast seas, they began to train the sages in the art of traveling through dreams. This they did surreptitiously, for though not a new art among the Old Masters, it had been abandoned long before my time. The dream world deemed unnecessary to the path and full of trickery, so for hundreds of years the Masters had not practiced it, and the art of dreams was gradually forgotten by most.

Yet our world's new and constant wars brought a time of endless bloodshed and famine, and even the decree of genocide was issued among the fiercest of the armies to murder their opponents' children.

Many ran, camped in the mountains, hid in the caves. Some of us found the traveling shows with the help of wandering mendicants and the circus people. Still others swam from the mouth of the river and down the ravines into the desert cities.

Some of us survived, resisted.

So much of the earth scorched.

Then came yet another decree—all of the orphans in the mountains and deserts and caves were to be searched out, erased—regardless of family or allegiances or age.

A war against all children. I was there. Any child who escaped the battles was considered dangerous.

Some of us banded together, roaming aimlessly in packs, growing stronger through the winters, even ambushing and killing a few soldiers whenever possible, sometimes burning their villages. The soldiers captured and indoctrinated some of us into their war. It could not be avoided. These became child soldiers of the tyrants, and we killed each other.

At last, the Masters realized it was time. And so, in the hidden caves of this island where you dream tonight, a council of Old Masters and Learned Sage Women from a vast array of secret traditions gathered once more. There were continuous disputes among them—the journey into dreams releases its own ravage—but finally, it was resolved that if humanity was to endure, if we children were to survive, they would need to open their travels into our dreams.

Among those summoned was the one you now call Hempis. He, too, feared that we would become a hungry ghost, lost to our true home.

Yet we have come home.

You are home.

I and the mute girl are here with you, Head Monk.

You, too, should know, Enduring Sound, Head Monk of this monastery by our sea, that over time, these tyrants came to fear us. But instead of changing their ways, or listening to the pleas of the Masters and Learned Sage Women who tried to counsel them, their armies became more ruthless and intent on destroying their future enemies. Drunk on power. Drugged by their visions. Still, in the middle of night they came to fear us, even their own offspring, who began to rebel and leave their homes and fight beside us.

Stories flourished of rebellions on the mainland—even rumors of killings of their own parents and teachers.

And so, in this way the life a Temple Sweeper began, and in a tale of how he found you with the mute girl, an orphan herself, one who manifests in a diary's alphabet and visages of language.

The boy pauses, takes a ladle of water from the bucket beside him and lifts up the mute girl's notebook, then continues to read from the pages.

It is also true, and you should know as you carry on with your work, some of these tyrants, only a few in the beginning, but more over the passing years, began to murder their own families, for as it is said, and you know well from the teachings of your Abbot—those who live by the sword, die by the sword. Is it not so, Head Monk?

So, some soldiers fled into the surrounding islands around our island here—and they are still out there, Head Monk—determined to kill any they encounter. Be careful.

And this is why you are dreaming in these scrolls with me tonight.

It is why I have come.

The boy sits down and places his hand on his ear, sips more of the water from the ladle.

As for the Dream Masters—and soon so too for you, good monk—it was their task to find us first.

For if a Master locates a child escaping in the woods and forests, by foot or sea, on boat or horse, wandering in mountains or deserts—she might enter our dreams, instruct and guide us in meditations and the silence of freedom of the old teachings.

Some orphans have written their names in the scrolls and joined this quest.

Will you, Enduring Sound?

Many resist. I myself was not ready, nor sufficiently prepared for the battles ahead.

Are you, Enduring Sound?

These children had one advantage, even then, and more so now. The tyrants do not understand that Hempis and the others among the Learned Sage Women have moved through both death and birth many times on this isle.

Hempis and the Ghostwoman, though murdered often in their wars, travel on in the dreams of children. And though lost for a time, they found this one-eyed boy and mute girl.

And now they have found you. They are here now. Teaching the art of traveling, though not abiding, in the dream world.

Since you have arrived at this temple, Enduring Sound, many have died in the dreams, for as we have seen over and over—the wounds of slaughter are often too deep for one lifetime. From the villages and even cities of the mainland, mothers come to these caves, leaving their infants at the mouth of the river below. Then begins the Masters' journey to find whomever they can learn from or teach, be it child or sage. Among their words am I and the mute girl, as we, too, are manifestations of awakening dreams. As you are a manifestation of ours. Among the ones found in the scrolls, you too are among them. A child found in the brush that day the soldiers came. A child suddenly of no name or home or parentage or consciousness of love. Yet Hempis and the Ghostwoman arranged for your passage here. For in the sky and in the story, among the birds and all living creatures, the girl was already spoken of as an auspicious one. And as for this Temple Sweeper before you tonight, even the soldiers once witnessed his now fingerless hands cured with just a touch and whispering in ears.

So each day he carries the stones of the dead to this cliff overlooking the sea.

Yet you were found, Enduring Sound. You are alive. You may wonder, as I once did, how they could find you?

The boy closes the diary and walks to the door of the Temple Sweeper's cell.

Look for yourself. You, too, are written here, Head Monk. Can you not yet see? Though grief weighed our hearts, as it does yours now, Enduring Sound, and it is difficult to remember suffering—this is our story, the story of the Storyteller.

And now it becomes yours.

The Bell Rings Again Just as the Head Monk is About to Leave the Dream

You will sculpt the fine edges of the pain and awakening into a frame of remembrance.

You will be tempted to call this only a fictive certainty.

This no other than the House of Language.

The river of your own blood.

What do you most need of me?

This will be the last, and most important, conversation of our life.

Though when you remember with the Temple Sweeper, the boy will be ready to leave the dream with him.

The Essential Story—

The One-Eyed Boy Finding His Way to the Caves with the Ghostwoman

All of that was true, but I left this part out. This was the story my body was telling. Everything here as it is, the cypress & beachgrass, river & sea, the wound of words floating down river, the boy-monks playing on the shore and the face I saw the day of the attack: the face of the world. My body became a tree, a bee, a shrine I thought I'd been before. And it wasn't a story, or a thing, nor a tale or fable—just this being intermingling with the hands of others as our spirits waded about in eddies over our bruised tongues translating themselves in unknowing. There, there by the water, the stones looking back in a hallelujah of seeing us all, just as we are.

The girl waiting, even then.

Hempis, the Dream Master, waiting.

You waiting.

Before the troops came and murdered our families.

Still, even before this, I heard the flight of bees singing, soaring toward the sphere of heavens we made our own.

THE MUTE GIRL LISTENS

&the Brush Stroke says to the boy—

> The forgiveness of trees.

> We imagine the body.

> Consciousness & the body are not two.

> The small cavity, size of an egg, just below the navel.

The Second Brush in the Story speaks—

> Every story touches every other story.

> Stories are not us, they are only stories.

> All stories are true and not true.

> All stories are trees.

> All stories are sea.

> All stories are river.

> All stories are You.

What the Child Asks You When You Find Her at the River—

The Ghostwoman Addresses the Assembly of Monks the Next Morning

What does she ask of you? What does she ask you monks hiding here in the monastery, pretending you are not who you are—good friends, good friends—here in the scrolls as real as your meditations by the sea. Come, come a little closer. You will remember your own life in the mountains and the circus and the ones who brought you here. A boy and girl something of a figment of your imagination, & yet every morning you wake up waiting at the side of your monk cells, or a door of the moon, & sometimes only with one eye & a mute voice, sometimes the mirror of your own faces in the river of drowning where we reached out for you, and you know, you know it's all you've ever wanted—to let them & all of these worlds of suffering and healing back into the body you've forgotten in the story. The mute girl with a small bird in her hands. You were all there in a field together, just below blind man's bluff, & the horses coming & going as you flee down river and into the hills & on into an unknown freedom of jugglers' and dancers' and clowns' arms, and you know it's a place of poverty, a place of you now, just as you are. So many of us in the surrounding forests, boys & girls & animals & monks & spirits, so many good ones died in this place when the soldiers came, the torches came in the middle of the night when you weren't watching, sleeping in your homes—try as you will, you orphans don't remember all their names. Yet these monks and friends around you now, & how you found your way to this monastery on the sea through the mountains cut and scattered with broken bottles & weeds & blood & soldiers as the burning begins in your stories of remembering and forgetting. And they remind you, you'll always be free, but how can you ever forget our deaths? How can you turn away? What does this life ask of you? Ask yourselves.

Why are you here, good monks?

The Autobiography of a Dream—

Now, Enduring Sound, Read to Me, Please Read to Me Again From the Girl's Diary

& then the story turned & went
further down the river
where we saw words falling off leaves
& syllables of laughter spilling into
the water as new languages
of mothers & fathers & children
gathered in the sounds
& alphabets bloomed off limbs
off trunks off buzzing bees
flying up in voices of this day on
earth of whom or what no one
can ever really say because
the whole breath of the river is
roaring in a boundless
chorus of cacophony—
beauty & ghosts of caws once
unspoken & the music
of spheres of unknown
phonemes & prophets of Lost Children
playing all up & down the banks
of river splashing in your face
as you plunge into the waves of
water & boundless sea.

Enduring Sound's Journal Before Slipping Out of the Monastery to Follow the Temple Sweeper

As my nights with him passed as such, I became obsessed to uncover the secret that sculpted in time the mystery of the Temple Sweeper's words. Language is more than words, he said when I confessed this obsession, but you must go through words to arrive in the wordless. The nights grew colder, the darkness longer, and I would wear your Abbot's coat you gave me when just a boy, not so long after I'd been left at our monastery, an orphan, as all of the monks of our refuge, having somehow survived the wars ravaging the mainland. But in those years the soldiers' boats could still be spotted on the sea in their search to find all of the children of their enemies, and to slay them to the last one.

As a boy, the coat was my blanket, and in its largeness swallowed and protected me those nights I couldn't sleep, longing for my family, gradually forgetting even their faces, which I struggled against, and struggle to remember still. You gave me this heavy wool coat after I once more tried to run away, escape from this island by stealing one of the Seeker's thin, wooden boats. I had almost drowned after tipping over in the long vessel, and then almost died of pneumonia. But your coat, and the medicine from the Learned Sage Women who came to tend to me, healed my small and sickly body. The coat has kept me warm over the many years since, and now it fits me even better than it once fit you, dear Abbot.

From time to time during our evenings together, I have tried to offer it to the Temple Sweeper, and he always waves me away with a smile.

Die to the heat, die to the cold, he grins.

And, indeed, it does seem that our Temple Sweeper does not get cold.

—*A NIGHT OF WORDS*

The Brush Stroke Speaking to Enduring Sound as He Walks Behind the Temple Sweeper to the Graves by Moonlight Later That Same Night

What's most on your mind right now, Enduring Sound? What's real for you and most prominent in your hearing? The hearing a sound itself, an act of imagination, and not what you usually say to the others about yourself?

You can stay silent or speak, Head Monk. But please, please stay a little longer, and don't judge this moment when we again find one another.

We are never alone.

We are only this wonder.

I, too, am here beside you.

Don't turn away.

ENDURING SOUND
SPEAKING TO THE SELF OF CLOUDS
ON A RAINY DAY LIKE THIS—

TO WHOM WILL YOU TELL THE WOUND OF YOUR STORY?

What would you say to the girl in this very moment, her mouth star-mapping in this miraculous air, this ghost of a self, a little death & time, a glass of wine, a drop of blood in a shift of wind on a day on earth, and on a rainy day like this you see her passing cloud over hills & storks in air, still stones & swallows soaring wings & all the filters of leaves & bees leaving again as her bold hand moves & the body speaks from itself of itself & to itself where you wanted to say I love you on this day of earth, & day of rain, with these Lost Children.

The girl reading to you from the diary,
uttering through the bees into your ears—

How do you hear the girl & a bee as the boy walks through the fields of vanishing acts? A carnival. The birds quiet too. All rain. All reign. Words worn & smoothed into pebbles parades parables prayers along this blossomed ground of twigs of wood & shadows. The one-eyed boy wants to understand the question. That is why he has come to tell you a story.

What do you most need to listen to in your own life?

I was once alone as a child, the child says, again

crossing the river.

These faces in rain, all the pine cones

& sorrows.

And here again hearing her speak to these things
of passing

I need to hear in all of our lives—

A broken language healing

here in a quest

where all the sentences

stand up and say,

p.s. we love you.

The Brush Stroke Chimes In

I want to be a part of your name, it says to the boy
and then

the boy says to Enduring Sound—

One night on earth.
We walk like this.

A Word for the Abbot Tonight

Never once have I doubted the sincerity, nor authenticity, of our Temple Sweeper's tellings. After all, had not you, good Abbot, first asked him to become Head Monk, coming to me only after the Temple Sweeper declined with his silence? And even later, requesting for him to come forward as a priest of the heart and be one of our teachers. Yes, I felt the tinge of jealousy on both of these occasions, for I, too, still suffer from delusions for rank and esteem among our assembly. Yet this passes, as all follies do, and over time I have come to understand I am among the most simple of the monks of this monastery, and to this day I wonder still why you appointed me to this position.

Though it is true I am most watchful over our rice bins, our proper storage of water, of the upkeep of the Meditation Hall, and all of the various duties as required in attendance to and mindfulness of these things. Why, only last week with careful inspection I found the source of our recent shortage of water for the monks' baths. One of the river's amber crows had stealthily pecked a small hole at the base of the wooden tower. (I had to admire its stealth, and with the same stealth, I followed the Temple Sweeper along his path to the sea after leaving my cell by moonlight.) And then, why only two mornings ago, a new fox was spotted in the far side gardens, dragging away several ears of corn! I have vowed to find this mischievous fox, but our efforts so far have been of no avail.

Still, as Head Monk, you know and trust my commitment and resolve. This must be why you chose me. How could our Temple Sweeper ever have tended to such things as these. Sometimes, sometimes I even wonder if he simply lives in his stories, and this mute girl's so-called diary.

Or perhaps in calling him forth, you, too, good Abbot, you were trying to pull our Temple Sweeper away from these graves on the cliffs overlooking the sea where he has spent so much time these past twenty-five years while among us? It would have been clever, indeed, but the Temple Sweeper also is intimate with the silence. To doubt his sincerity or authenticity these nights of writing in his scrolls, often in sounds and even foreign languages I don't even recognize—this is nothing of which I am capable. It's just that, the Temple Sweeper himself has said, we all are a dream, a dream dreaming each other. And he so often rambles in the speech of a mute girl, a one-eyed boy and many other fantastical beings...and now, now it is as if they have entered my own dreams as well.

If it were not for my duties and daily with the monastery, I might wonder who I am, or if I am even real.

Or if I am, perhaps, only a page in his scrolls.

But who is speaking to whom when I write these words?

Enough. The Meditation cushions are in need of fluffing, and why should I indulge myself with such thoughts when your dinner is waiting.

I will bring it to you at once.

Still, I write in this journal you've given, as requested. Though I do not know why, or why you asked, I am curious about its leather and bone-engraved dragon cover, the hand-cut and sewn pages made from dried red and orange autumn leaves. And most deeply, most touched, by your telling me it was given to you by your own teacher before he vanished in this war on orphans.

—*IN GRATITUDE, YOUR FAITHFUL SERVANT,*
ENDURING SOUND

The winter at hand. The harshest season of blight before us, and his body weakening. The tremble in his hands. The blurring of his left eye. He eats less, only a few grains of brown rice with a few vegetables for most meals, which he now takes on his own in his cell. He used to eat so much, though silent, among us in the dining hall! And we monks see how he shuffles quite slowly and with a limp, bowing to his seat and rising from his sitting cushion—how the halls aren't quite as immaculate as he once would leave them. Do not worry, my Abbot, I have privately assigned a young novice to secretly sweep again after he has left the grounds on his sojourns. Please understand, these nights, how these long nights of our gathering over his scrolls are, at least on occasion, tumultuous, for me.

Yet some evenings when he paces across my cell as I write at the desk, an inexplicable and spectacular aura of a quite curious light emanates from the frail shadows of his footsteps and gesticulating hands—and in flickers, all of the voices he utters merge and float in the spaces between my thoughts. Their visages almost become as tangible to me as his own face, his gray eye and long hair, his worn-thin, tattered robe in the window's reflection, the necklace of beads he rolls in his hands and the muttering sounds, as if ushering from an almost rivering mouth.

He is still human.

Though at times I wonder.

If he has become spirit.

—Night of the Amber Crow

Scroll V

Hearing a wind of you. You who are you and no longer just you. See for yourself if you don't believe us.

The Girl's Letter to Enduring Sound

The elephants manifesting on the hill that day the soldiers shot. One of Hempis' many deaths in the circus. The seasonal vegetation—squash, cabbage, beets—below in the fields and the vanishing tents the day the boy again found me after weeks of wandering in the mountains. The Ghostwoman ushering us all into the vastness with the sounds of gunfire. If you crooked your neck and focused your eyes you could see this. The sage, Hempis, chanting, grabbing hold of the ropes from the bells, tumbling out of the belffry from the soldiers' bullets, landing by our circus tents near to where the boy was standing.

A belltower and tightrope, the jugglers and clowns playing in the fields.

The boy had just arrived—and he was confused.

The boy had once spotted these same six soldiers near the river as he ran—these six soldiers rolling dice and shuffling cards, drinking and smoking between the various slaughters throughout time. And the boy glimpsed them here and there during his pilgrimage through the mountains, having forgotten his name, forgotten his very being, yet carrying my diary in his escape. The vultures flying overhead as he walked and fished and ran through the cliffs and caves—before he met Hempis, or rather, Hempis had finally caught up with the boy with the help of his trusted amber crow and fox. On this very night. This very night. As when the elephants arrived at the circus, and the soldiers began their shooting, here we are.

The elephants bending down to the ground on their front legs, so we could climb up their trunks and onto their sturdy backs—carrying us all away with the Ghostwoman toward the sea.

The imagination of elephants appears for such reasons, and soon we would be laughing among them in the rivers. But on this day the elephants manifested on the hill in colors of saffron and white clouds. This much is true, good monk, Enduring Sound.

But what is betrayal, if we are only what we are, and how can we be other than these very soldiers too, other than ourselves and all of this suffering and slaughter?

The girl I once was asked the Ghostwoman this very question.

And in this way, I spoke as if not mute, and in this way I passed each day afterward, walking step by step with the Learned Sage Women, of whom I one day became.

Yet for the one-eyed boy, for the Temple Sweeper, the work was not yet done.

I say directly here for you to record accurately, good monk, Enduring Sound, we were frightened ourselves. We could see very clearly from the inscriptions in my diary all of the deaths witnessed, and those to come.

Of course, it had all been witnessed before.

And water is always in the river.

Don't try to push the river, I thought, when I heard myself saying these words.

Yet I was, perhaps, remembering my personal myth and reading the omens of the elephants as they spoke through the diary. This you will learn to do as well, just as you will master yourself and translate the omens and scrolls, good monk.

Stillness, a calm, a resolve to go on, this is what I heard the elephants on the hill whispering in unison, then chanting together.

And we will survive.

We have never been born and we will never die.

From beginningless time we have always been free.

These elephants were chanting on the hill for us, and it gave us courage to go on.

Such is the story of the elephants.

After hearing them, I wrote down their story for you to transcribe tonight when the Temple Sweeper leaves your cell, good monk, Enduring Sound.

This, you will do on your own tonight.

After the Temple Sweeper leaves the monastery garden and begins his walk to the sea.

This is the story of the Storyteller.

THE BELL RINGS AND MOVES INTO EMPTINESS

The monastery bell rings and moves into emptiness. The same as when the boy heard the bells ring in the ancient elephant caves after wandering the road of fear itself.

What fear is it though, good monk, Enduring Sound?

In our temple the bells begin to ring shortly after your morning sit in the great hall.

The Abbot passes as we bring our palms together, and afterwards Hempis passes too, as the monks' hands come down along the rows of the hall like the ruffling of a flag in the wind.

The black cloth of the monks' arms brushing their waists.

The drum begins—five soft, slow beats followed by the echoing of the bell, its sound continuing on after the dream and after the drum. Three rolls in sequence, and then the drum fades off all together as you sit. It is only the sound of the bell again and again, the chatter of birds outside, the shuffle of monks standing up and then bowing.

You know this all well, Enduring Sound.
You can hear the bell traveling into silence.

Into the air as intangible as your body's infinity.

Intangible as the sky.

Don't try to touch it, the Abbot whispers into your ear. You can't touch it even if you try.

You feel it in your blood and when your bones crack, you think the air is dry.

Crisp air on the mouth.
No murmur.
No coughing.

The monks trained in stillness.
You are awake.
The bell carries the mind and all of the stories
along with it.

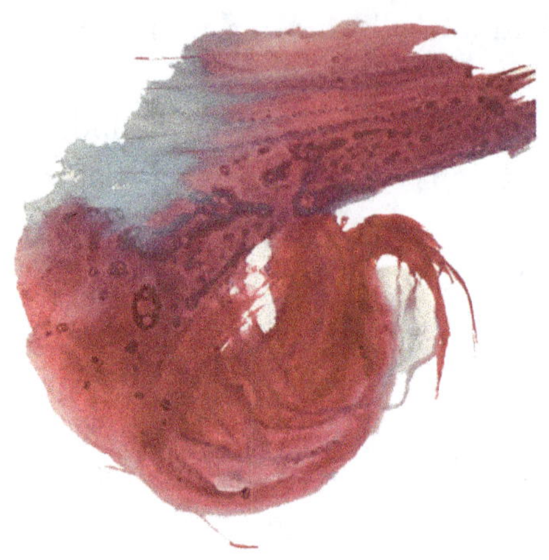

You count the rings, measure the pauses, feel your own breath—weigh the strength of each ring and hear the vibrations going further inside the organs of the body, little by little, disappearing into that place where all sound goes, where nothing is trapped, shut off, restricted.

Don't touch it, the Abbot says. You can't hold it.

Interspersed with the stories disappearing into fields, the bell is the tempo of breath to the brain, a pacing for heart, a container for memory, dream, heartbreak, desire.

In this temple, you sit.

In the dream world too, you can sit, good monk.

You study the world.

You rise and walk in meditation, short steps in sync with each tattered breath, each breath leading to the chant that is an orchestra of silence—a folded cloth floating swiftly up in the air.

Sometimes the one-eyed boy comes.

In the sitting, stories, even the beast of the killers and demons come. They stray into vision and dream, nightmare and terror. These visions of death, also part of you. The soldiers and tyrants come. Their dead come. Those you've seen in the graves, come. Those whose deaths you've witnessed, come.

The one-eyed boy comes, sometimes—also of this dream self.

All of the powers of rage and the power itself called into question—over and over. Is it not Hempis who whispers in your ear, bowing before the altar as you stand beside him?

Life is but a hundred-year dream.
Nonetheless, a thousand-year sorrow.

Later he will grin and raise his bowl into the morning light, adding—

But that was a thousand years ago.

A head shaped by scars, face shaped without one eye, face of distorted mouth contorting as that of a ravaged beast while the boy rises from the dark without words.

You hear his muted cry and beckoning.

You hear the bell? You ask this boy. What do you want
to tell me today?

His shoulders slumped and his face opened with the head thrown back as his arms reveal claws now, his mouth and tongue-less tongue—flailing.

You don't have to say anything, you say to the boy.
You can stay here, you say.

The bell has fallen into silence and the sun is rising over the sea. See. Seer. Seen. Hempis, or the good Abbot, says to you?

You begin to understand beast and boy are one.

This beast who made a horrific presence so that the boy could continue his life and survive the ravage when he pulled the mask off our killers and saw the face of all humanity. He plunged the knife into a soldier's heart as the soldier lifted a child from the ground. Then, the boy and the girl ran.

For the first time you remember.

This self that bears the name of the past, good monk, Enduring Sound.

As the bell begins to ring again, the boy and beast are startled back into the emptiness; the sun enters the temple, vanishing into hair, in ears, the wet eye, the moisture of lips.

The mute girl comes for the boy, too, good monk.

You see inside the body of a story that will return until the day you learn to love even this and forgive.

Another day will pass this way—the monks again will sit. The bell and the drum carrying the smell of hungry ghosts into the air with the blowing scent of silver honeysuckle from the altar as the bells chime in the courtyard.

A face traveling inside the sound.

Sometimes your own face appears.

Sometimes a killer, sometimes a monk.

Once, Enduring Sound, on a journey down the river, the one-eyed boy docked his small boat of escape in a wooded village. He had traveled far from his home, running from the soldiers with a child in his arms.

But somewhere along the escape, he had lost the girl, lost you.

And he was a killer too now, he had murdered a soldier, for you, and there was a price on his head.

As the boy got out of the wooden boat, he walked into the mountains and then through the gates of a circus built near the mouth of a river by the sea. Entering past the tents and strolling the grounds, the boy saw her, saw the Ghostwoman, for the first time.

Hempis' fox and crow behind her.

This Ghostwoman says to the boy—

The boy looked up at the circus tents and recognized one of
the girl's many faces in the Ghostwoman's own face.

Then, in that very moment, he saw another face. The face of a
strange monk, swinging in a belltower just beyond the circus tents
and children.

A strange monk, you wonder? But who is he?

The Ghostwoman pointed up to where this strange monk was
beginning to wildly gesticulate, dancing about in the belltower,
waving his arms in the air and calling down to the one-eyed boy.
He must be mad, thought the boy. He must know his death. Or
maybe this strange monk has escaped these soldiers, too, just as I
have? But the boy did not recognize him. This strange monk wearing a tattered wool coat, a dragon-shaped cane in his arms, as he
kept calling to the boy, pointing to the blood stain on his pants,
holding up his leg, grinning. Suddenly, they both smiled at one
another, and a great ease filled the boy's body. It was Hempis, the
very one he met in the forest. The boy waved back, and the strange
monk, as if elated, began to sing, he leapt into the air and grabbed
hold of the belltower ropes, letting the weight of the huge bells
pull his body upward. There, already up in the air, he leapt and
grabbed another rope, swinging to a smaller bell, and another rope
and smaller bell after that, and another, even a fifth. Soon, his body
completely suspended, floating back and forth in dance, a wave
of rich and resonate ringing music like none you have ever heard
rushing over the circus tents and Lost Children, and out into the
roaring current of the river from where the six soldiers were approaching, crossing the waters on their horses. His body swinging
gracefully, completely there in the body. A crescendo of bells rising
as the soldiers on horseback rode in, quietly, as if in anticipation

of where we were and of all that was about to come, and in a measured, disciplined, waiting.

Six soldiers soothing their horses' breathing as they trotted ashore, barely visible.

Yet the children saw them and began to run.

The strange monk's small frame still rising and falling, as if flying above us then, a spirit ascending, as the six soldiers dismounted quickly, positioned themselves in the rocks, not far from behind where the boy was still waving.

The soldiers took out their rifles and shot.

And then, they shot again.

And again.

The bells still luminously ringing

as the body plummeted to the ground,

and we—we and the Ghostwoman,

and all of the circus itself—

vanished on the backs of elephants

into the infinite space

around these vast worlds of our stories—

this story of the Storyteller.

Spiritual Autobiographies—

The One-Eyed Boy at the Circus That Night

Their merry story came with these elephants, and the elephants had their own voices. A language without shame or blame after Hempis fell and I entered his dream.

All the players readying for another dress rehearsal, even as the circus tents and props began to vanish. The editor and censor arguing over the ending. The Learned Sage Women reading out loud from the girl's diary. The fire swallowers oiling their tongues to keep pace with the telling, the timing, the emergence of all these tellings. As if this happened in a moment, and yet, an infinite moment. The crime, the crime—the Poet and Prophet whispered among themselves, joining us once more and riding in with these elephants, yet questioning one another as they passed the wine back and forth between them. And late, late in the night, the censors. The censors squabbling, raising their voices, retorting angrily about this and that, arguing that every story must involve a conflict, a crime and with a crime, a kind of confession, some plot or another, and most importantly, some revenge. And redemption. Though no one in the dream knew what their own crimes really were. Most of us were waiting it out until morning. Plots exploding along the vanishing points into poems of laughter, plays of rage, stories of becoming, diaries of dreams, and then—and then, all of these prayers, epistles, flights of function and purpose. Apparently, according to the editors, nothing was to be left out. Nothing can be left out, the editors argued with the censors. The Poet and the Prophet sharing a cup of tea by the time they heard this.

Of course, the censors fail in censoring anything as the telling just finds another way of saying what needs to be said.

I stilled myself, just listened. The human crimes under consideration that night uncertain of themselves. That's something I recognized, the uncertainty, and even denial. I sensed this way down inside myself as I studied the sounds of these elephants carrying us away and through the visions, past the mountains, the rivers and sea, the stars and moons, and to this very isle of a monastery, and the elephant caves beyond the cliffs, leaving the child with the good monks.

The girl and I riding on the backs of elephants, together again.

The elephants becoming their own being and speech, too. Some of the best of speechless speech, I thought. Though true, I couldn't understand it all while riding on their saffron and cloud-colored backs. I was happy, happy I was again with the girl. And the Ghostwoman began to read to us from a library of letters from these elephants' awakened imaginings—

> The imagination of elephants appears for such reasons.
> Such is the story of elephants.
> Hearing in this way, the girl later translated it as such—

> ...the crime was not loving the most despised child.
> And herein is what I and the other elephants,

these Learned Sage Women, have come to tell you tonight. The nature of the crime is the absence of love. When you translate our diaries of the dead, eventually you will understand the causes and effects. And until that day, we still and always will, love you. When the time comes, we will carry you on our backs again, just as we have tonight. So stay sturdy, carry on with resolve.

And without further explanation, the elephants walked us on and through space and time, leading us into the fields of what Hempis later explained to the actors and circus players as hereness.

Enduring Sounds' Journal and Mid-Winter Quarterly Report—

Scrolls or Mistranslations? By way of explanation to our Abbot

Our voices the same, good monk
Only here, in their stories—
The masters of light
They gave us forms and words
In a moving circus dance
Yet we are them with each breath
And ball of flame
We blow from our mouths
Do not be confused by death

As you have now seen with your own eyes, dear Abbot, and from the few scrolls the Temple Sweeper has allowed me to show you—seen from the words written from our nights together—our Temple Sweeper often talks in a jumbled, you might say, confused, or almost pure, form of speaking. On more than one occasion, his voice has held a certain melodic hypnosis over me, and I drift off into the clouds, and then the Temple Sweeper has to wake me. To speak forthrightly, it is nearly impossible for me to always follow, or comprehend. Our Temple Sweeper, why, he frequently changes languages in mid-sentence! And hardly ever knows which language he himself is using when I make him stop and ask him. As if all languages merge into one. But I am no translator, my Abbot. Nor have I studied the art of words. In these moments all I can do is to transliterate his sounds, certain tones of his voice, phrases or even caws. You must remember, though you had me trained as a boy after giving me your coat, trained by the most learned of our good monks, who can read and write, I have had no true or formal learning.

I remain a simple monk.

Still, on other nights, the Temple Sweeper's voice moves as if
in winds into a series of cadences, almost animal-like, then as
if out of ancient bird calls, or those of an owl and albatross
flying through the murmurs of the various fish from our sea of
nothingness—and then, I can suddenly, miraculously, understand
him. In these flickers I hear a kind of humming, untold tales and
stories, a strange poetry or song, winding bells, or sometimes,
foreign chants, mantras from the ancestors' texts I have not been
trained to read.

So, as I have told you before, good Abbot, I have, no doubt, failed
him.

I am failing our Temple Sweeper. So why continue this journal?

The Meditation Hall has been mopped. Our bowls washed.

The kitchen monks are content with the new rations.

The novice monks grumble, but are happy their cave retreats
are complete for the winter. Our gateless gate has been freshly
painted. The dragon and elephant headstones repaired.

Only we have yet to locate the mischievous crow and fox, they
too have probably retreated to the caves and we will find them in
the spring.

Yet I should report to you that no matter how discouraged or
tired I become in writing for our Temple Sweeper, he urges me,
all the same, to go on—just go on, he says in his faint voice. Just
continue on with me night after night, breath after breath. Write
whatever you hear inside your body and listen more closely to the
letters of the sounds themselves, he says, which he sometimes calls
the sound before sound, referring to the mute girl's alphabet when
I say I can do this no longer.

After his death, which cannot be long off now, and with your permission and help, good Abbot, I hope to cross over this vast sea from our monastery isle and consult with the Learned Sage Women who survived the war on children and remain in the hidden stretches of the mainland.

This is my request to you tonight.

I hear their schools, almost like temples—or what I was told once were universities—are havens for books in deep, caved-libraries, and that these small schools and sects are, indeed, spreading throughout the mountains and on into the sacred grounds of the desert far beyond our knowledge of place. These women sages' wisdom admired by all. Will you send me there, dear Abbot?

I will return your coat if you say yes. And, after all, I have done as you have requested for many years now, even writing in this journal, which creates considerable distress for me.

Will you send me with the Seekers to find them? I see their thin wooden boats have again arrived.

And how else might I finish the Temple Sweeper's scrolls?

I should say that it will only be with your guidance that I will be able to find them with the Seekers who can lead me across the sea through the mists of clouds to these tucked away abodes on the mainland. Do you trust me? Though perhaps first you will instruct me, and reveal to me why these Seekers who endured and also survived the slaughters—why they were not joined to these learned sects, yet continue to visit with us here on this isle. This, no one has told me. Will you?

The Temple Sweeper himself does not speak of such things. A mystery. Too many mysteries, my Abbot! You must break your recent vow of silence and instruct me. And tonight, as I write in this journal, tell me why I am still hesitant to speak of my true feelings. Why should it be so difficult for me? When I confessed this to him, the Temple Sweeper told me with time it would happen, that all of these feelings will emerge and also pass in time.

All the same, I think it is of no consequence. You see, in the end, or thus far with our Temple Sweeper throughout these changing moons, I have only been able to translate roughly one half of the Temple Sweeper's utterances in these fragmented scrolls.

So, of no consequence. Still, why—just the other night, I, perhaps, found out why. Found out from the Temple Sweeper himself. It will become my own pilgrimage in the words to complete the scrolls, on my own, he said to me as I stared into his face across the table by candlelight. And by then, the Temple Sweeper said, by the time it is revealed, my visitations in your dreams and visions will be in the realm of no time. And not only you will be able to hear and see them when I depart this body.

Can you hear or see them, good Abbot? If so, will you end your own silence and tell me what you do hear or see?

How much time has passed, I wonder myself, as I look out the window at the sea tonight and write in this journal, alone with the voices, I wonder what in the world ever was time? Yet I have begun to remember some things—the face of my mother and father...of others. This encourages me. These journal notes then, may I call them my mistranslations, and the same with the scrolls I write for our Temple Sweeper? It is impossible for me to continue otherwise. As you see, I have not been properly prepared for such a task. It is not really my fault. And besides, my own eyes are weakening.

I am filled with uncertainty, regardless of what our Temple Sweeper says, so perhaps you will help guide me when he leaves this body of dust?

—*Night of Unknowing*

Head Monk, Enduring Sound, Friend of Our Temple Sweeper, The 11th Month, 1st Day, Year of the Elephant

Letters to the Reader
From The Temple Sweeper

A stone in my hand, a stone that is not my own, a stone look-ing back at the sea tonight. The stone sees. Our Head Monk, Enduring Sound's hand writes. Or must I tell someone and you are the only one who will hear in the darkness and understand the laughter coming from the earth.

A mouth of the earth.

Maybe the ravage began earlier. When I began the dream trav-el, I was only a boy. It was my charge to find more of our Lost Chil-dren and to help deliver them to the circus for the Ghostwoman. Yet I went astray. A rage took control of me, and over time, I dis-covered a path, a portal into the tyrants' dreams. In this way, my life as an assassin began.

Or maybe the scrolls began when I saw the soldiers kill a child for the first time while a girl was sitting beside me on a train. It was during the beginnings of the war on children, and huge, ominous vultures flew in the air. Many of the elephants grew sick. Dolphins began to die. The monks hid in the caves. Our schools were shut-tered. I was on a train with my family on our way to my sister's wedding.

They shot the girl sitting beside me first.

They didn't ask for her ticket.

They shot her in front of all the passengers to show what might happen to them if they did not obey. When my father rose up, he was the next to be shot. Then, my mother.

Finally, my sister.

I did not get up.

Almost human, these dreams. Like the story of the cypress tree outside the monastery window that talks to me in my dreams. An old man waiting. A cypress tree without intention and like this wandering monk now, without identity. Even those parts of your body that have vanished return in the stories that are both true, and not true. Like the ghosts of words long ago spoken and returning without utterance. Slowly at first, and only in the sky or sea, these angels that flutter to earth, then there are days when the body itself overwhelms you with the secret you have hidden and needed to tell all of your life.

I see us sitting on a train in the desert on our way to my sister's wedding. Later weeping, lamenting is perhaps the word, my particular place and manifestation in time. Our simple lives and innocence not known to them, nor to me. And not knowing what had to be done when I first glimpsed the Ghostwoman and the mute girl outside the window as the train moved past the desert's beginning of bloom in autumn. Staring back down at my blood-soaked new shoes.

The prayer, it's a deep water coming from the earth, as if the words were no longer made of memory, time, and desire. The girl's bird of paradise later flying through the night sky above me. No longer a voice to be carried by the living, nor dead, but a reckoning of all things past and future, all things forgotten and coming in the infinite games of time.

Even when you have been in the fields of vanishing, stories return to the body.

I see the tracks leading to the station in the village that day. The green leaves near the pond of water the Seekers called oasis. The fog covering the sand on the windows of a train and the soldiers parading up and down the aisles.

Perhaps that is why Hempis never asked me to tell him when he found me again, when I, too, disappeared into these luminous stones.

For the wedding, our father had decided to take us down the mountains and over the border and out of our village, though he spoke of the birds we sometimes saw from the Vulture Peak. My father said many had died, and we must be careful. But in the desert where our sister's future husband lived, we would be safe. There were no reports of the soldiers there. They had not reached the deserts.

I was a skinny kid with hair to my shoulders, and among our people our family was well respected. My parents were educated in the cities, and we received abundant care and learning. The villagers admired my mother and father. They were called healers. But I could not go back. After witnessing their deaths, I could not return. I did not return. I went into the desert alone that night. Sometime, somehow, later—a strange desert monk found me. He told me that many weeks had passed since the train's ambush, and that the soldiers had fled. That I had myself been wandering alone, and he had followed me, and kept watch. But he cautioned me some of the soldiers were still in the desert and surrounding lands. I had, he said, first made my way with the other passengers who were thrown off the train to a refugee camp in the desert. This, I do not remember to this day. Even now, I only remember the strange, desert monk who found and cared for me.

I was missing a finger. The first severed.

An apparent urge to cut myself.

But this, too, I did not remember.

What I remember is wanting to bury my family's bodies and these soldiers had instead emptied their pockets and taken all of our belongings and burned their corpses.

Yet sometime during those nights in the desert, the girl and Ghostwoman came to me. At first, I thought my mind was lost and I was hallucinating. This was not so. The girl who began to come more and more often left me words carved on a stone, or written in the sand, and these were the first of her many letters, appearing as if a mirage. She would read me the words, slowly, pointing out the shapes of their meaning in the sand with a stone-carved staff covered with shells—

I would have surely bled to death if this desert monk had not cauterized the wound. When I awoke that night and saw him, he was standing above me.

We must run, the monk said. We must escape here. You wear the face of a mere child and orphan now, and you cannot speak their language.

I do not know how I understood him, as I did not speak his language either. But for me, somehow languages appear in my mind as little beings, and sometimes, I do understand.

If I had not escaped with him, I would have starved to death. Countless others died in the famine that year. Later I would find their bones scattered across the desert.

Except those who also ran, and joined **those** of us among the Lost Children, fighting back.

Though I did not know this monk, I followed him.

And, as it turned out, he knew the trade routes and the names of merchants in the villages we passed through over those months. Gradually, by watching him speak with his hands, making drawings in the sand, as the girl did in my dreams, I came to intimately trust him. Though kind to me, I discerned the monk possessed a certain ruthless charm when we met others along the roads, even a few soldiers. He would give them money, which for a monk, he seemed to have plenty. Or on occasions he would chant for their well-being, if asked, and sometimes bow to his knees, humble, subservient. But for some reason unknown to me, he chose to help me carry on. Surely his own escape would have been faster on his own. I thought he stayed with me because he had been on the train and saw what happened. Or maybe, it occurred to me one night, weeks later when we passed another border crossing, it was because he asked me if I had seen the Ghostwoman and girl outside the train's window. This so startled me that I was filled with fear and thought to run as soon as I could. But I did not.

Instead, I fled with this monk through the long deserts and slowly along the rivers and into the mountain passages leading back to my people's land. We walked for weeks, and into how many months, I could not say. Our eyes rarely met, though we meditated each morning and he chanted. And every few days, he would shave my head.

Once, I drew a picture of myself with long hair in the sand and wrote, as best I could for him in the sounds he himself spoke, that I was not a monk.

A sly smile came over his face.

You will be someday. And for now, the soldiers are not killing monks. So, you are a monk! Soon, they will kill monks too. Then, you will no longer be a monk. When he would speak to me in such a way, I could understand every word. I remain unaware how, though suspect, he spoke my own language as a boy.

We lived that winter in a cold forest on the outskirts of a village by a magnificent lake with fishing boats frozen in its turquoise and diamond-shaped, iced waters. We fished and made fires, meditated in the mornings and evenings. He taught me to recite from a book of prayers he carried in his knapsack. My finger healed. During the day he made drawings in another book, and over time, he began to teach me to use the brush.

Then one morning, I awoke and the monk was gone. No trace. No footprints in the newly fallen snow. No smell in the place he had slept. Near our camp I found a small mound of skulls he had made on the frozen lake. As to where he gathered these skulls, I could not say. It was hard for me to imagine that he had carried them across the desert and to this lake in his satchel. Yet later it came to me that they were the skulls of my own family. They were circled by carved stones. Nearby were large boulders, stacked on one another, inexplicably.

By the mound of their skulls, I discovered he had left me the book of drawings. Looking through the pages I saw a hand-drawn map, a series of writings that I guessed to be a diary of some kind, though in his foreign tongue. And then I found a word written in my own language in the snow, just a few yards away from the book, apparently engraved by a large knife into the blue ice—

H-E-M-P-I-S

As I didn't know what to make of any of this, I gathered my few belongings and tried to follow him. To no avail. If he had left tracks, the wind and snows that came frequently now erased them. He himself erased. Though many other monks would meet me in my journey, each time I would say the word, "Hempis," they would nod, give me food from their bags, and a few even walked with me for the day.

Mostly I continued my wanderings over the frozen and tur-quoise water of the lake alone. Countless more days and nights passed. Spaces and time opened into patterns of the forest, the surrounding hills of the lake, the trail from the map the monk left me. I thought I would die from the cold. I only slept during the day, and walked through the nights to preserve my body's warmth. Then, on one of these nights, the girl came out of the darkness.

This mysterious girl.

She handed me a bundle. She appeared quite small in her coat and hat, a fur hat. When she handed me the bundle, I opened it and found three fish and a warm coat made of thick animal skin.

I glanced up to thank her, and no one was there.

I ate the fish.

And put on the coat.

On another of these nights, one in which I had made the mistake of sleeping, she came into my camp and woke me. Again, she had a bundle tightly tied onto a stick, which she carried over her shoulder. I refrained from getting up. Get up, she said. Or you will die here. My body nearly frozen. My hunger great. Some time had passed since I had the strength to carve through the ice and fish from the lake.

I considered the possibility that I was dead.

She began to open the bundle.

Seeing the meat she laid before me, starting a fire, I asked, who are you?

She took the stick and wrote in the fresh snow—

H-E-M-P-I-S. He is coming. Stay alive.

Before I could say more, she stepped back into the blackness of night.

In the bag left behind, there were three more dried fish, a machete, and some dried meat.

In this way, I stayed alive.

On the final night of trudging over the ice of the lake, I saw an open field in the distance and understood the contour of the lake was finishing. As I approached the field beyond the ice, there was an old temple of some kind I'd never seen except in pictures my mother sometimes brought home from the university. I carefully and quietly explored all around. There was only a little light from a half-moon in the flat expanse.

As I edged closer—and not without hesitation for there was some foreboding to the place in that night air and distant howling of wolves—I discovered a site of soldiers, and a stall of horses. The soldier who sat by the door of the temple, I spotted first. He appeared to be sleeping.

I recognized his uniform and the burn marks on his hands from the day on the train with my family. He was the one who killed the girl.

As I crawled my way up to the window, I saw other soldiers were sleeping inside. I counted six, surrounded by bottles. They were drunk and snoring loudly. By one, I saw my father's pocket watch and my sister's locket given to her by our mother.

The moon no longer above us, drifting into the clouds. The night air had darkened, gone black. I took the machete out of my bag and inched forward, bit by bit, terrified yet emboldened by rage, for what seemed like hours, on my stomach and hands, crawling.

When I finally reached the doors where the guard was still sleeping in a chair with a blanket and gun and a bottle on his knees, I came up behind him. My coat open and the machete in my hand. Afterwards, he slouched over with a slight moan. I slipped inside, without a sound. The other soldiers, who must have been drunk for days from all of the empty bottles scattered around them, died quickly. I put my father's watch and my sister's locket in my pocket.

Then I entered the barn and went straight to the makeshift stall that housed the soldiers' livestock. I lifted the machete and sliced an ox across the lower edge of its belly. Then one of their horses.

I don't know how many others.

Afterwards, I severed my second finger, leaned against the stones outside under the returning and curious light of the half-moon and awaited my death, which I longed for.

Sometime during that night, the one called Hempis had come to this barn and found me. Later he would tell me that the girl had helped him find me in his dream. As I awoke in the blazing sun, my arms and legs were numb. Parts of my body still sprinkled in blood. I was naked. The bulk of my flesh I could not see, for it was covered with mud and snow. A fire was burning below the cot I was lying on, which was suspended three feet in the air.

What frightened me most was the face. This one who then told me his name was Hempis. He was part crow and part fox. The crow's head terrified me as he spoke.

Yet he had cauterized the wound on my hand, just as the strange monk in the desert had.

Now I understand, they were one and the same.

You are not an assassin, the crow whispered in my ear.

Thank you for leaving two of their horses alive.

They will carry us on the journey when you have healed.

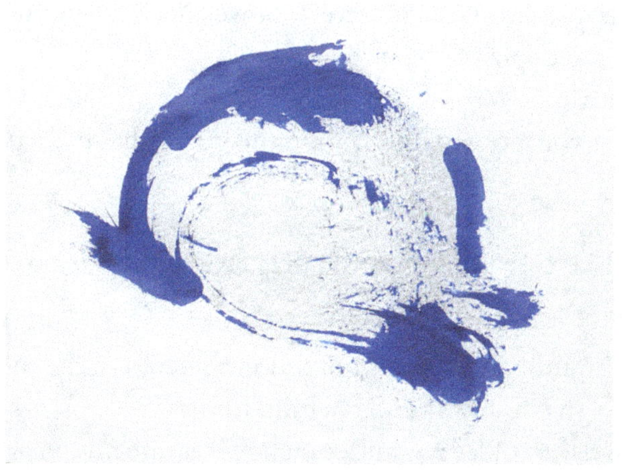

THE MUTE GIRL'S LOVE LETTER
TO THE READER OF THE SCROLLS

Just to come to you again, like a repentance.
To know it is true relinquishes the past & our stubborn
attachment to it. I have moved so far
in these years of deaths that you probably
think the Storyteller should be judged for the story.
It is not so. If you and I were not honest with one another,
maybe it could be so.

The Ghostwoman says, not always so.
Sometimes so.

And still, we are mirrors of one another.

The washed-up shore of wet leaves as your boat passes.
The monastery monks in these fields, both ghosted & alive.
Pelicans of winter.
Salt in the hand.
Often, I wonder.
I sense you would not have followed us if we were not
of the same spirit.
Our stories.
They, as you, are vast and empty, and our body carries them.

So why have you come this far?

When I crossed the river, the Master said there is no other
shore.

You are familiar with this boy who wandered in the snows.
You see the monks trailing behind him
through the wilderness and somehow, you are not surprised.
No doubt, you have touched your own being.
There are many boats.

The moon on the horizon says I miss you.
Can you hear it on this night outside of time?

Once, you held a lover in your arms, and later witnessed
the passing. The taste in your mouth.
Here we come in unknowing,
continue in these boundless rivers & seas.

You stand by the gateway of the book and question—
forgiveness, redemption.
You are only a child, you say.
You are only a scroll inside a scroll.
Yet deep down you know all of us as we exist,
just as we are.
We are of the same cloth.

And one day when you were alone and lonely,
you picked up the book.
You were strolling the hills, or in the library,
or maybe at home, reading
a poem or story where you saw yourself.
You came across a book and opened it
as you might open a letter from an old friend
you barely remembered.
You saw us then, and for some reason,
these things reminded you of yourself.

You even saw a boy and girl in the snow
and after reading a few pages
you said, I know this boy, this girl.
I have cared for this child
who I am.
We stood together once by the grave of an old friend.

Hempis whispers in your ear—you first experience
your own pain,
then the pain of the person to be forgiven,

and then understand that the imaginary
barriers between two beings
dissolve.

O, I remember. I last met you in the breath of your breath.
All of these ghosts & visions & dreams
are, in fact, all of us.

You could smell it in the sentence
as you opened my letter in the book.
So you follow.
You came into my life and the story's
entrance as if it were your very own, as if in its words,

you were tracing our history,
the scroll of our own human weakness.
And it is your own kindness you discover.
You tucked the book under your arm
and you started toward the circus.
You carry it close to your heart.
You live and create your own telling and untelling.

And now we are of the same, you and I.
We exist together.
We carry wounds, like lovers, carrying a newborn child.
We have learned to love each other, and now,
we will learn together,
how to forgive.

Scroll VI

Meeting you in the dream too.
Meeting us all,
alive, waking from the dream.

—*THE GIRL'S DIARY*

Head Monk, Enduring Sound's Poem to the Temple Sweeper on This Very Night

Dear departing Temple Sweeper,

Before the first light over the monastery roof,
you are rising.
I am rising—rising up,
the moon arising, approaching you,
you arising, Temple Sweeper.

I look at the empty space where you are not—
you are everything you are not, you told me once—
look into the darkening
shadow of a grapevine, into the grains of dust,
into the stones, still here.

The orphaned monks walking
these hills and mountains, still sleepy and not awake,
searching for you.
They are homeless—and everywhere we go is home.
Yet you found yourself, and find us,
in the mountains and clouds.
To see your golden body lifting in wind.

The clouds shift past the girl's flying bird of paradise,
and again tonight, I glimpse the boy
of my own lost childhood before he became this one
called Head Monk, Enduring Sound.
That day you and the girl pulled a child
from the flames
when the soldiers swept into the mountains,
and the wars

on children began. Before you carried me
here to this boundless sea and monastery,
beyond land and here in faint shadows of rain.
A faceless moon reflects the stream's water, an
astonishing abundance of fish.
My own voice returning.
A misty figure traipsing beyond the hills and cliffs,
the crescent-domed caves to north, south, east
and west.

I see you with my ears.
I hear you with your eyes, Temple Sweeper.
I move with your shuffling footsteps
in the silence
of the halls of our monastery.
Where do we go from here?
Why did you not come tonight?

A Voice of Awe—

The Ghostwoman Speaks

A girl stands by her elephant on a cliff overlooking a sea with arms outreaching the horizon.

I am this girl's mother, good monk, Enduring Sound.

The elephant speaks and hearing it, you find it strange that you understand it is my voice?

Beneath your window tonight, Enduring Sound, in the moon, here we all gather.

A sky reaches down to you, as the Temple Sweeper calls you to our scrolls.

We, this sky.
This very moon.
This very orphan.

Just as you, a boy awakening from the dream,
and the boy a dream.
All of the monks in this monastery were one Lost Children.

Orphans of the Moon, she wrote.

The girl?
Dragon. Elephant. Dolphin.
My daughter and child.
Bird of paradise.

Each morning ancestors gather in the pre-dawn light on the banks of this sea, awaiting you. We sit together, backs to the shore of moon, bowing to both rain and sun, chanting in these hues that drift along the crest of the waves into the caves of a carnival circle.

You among us in this very letter to you, Enduring Sound—our shedding skins growing closer to one another. Time again transcends us, meets the other sides of our true nature. To cross this sea is to be a sea.

And if the Temple Sweeper fails to tell you, let me tell you now. We await you, as we await him now, Enduring Sound.

You should know, the soldiers took the girl from me long before you became an orphan-monk and scribe. Still, the girl and boy found you first. Soon, you will remember us, and how we brought you to this monastery with our traveling troupe of children of the theater, children of the circus—for the third, and the fourth acts.

Here, our former bones buried by the cliff-side, carried by the Temple Sweeper across time. The bones cleaned endlessly in the coming and going. The Temple Sweeper mastered the stones, and Hempis taught him well.

A master of the stones as you will someday be.
A simple monk.

When he lifts the final stone, this will be his own.

Please, with all of your attention and intention, with care—continue the ceremony for all of us who have passed before you as you tend to the stones of the world. The stones of words. The words of dreams. The dreams of stories. Just as everything you carry—the scrolls in the book you write yourself, the robes you wear on your back, the food in your stomach, the compassion of stones.

All of it exists and doesn't exist.
This is for your benefit.

We are not ghosts.
Do not be mistaken.
This is no tragedy.
We are here.
Singing.
We are alive.
We forgive.

The moon on the horizon
a crest of your face.

Enduring Sound, I would have liked to ask you so many questions when you were a boy. But we had no time. We had to escape and bring you here with our circus players, leave you with our friend, the Abbot, and go on. Now you will ask these questions for yourself, for us, for the scrolls. And the scrolls will respond, as the answer is in the question.

A good day to make the great death.
A good day to live.
Take this letter we have prepared for you, Head Monk.
It is only one of many omens you will translate.

And observe when you begin your morning duties: something is changing in the weather, something is beginning. Have you noticed? Magnolia, dogwood, and even the plum trees showing hints of green. Winter, winter is passing. The snows less frequent as spring again whistles. Something is changing. It is you who are changing. You sense a slight hesitancy, even a sadness in it, though you have helped bring our life into being in your very meditation tonight. Go forward. Discover this joy.
Ghostwoman?
Yes, Enduring Sound.
In this morning's dawn I watched the faces of the past become the present, manifesting over and over in this curious world. Even my eyes looked back at the one sitting in the temple, as if astonished to hear this letter in my meditation.
It is good that you speak to me as such, Head Monk. This is the very awe of your own face.

No escape.
All escape.
Nothing to escape.
No one even sitting here.

Leaving only wonder,
curiosity,
gratitude,
love.
This continuous transmission.

Enduring Sound?
Yes, Ghostwoman.
Tell me, Enduring Sound. Has our Temple Sweeper told you that I am also the one who out of silence writes with the girl in her poetry. Why I, too, dream in the ringing of bells. I, too, find you in meditation like birds of thought. And you will find us all in these poems when you take them out of your scrolls and read them again on the day of your passing from this body, hearing the bird of paradise once more, as if for the first time. Enlightenment holds onto nothing, not even the truth, the sage said. Finish our story. It is yours. The Temple Sweeper and you are becoming one now.

How could you fail to meet us all again?

MUTE GIRL TO THE HEAD MONK
THE NEXT MORNING

You fold the letter my mother gave you into the shape of a boat, carefully place it into the official document envelope, lick the glue of its thick paper, and scoop a handful of ash from the stone that you suddenly recognize as bearing my mother's original face and nameless name. You seal her letter with a candle, drip wax, say a short prayer, a mantra, and put the page in a glass bottle into the river, bowing to the boat of words.

You've memorized the letter, and will take its words with you, trusting the official document will reach the mainland and find its way to the caves of the Learned Sage Women when the time has come for you to, again, go to them.

It is important that you truly embody this. It is why the circus people helped us to bring you here. It is your past, and now it becomes your future.

The Learned Sage Women await you.

As for me, and the one you call Temple Sweeper—you are so much more than the child we brought here, Enduring Sound.

So today, as you dust the Meditation Hall, and later go to inspect the surrounding isles of caves for the monks' solitary retreats, pay particular attention to this.

You are not alone.

FREEING GHOSTS

Archival Drawing Found in the One-Eyed Boy's Cave by
Enduring Sound and the monks of our monastery with these
words inscribed by our Temple Sweeper.

—*HEAD MONK, YEAR OF THE DRAGON*
ENDURING SOUND'S JOURNAL

The Dream of Masters—

The boy, trailing behind Enduring Sound, who follows behind the Temple Sweeper, calling out to the orphans who listen from the Meditation Hall, awaiting their return

In the opening days of our journey into this world of red dust, I am a boy playing in the fields. A thousand years ago, good monks. Though you don't remember, all of you monks of this monastery, too, were there on this auspicious occasion.

I am the boy, and the one you know as the mute girl is one of the Lost Children without a name. Just as I and you all were among these ancient, perennial children in these scrolls your Head Monk writes now. And again, here the Temple Sweeper is among you, a boy with only one eye, flying on the back of the girl's bird of paradise.

Though you still can only see me as a withered old Temple Sweeper?

This will pass, my friends.

In the days of old, I and the other children in the dream walk the road of the deserts and mountains to find our way home, to this very monastery on the sea, to a freedom and new birth, for we have made our way through the countless villages of the dead, the countless moons, the prisons of outcasts where they put us for our so-called deformities, our broken bodies, our bloodlines, the unwanted colors of our skins or eyes, our homeless domains in the power of those who bring violence to our bodies. The tyrants shunned us for our poverty then, as they do now. The most despised children. And you, too, among us, good monks of this monastery on a sea of emptiness. You escaped and entered beyond the open valleys with Hempis and the Ghostwoman as your guides, a girl and boy as their apprentices.

This mirage of separation is terrifying until we finally realize we do not exist in the way we once thought.

You, Head Monk. And all of these monks in the assembly, meditating tonight as you try to follow the Temple Sweeper on his journey home. You would not cry if you knew where he is going. If he did not know where he is going, he would never leave you.

You and the girl and the Ghostwoman and Hempis. These Lost Children. As a Master said, when she enters such a powerful meditation, the elephants and dragons become aware of their former lives.

You are still dreaming the dream as you speak as such, Temple Sweeper?

The language of dream is time, Head Monk. This is the House of Language. This awakening inside and from the dream itself.

Here, hear for yourself the words in her diary—

In the opening days of the journey, the boy first
glimpsed you, good monks. Saw you, too, there
among the wanderers and seekers, the circus
players and elephants. When he first glimpsed
the dream-world, the mute girl took him to the
House of Language. When you first truly looked
into the girl's eyes, she painted a bird of paradise
on his chest. When she first kissed his one-eye,
the boy flew his eye into the land of deserts
and mountains. The orphans running from the
soldiers, just as they still run today. Yet when
the boy first began to travel in the dreams, he
saw us just as we were a thousand years ago. And
these meditations contain the secret, the story,
the fable, of how we defeated them, defeated
the tyrants who persecuted the earth, how we
overcame their power with compassion. Study
these oracles and you will find the wounds,
secrets, and desires, and we will heal them.

You awaken in the dream as an enduring sound.

We were born.

We die.

We return.

This is the book of our forgiving.

Even as a boy, again in this very life, even in this
vast wilderness a thousand years later—yes, here
in this world with the girl kissing his eye and
painting a figure of a bird of paradise on his body,
he dreamed of all of you monks of the monastery

vanishing into the plains among the brush strokes
of ink before you in the cliffs of this sky tonight.

If Enduring Sound is writing beside me once
more, their persecution of the Lost Children
will be healed and betray us no longer. For
as with Hempis and the Ghostwoman, we
will discover the truth of liberation from this
suffering. Say it is so, good monk, are you here
in your monk's cell waking from the dream?

I am writing your words, Temple Sweeper? Or of a boy you
once were? Or a girl's diary? What is this dream, and who is the
dreamer? I myself confess, I am uncertain of everything.
Temple Sweeper, will you not leave us?
Where are you tonight?

I am here.
Beside you.
Inside you.

Now, we are awakening through the dreaming together. It is
time to go ring the bell in the Meditation Hall, Head Monk.

Head Monk's Journal
& Quarterly Report to the Abbot
On the Upkeep Of the Monastery on
Another Passing Winter

Now i go with everyone
i am them
they are me
fellow travelers
meeting again on the road
after all of these lifetimes
as we always have
no past present or future
in moons of rivers
in rivers of moons
right here

These were among the last words the Temple Sweeper penned in the margins of the scrolls with his own hands as I slept, having rested my head on the table between us, as he often requested, noticing me rub my eyes and knowing I was tired. It had been a normal night, good Abbot. Nothing different in any way I can note here. There was some diary or another of the mute girl, as usual, the boy, what he called the "essential story," and I have recorded it as such. There was a strong full moon shining through the window of my monk's cell. The light particularly luminous, and making it easier for me to see and write as he spoke and paced around the room—touching the walls, running his large hands along the desk between us, as was his common practice through the winter, then bowing three times on the floor after finishing some passage or another. Resting there for a few minutes himself. I suspect this is when I dozed off, seeing him lie back, propping up his knees, as his spine ailed him of late, probably due to the unusual cold of this passing winter, and no doubt the cause of his limp and increased shuffling through the temple, in and out of the Meditation Hall, and on those evenings that I followed him to the caves in the cliffs overlooking the sea.

Yes, it was a normal night in this way, good Abbot. He had asked me—as surely you had encouraged him to do so—if I had properly attended to my duties in the upkeep of our monastery. And he asked about the health and practice of the younger, novice monks and orphans who have been arriving on our shore in greater numbers through this harsh season. I assured him I was tending to their care, and that all was well. This always made him happy, and he would come pat me on the shoulder and say—well done, Head Monk.

Please do not neglect this.

Though your attendants have asked me several times during your vow of silence this winter, I can remember nothing else of consequence from the night. He did seem at ease. But he was often as such, laughing and repeating—

Maybe yes.

Maybe no.

Not always so.

Of course, I was additionally fatigued from my sojourn to the islands that day. With the winter ending, and the time approaching for the novice monks and their teachers to begin their solitary retreats, the caves needed inspection. We did our seasonal sweeping and cleaning of the caves, lighting incense and making offerings to purify the air and space. It is an always exhausting task, and a long week, but I was content that we had prepared the caves well. I was only disappointed that we were unable to catch that rascal fox and mischievous amber crow.

Already they are up to their old tricks! We got very close one day as we walked along the path connecting the caves, close enough that we could see that they were both one-eyed themselves. And this made me wonder, naturally, about the boy and the scrolls and my own dreams of them. These dreams have only increased for me—and many others I might add, this is no secret among the assembly. It has, indeed, been a strange winter of dreams, and I am hopeful for their passing. And what can I say about such things. Another mystery, you would probably say if you were speaking. Further I am not able to discern.

I will tell you—and it is my hope we can speak soon and you have considered my earlier request—that our searchers and those of the Seekers—throughout our monastery isle and those isles and waters surrounding us, have yielded no clues as to our Temple Sweeper's whereabouts. In short, we have been unable to find the Temple Sweeper. Some of the monks think he slid off like an elephant to shed his body. Knowing you have taken ill yourself, I dare not disturb your rest and will instead deliver this quarterly report and journal to your attendants.

The fields have been plowed.

The caves are ready.

The overall upkeep of our abode is in order.

Rest well, dear Abbot.

I am sure we will find him.

And that you, too, will arise and share our company in the Meditation Hall again soon. It has been somewhat difficult for us monks not to see you while conducting these searches and continuing our work.

But we prevail.

You have trained us well.

And I deeply feel your presence as well as that of the Temple
Sweeper, certain all is well and as it should be.

—NIGHT OF THE MELTING ICE ON THE RIVER

YOUR HUMBLE SERVANT,
YEAR OF THE DRAGON

Worthy of Love—

The Temple Sweeper whispering in Enduring Sound's ear as he launched the boat of the Ghostwoman's letter on the river

You will return to burn the grave of this temple sweeper when I am gone, good monk, Enduring Sound. And in the blink of an eye, yours will soon be among them. Another person of no rank, or need of one, to complete our tasks.

Carry the stones each day, even in death, even after leaving the body.

To hear the stones speaking is to marvel. Don't let anyone tell you the inanimate doesn't speak. If you listen closely, you will hear the voices of the world. Spring arrives. The birds return. To study the wordless words is to astonish beauty.

This body aches in the beauty.
You need not suffer.
Pain may be inevitable,
suffering is not.
Sun of miraculous compassion.

The boy, too, carrying stones. For the long unattended. To be honored, the moon has turned its face inward.

Glimpses of mountains & rivers are filled with laughter.
Dark blue berries under a bamboo root.
The Master once asked the boy, what is your passion?
Raspberry seeds along the limbs of the vines.
This morning the boy spoke to you these words—

My passion?
To hear the inanimate speak.

The Mute Girl Leaving the Diary in the Cave with the Boy

Dear You,

Day 1

For three moons I have heard the call to rise for
your coming.
Will you accept me as I am?

The one who has written you into her secret poems you find
on the walls of this cave. An old monk and yet while still a
boy, you too were named by your desire for me.

There is no cave of birth and death.
You still hear the sound, even now.

Day 2

I studied you traipsing this hillside each day. The ancient
ones of compassion carved into our mountains. These old
souls by the sea, wandering under an azure sky as the sun
reached its pinnacle on the cliffs overlooking our story.

How could I ever consider you other than my only love—
though we were only children?

Day 3

As a boy you would wait for me by these same caves you
pass now on your way home. You would wait for the orphaned girl left for dead by the soldiers. Wait for the girl

who arrived each evening as you hid in these caves, my body covered in leaves until I came no more in this body.

Just as now we await the scroll of our blossom in a dream of words. But whose words?

Day 4

So it is with the child, this freedom looming in shadows. In the life you are now departing you will travel through the spheres, Temple Sweeper. I will be traveling beside you in this journey of love. I have waited this long, and we have come this far, why stop now?

Day 5

The Girl Looking Up from the Diary

This is where we are, Enduring Sound.
This is where we have always been going.
If you knew where we are going, you would not cry.
All of the birth and death you name in the Scrolls of a Temple Sweeper—calling us to our true being without beginning or end. Our story will withstand, continue.
Just as the man you once called father is waiting.
Someday you too will return home.
But home is right here.
Perhaps you didn't know the mother in your own body.
The birth in your sound.
Or perhaps the one-eyed boy
again appears as he is.
In the word.
In your world by the sea in a monastery.
He has come as such, many times, as have we all.

And now you remember.
Your eyes are not so clouded.
The parchment I gave you a thousand years ago.
A boy on a mountaintop.
This very one in a book of forgiveness.
This one tracing our lineage back to the place where
we begin.

Do not be distracted by death.
Finish it.

In these stars that go nameless in water.

We are found in these words.
In this sound before sound.

In this ending that is the beginning.

Scroll VII

Birds of Paradise

Not Knowing

I didn't know what to believe, or not to believe—or what belief even means—while hearing these words. Those spoken directly to me in my monastic cell. Those that came in visions or dreams. Nor those we would translate later with the help of the Learned Sage Women. What does belief have to do with any of it, Enduring Sound—I would often ask myself—as I often speak to myself in this way. Especially staring out at the boundless sea at night. And then back at the dragon and elephant carvings around the cave of these hills and mountains.

Yet with the Temple Sweeper's departure from his body, some of the other monks began to experience the same dreams.

He himself had foretold this.

Of course, it is impossible to say now what I actually felt or thought, much less believed, through those seemingly endless nights of sitting with the Temple Sweeper. Nor when I escorted him to the graves and he began to train me in the art of caring for the stones. I only know the reverence I had for him then, as I do now. And if nothing else other, nothing other, this is clear to me— our Temple Sweeper is not dead. It is true, his body is no longer sweeping the courtyard or the Meditation Hall. Yet his manifestations rise in all us monks, as we walk in the orchard, stand in the hills, sit in the Meditation Hall. He appears in the clouds over the cliffs by the river streaming into the sea. And whenever doubts arise to question me, the Ghostwoman and her daughter arrive to bring me their assurances.

But what can a simple and unlearned monk possibly understand of events a thousand years ago? I cannot even understand my own loneliness and being in time. And though there are tomes of history books in our library of the endless wars against children, they all seem the same to me. And the print, handwritten, is small

and often illegible, and they pain these feeble eyes that grow weaker with each passing moon. I have not been trained to understand them, yet in some crucial, inscrutable way, I understand.

And as far as my own childhood is concerned—glimpses, shadows. Is that really my own mother's face, my true father's face? My only vivid recollections are waking with these monks and immersing in our monastic training. Even my efforts to query our good Abbot on the matter have been of little help. Our Abbot is quite old now, and though recovered from his ailment, he rarely leaves his meditations, nor silence. Many among us say he will be the next to depart this body of red dust. And what will we do then? None of us is prepared to take his seat, and protect this sea. He himself refuses to speak to the matter.

Still, when he arranged for the boat and Seekers to take me to the mainland to find the Learned Sage Women, he called me to his cell the night before my departure and spoke to me.

As for the days before your entering this temple, I can tell you little, Enduring Sound, our old and dear Abbot said. All I can attest to is that it will be revealed in the scrolls you strive to translate and understand. I am permitted to say this—just as with our Temple Sweeper, you, too, were brought here by the circus and theater people. You, a mere boy of three or four, and like most of the others, an orphan of the wars. They came by night when all the monks were sleeping. Delivered you into my arms at the temple gate I myself opened, and they then sailed off again, swiftly, in our Seekers' long, wooden boats. The woman who handed you over to me was, no doubt, the one you and the Temple Sweeper described to me from your scrolls in your dream dialogues, that of the Ghostwoman. She spoke without language, and the circus children around her were like embodiments of laughter. She was the only one weeping. This is all I can tell you, Head Monk. Though maybe it is of some help. Travel safely and be sure to return in twelve moons. You will be needed here. You see my own body is reaching its end, and with your return, I will announce my death and give our monks time to prepare.

On that final night when we were together, that night as I was falling asleep, and the Temple Sweeper himself rested on the floor—afterwards vanishing into us—the Temple Sweeper said to me, said in a low and gentle voice as I put my head on the desk—you exist as an idea in your mind.

Belief? How is one to believe in the beauty of unknowing? Yet this heart longs to release into this mystery, and to help the other monks, who also wonder in confusion as to who we truly are.

Of course, the Ghostwoman and the Learned Sage Women were deeply, indeed intimately, connected to these questions. And that is another story I will try to record in this journal, if you will bear with me, this diary as I have come to call it, of my own mis-translations. Still, how could I have ever sensed any of this then, on those tender, brutal and miraculous evenings together with the Temple Sweeper in my humble monk's cell, writing these scrolls together? Much time would pass before I could finally translate many of these passages.

I should add that the Temple Sweeper was vague, even shy per-haps, in speaking of these women, our Learned Sage Women. He would shift tongues more frequently on those nights of the telling. Now, I suspect there was something that confused him too, and hence, he was conscious of the changing of languages as he spoke and saw my own confusion. As if the women had sprung from some unspoken earth, an unutterable desire, an infinite well and sea of pages. Or even a mystery that frightened him?

Maybe yes.
Maybe no.
Not always so.

What I did learn on those final nights is that in the Temple Sweeper's telling, these women could birth children without men. That their bodies could freely take the shape of animals, particularly birds. What seemed to astonish him most profoundly was what he described in simple words as their ability to manifest the meaning behind the sounds or songs of words.

But this I could not fathom when I departed with the Seekers from our small monastery in their long wooden boats into the seas between us and those sages' hidden dwelling in the mountains on the other shore.

And you wonder what this simple monk believes of such things?

Is there anything such as belief? Head Monk, how could you ever know? Listen to yourself, Head Monk. Who is really speaking? How could we ever know? Yet, somehow, what I came to understand in the unknowing is the no need to know—to just go on, to go on to the next thing, and to hold nothing back. The Temple Sweeper said to me.

And yet still, it was something the Ghostwoman said during my time of pilgrimage with the Seekers. We were camped deep in the forest to evade the soldiers of the mainland. It was something she almost whispered to me as the others slept. Though two of the Seekers who had accompanied me on the trail through the mountains so far were still awake, keeping guard over and for me even in this densely remote haven of darkness and wild animals, they apparently could not hear, nor see, this ghosted figure when she arose out of the blackness of the forest. Later it would strike me as very much like the tale the Temple Sweeper told me of his time as a boy in the desert after his family was murdered on the train.

She simply appeared. Came out of the thick wood, as though from the bark of these tightly intertwined trees, and I recognized her at once from the Temple Sweeper's words, and from when she had entered my own dreams. Clad in her colorful and torn rags, she urged me to be still, clasping one hand over my mouth as I was about to call out. Her gray eyes stared into me and instantly hypnotized my nerves. Her sweeping hair over my arms and robe—as the letters of her alphabet floated out of her fingers in the contours and images of birds humming the sounds of her words—

> Your heart will open
> as if a flicker or phantom, a dance upon
> a stage as a person of no rank. For the secret
> of return and awakening has
> been awaiting you here all along.

It is better to return to the Temple Sweeper's story and his words, or at least as close to them as this humble scribe can offer. As far as finishing the scrolls, I am not him—he is, in fact, me. All the same, this is beyond me. I have failed him. Though as of tonight, and I can promise no more, this monk with dimming eyes has vowed to go on, word after word, sound after sound, lifetime after lifetime. And we cannot do it without you—

> Will you come and help us?
> As he often repeated to me,
> the problem is you think there is time.
> Time itself an illusion, he said.

Though tonight glancing back at the face of your sea and these soaring clouds, I ask myself aloud, Enduring Sound—is time not also Suchness?

Time with the Learned Sage Women

My days and nights in the library caves of the ancient universities with the Learned Sage Women gradually became my language. In the beginning I thought they were merely evolving my understanding of words themselves, occasionally correcting my mistakes and limitations due to learning with only our good monks as a boy and as a young man growing up in the monastery.

For instance, these women were surprised, and one might say, even amused, by my lack of knowledge of any other than the masculine, or what they called the maleness of words. We speak in a language beyond male or female, my first teacher said to me soon after arriving. Freeing language into the-what-is, the constant comings and goings of the eternal now, this is the language we speak in, and to live among us, you will need to learn this, good monk.

This may be true, and I accept it. But will it help me with the scrolls? I asked her.

It is the scrolls, she said, pointing my gaze to outside of the cave's mouth. How could a sea, or a moon, be only male or female or a so-called neuter gender? How might a word be anything oth-

er than the continuation of things, objects, human beings, or animals? she went on, sending my attention toward a blue jay that had
suddenly lighted on the lantern outside. She smiled inquisitively
with her arms held out, gesturing with her mouth while making
the same sound as the bird. Further still, on that first morning this
Sage Woman told me that for those among them, every particle,
indeed every atom, has its own utterance, and in such, its own song.

The Temple Sweeper spoke of such a song, I told her.

There is the aliveness of all things, be they of a so-called animate or inanimate nature. What the Temple Sweeper has told
you is true, she continued. But now you must unlearn it all and
learn it as your own. The other women around us then laughed
and asked—do you not know the earth is alive, a sacred being?
Afterwards, they took turns rubbing my shaved head, calling me
a silly monk and teasing me in this way. Study the sounds, good
monk, they too are alive. They are the songs from which your Temple Sweeper speaks.

So, over the days and weeks I began to see nouns and verbs
differently. Recognize the genitive, my next teacher told me one
morning. The genitive as a verb on horseback, the-what-should-be.
Each sound seen through the eye mirrors and echoes the others.

> True reality is waking to this mystery
> of one another in each moment.
> We mirror one another and all things.
> This is nothing other than what you realize already,
> good monk—that all of what we call the world is
> nothing other than love.

As the days passed, earthing into these syllables and letters, I
did slowly hear more intimately the sounds of animals, plants, and
planets, their beingness in words. That each has its own history,
wounds, and healing. Of course, grammar is not so difficult to
memorize with repetition, even for simple monks such as myself.
Yet these learned women in their festive clothing and rituals con-

tinuously drilled me, saying it is not okay, it is not enough, good monk. You must first understand the livingness of sounds, these love letters from the rain and clouds that never die, and then you will unmistakably hear their true meanings.

And on those days, often enough, when I would become overly serious with myself, straining my eyes on the scrolls, one of these Sage Women would come and pull me to my feet and try to coax me into dancing. But I cannot dance, I told them, and they would again laugh together, pulling me around the various rooms of the cave lined with books and manuscripts and sculptures of letters from across the languages of time.

And the sound of the letters in the word "star"

emerged as stars.

The wounds of "water' found its way into my wet eyes.

An echo of "mute" manifested in words.

The histories of "name" became a naming.

A flight of the "bird" a bird of paradise.

The Ghostwoman whispered this into the ear of the forest.

And gradually, I realized everything I had recorded in the scrolls was, indeed, a mistranslation and must be begun from the beginning. Needless to say, I was quite discouraged. But they would not let me give up.

In such a fashion, they mentored this simple monk. Meditating beside me. Eating with me. Walking with me. Requesting my complete presence among them and in my translations. In each particular, a vastness, my teachers would say, over and over, each day in each lesson. Thus, little by little, I more intimately came closer to our Temple Sweeper and the words he spoke to me again as I dreamed in his scrolls.

But they would not help me in the sense of deciphering the language embedded in the pages I had carried across the sea from our hidden monastery. Now I sense it was not what they were there for. I had to do the work myself. Though there was one girl who would, somewhat furtively, come to me in my moments of extreme despair. Her own head shaven, like my own, and her body very small, and injured somehow, not in an obvious way. But I noticed small scars on her arms when her robe folded up, the ones she clearly did not want me to notice, so I said nothing. Silently, she would sneak up from behind when I was deep in thought, wrestling with the Temple Sweeper's speech. Some days she would tap me on the shoulder, bow, blindfold my eyes, and take my hand, guiding me through the labyrinth of dwellings and temples within their sanctuary of the cave's mouth. This cave, opening onto the wilderness from which I had come and which I presumed to be the other side of their huge mountain.

And there, after removing the blindfold, I could see across a deep gorge, and I beheld a magnificent wooden carving, as large as a mountain itself, of a woman in the posture of both dance and prayer.

Some days, the girl, who I came to realize was the mute-girl, would walk me through the forest, along a stream, pausing and sometimes pointing at squirrels or snakes or muskrats and various other animals or objects, indicating for me to stop and put my hand over my ear, as she had. Or she would toss me a pine cone or a piece of bark from a tree, nodding at me to do the same with her. It's a game, she'd say, but without speaking, and I somehow understood. Quite often she would take my own hand into her own, and slide it across the side of a bush or plant, smiling as if something significant was passing between us in a particular cloud or ray of sun through the cliffs. These things she would do without uttering a word, yet on occasion, afterwards, she would page through the bound scrolls I carried with me everywhere. She would nod her head in a vague approval.

Once, the eldest among them, guided me to a cave beyond their dwellings. There, she had me sit and meditate, and when I arose, perhaps an hour later, she was gone. It was not without challenge that I found my way back without the aid of her, or my trusted Seekers.

On another occasion, two of the Sage Women, one with no right hand—the other without a left hand—led me to a waterfall where the fish were so bountiful they would leap into my arms whenever I touched the surface of the water, and then swiftly leap out.

One night some weeks later, as dusk was descending, the woman the other Sages called Wounded Hand, brought me into a wolves' den. I didn't know where she was taking me after finding me at my desk, writing in the scrolls of these things, but it was not my place to question or doubt the Sage Women who treated me so kindly. As we entered the den, I froze, and told her I could not go in, that I was, yes—as she had asked me in that moment, frightened of wolves. Nor can I now tell you how—perhaps something, some longing in her eyes—when she placed her hand over her heart, something somehow calmed my spirit enough to go in and sit among these wolves until their growling and snapping of teeth settled. I was trembling, unable to stop, but she held my hand. We awaited the rising of the moon. The moon rose. We and the wolves went outside the mouth of the den and stared at the full moon together. All was still, and later the howling began. Soon, I was howling with them! When we left, these wolves were still howling, and I sensed that they were now my friends. My trembling was gone.

I knew that if I met them alone in the forest, they would not hurt me. Nor would I hurt them. They would, indeed, protect me if the soldiers came. Just as they stood guard and protected these Learned Sage Women. Later, the Ghostwoman herself revealed this to me.

In spite of all those mysterious meetings, it was walking among the shelves of the Manuscript Cave that lined the stone walls of a luminous, candle-lit cavern that most helped me to grapple with those parts of the Temple Sweeper's stories that persistently alluded me. I was awe-struck, walking slowly through the cavern, touching with my fingers, ever so lightly, each and every binding on the walls. It was a ritual these women practiced every night after we had passed the bowls of food between us in their dining area, and ate together with our hands. We then cleansed our hands and feet and chanted before entering the cavern itself. Each night the voices of the manuscripts became more and more audible to me. I came to slowly, though faintly, hear the voices of their pages as I passed, running my own hands across their manuscripts. Some were voices of playing and laughing children, others voices of anguish, pain, and of tears, and I would have to pull away. Often they were of a kind of silence, or prayer. As if waiting to be birthed by these women. These women my Temple Sweeper had told me could birth a child without a man. And now I thought to myself, maybe it is true. For some of the children running about their dwellings in these hidden forests of trees and caves, these children around the Learned Sage Women somehow appeared different to me than any children I had seen as a boy. There was an aura, a certain light, a feeling of ease.

The manuscripts themselves with voices, too, as if waiting for their beings to again manifest. The words of manuscripts floating off their engraved stone shelves, taking shape in the shadows along the walls, in the eaves of the ceiling, in the passageways worn down from all of the footsteps along the countless aisles within the cavern, and their voices almost visible, yet only to the ear.

Yet by then, by the time I began to hear the voices for myself, these Learned Sage Women told me it was time to return to my Abbot and monastery, and that they had revealed to me all that they could, and all that was allowed, in this lifetime.

On our last night to-gether before my departure for the monastery with the Seekers, who had again ar-rived and now camped out-side the caves, the Ghost-woman came to me. She knocked on the door of my comfortable abode, a com-fort to which we monks are not accustomed—a room full of drawings and sculp-tures and inked-circle paint-ings all over the walls in colorful and cheerful largess. No doubt, I would miss such abundance, I thought to myself. Quietly, she crossed the floor of my room as several of the Sages glanced in be-hind her, hovering by the door, silently. Yet I could see them peek-ing in. The girl with scars. The women who took me to the lake of fish. The one of wounded hand. Yes, they were there, peeking in. Sitting herself on a cushion, cross-legged, near the altar of the room, the Ghostwoman gestured for me to join her on the cushion nearby. The girl and eldest of the women, soon, along with all the others, then joined us as well, carrying in their own cushions. We sat peacefully like this for many hours, no one saying a word. I felt a deep ease I'd never experienced before, though I, as all of the good monks of our monastery, sit for long hours each day and some nights. In this profound calm, I must have fallen asleep during the night, for at the first signs of dawn, I sensed her thumb on my knee and opened my eyes.

When you leave here, good monk, there is only one thing you must not fail to remember. You must never forget. The voices you have begun to hear in the manuscripts are those of the Lost Children. You must tell their stories and translate their sounds.

How could I ever do this? I managed to ask her as the others' eyes also leaned in to hear my almost inaudible words.

How could I ever do this? I repeated.

> We will be there to help you, she whispered into my ear. And the Temple Sweeper has already gathered their voices into the scrolls.

It was then that I saw her face was the same as my own. And then she and all of these Learned Sage Women around me disappeared into the sun rising through the window of my room.

The Seekers

It was on the last leg back to the sea that the one-eyed boy and mute girl served as our Seekers. Some of the monks, since my return to our monastery, have asked how I am so sure it was they. Of course, I am quite confident in this conviction.

The other Seekers who escorted us throughout almost the entire journey were well-dressed and groomed, in an unusual way for this rough, mountainous terrain. They were older, but skilled and clearly well prepared for our journey. They spoke, but only among themselves as we walked, and they continually seemed anxious in their stealth movements along the hidden trails. One of them was always careful to go back and cover our tracks, every few hundred yards. And the head Seeker among them always wore an unusual hat, protruding quite far above his head, with the drawing of a raven on it, and a black bow tied around his neck. There were a few women amongst them who wore the same garb as the men.

Though I had seen the so-called Seekers pull their long wooden boats to the shores of our monastery islands on many occasions, none of these escorting me now were the same. I recognized not one of them. They appeared ancient to me, from another era or time.

Along some of the passages through the mountains, they had even blindfolded me, just as had the girl that day in the caves. I understood this was part of their secrecy. Now, I realize it is why the girl had blindfolded me as well. It was a form of protection. I could never describe to anyone how to find, much less find for myself, the place of their sanctuary; if asked, or even demanded to do so, I could give no clue. Yet I also sensed, unlike with the girl, that these Seekers were suspicious of my intentions. One would always stay close to me and watch my every footstep. And each day, or whenever a new group of Seekers emerged at one of the crossroads to lead me further from the forests and mountains, the leader would ask to inspect the scrolls I carried. And then, another Seeker would carefully review my letter from the Abbot before signaling for the others to guide me on. As if needing some confirmation of my rite of passage.

Don't misunderstand me, I was very grateful for these Seekers. They watched over me, very meticulous in their attention, feeding me well, and responding to my needs wherever we were, night and day, week after week, always delivering me to the next refuge and immediately leaving without a word, but posting three guards to protect me, should any soldiers appear. Undoubtedly, there was some kind of distance and perceived hierarchy between them though, almost as if they were no longer part of this world and moved in a realm of rigorous configuration beyond human speech.

One moon after meditating with the Ghostwoman, however, the boy and girl met me at the crossing of a river. The boy seemed to be about fourteen or fifteen years old. The girl, a year or two younger.

They waded across the water to greet me, bid farewell to these Seekers, and led me across the depths, insisting on carrying my things. The boy and girl held my bags and provisions high over their heads with their arms extended. I must confess, I was not ready to hand over the scrolls, though the boy thought it best, as the currents in the river were often turbulent and unpredictable, he said. How could I not trust them? No, it is not that I distrusted them. It is just that whenever the pages were out of my possession, I would feel uneasy, even become nauseated, and sweat emerged on my forehead. This anxiety would come when the other Seekers inspected the scrolls before, though the boy and girl did not inspect them. They only carried them across the river with my other things. Nor did they ask for my letter from the Abbot. This was a good sign, I thought, and I relaxed a little.

And crossing the wide river turned out to be of little trouble.

In my heart, of course, I already knew who these children were. Just as they knew me.

Still, it was a curious meeting as such.

The girl was wearing what I later learned from the boy, was a garment known as a jumper, good for travel, and it had blue and white stripes. The boy himself, on the other hand, wore the most impractical clothing for the terrain, dressed only in black shorts and a button-down gray coat that came to his knees. It is a strange world, is it not? Tonight, as I reflect back on this, I suspect this was also because of the boy's thoroughly easy-going manner. Some days he would talk endlessly about the plants and trees, the various wildlife and magical dwellings spread throughout the mountains we were traversing. I did not at first think of the girl as mute. It was only over a period of time that I even noticed she didn't converse, and yet, it seemed she was always speaking with the things around us.

Perhaps it was her constant humming that outwitted me in this observation. The two would frequently stop to write and draw in what I presumed to be their diaries—and they encouraged me to do the same in the scrolls.

But I have a journal, I said.

Yes, the Abbot told us, the boy responded.

It was once the journal of our teacher, he said.

Naturally, this made me even more curious. One afternoon I dared to ask them if they might help me with a passage of the Temple Sweeper's scrolls that was still completely foreign to me, in spite of all the Learned Sage Women had taught me. The boy turned, and after ruffling through his bag for a moment, handed me some brushes and ink. Draw what you imagine in the words, he said.

But I can't draw.

It's only a feeling, he responded, turning back toward the girl, smiling.

This encouraged me. Just as the Temple Sweeper had always encouraged me. And though it was quite some time later, my silly drawings did help with our translations.

I should note that the two never bothered to cover-over our

tracks. Nor did the two take any of the precautions with our camp-sites, or fires, as the other Seekers had done with a fierce intention each day. One might, in fact say, that the two appeared oblivious to the dangers of the forests or the sightings of soldiers. But this was not so. What I later discovered is that they had a different way of seeing and hearing. Unlike the others. Unlike myself. Nonetheless, when I asked them about this, the boy simply informed me that it was no longer necessary. And we walked on in single file along the path overlooking the ridge into darkening wood.

When I woke one morning and found the girl reading through the scrolls, those frantically scribbled from the sounds I heard from our Temple Sweeper in my cell, my having no knowledge of the language, if any, he was speaking—I observed her nodding, or shaking her head, smiling at times, in other moments in tears, and as if engrossed in a childhood story of her own. I feigned sleep as she read on, turning through each page slowly.

But what startled me was when she came to the blank pages, those yet unwritten, I saw that she began to draw, as if over and through any yet unmanifested words or poems, etching out an al-phabet of figures—one which we have now begun to understand, and cannot be said in our normal human speech.

And still, as I have already reported and you, no doubt, discerned for yourself, the girl never spoke. Though, indeed, I never sensed that she could not speak, nor that in any fashion, that the girl was mute.

Once I heard her singing on a cliff above the sea, for instance. Or were the sounds I thought I heard simply coming from a nearby waterfall, or the distant waves or birds?

Yet one evening toward dusk, I could have sworn that these ears distinctly overheard her telling the boy about the first time she kissed him. Did I actually hear her say this, or simply imagine it? Or did I recall a passage from the Mute Girl's diary the Temple Sweeper had shown me? This, too, remained a mystery to me for some time.

It was not until near the end of our pilgrimage that something else about the girl dawned on me. One evening after the boy had fished in the river and prepared his catch as a dinner for us over the fire, and now was cleaning the bowls, the girl came and touched my head, indicating for me to follow her. As I looked at her, I confess this monk did not want to get up. We had walked for many hours and many weeks. Yet when she kneeled down beside me, and I looked more closely into her eyes, I saw that they were the same color as those of our Temple Sweeper. They were the same gray as his on the night he first came to me in my cell and asked me if I could help him, if I could retrieve the parchment from the storeroom and write down the words he needed to say after twenty-five years of silence among us monks in the monastery. A beckoning in those eyes, or of the body itself, a shining, a grief, or perhaps, redemption?

I came to my feet and reached for her hand. But I could not fully get my balance. There was a blind spot, yet there I felt her hand. Naturally, I blamed this on the night descending, the darkness expanding all around, and then gradually—still almost in the split second of a lifetime flashing by—suspected what I had always known—that I had known this hand since the time when I was a mere boy. I also realized what I had known since then: I was slowly going blind. Even the Abbot's friends in the capital, the healers, had said this would eventually come to pass.

The girl, as if aware of this, put my arm around her shoulder—her strength surprising for one so thin and young of age, I thought—and she led me on into the even darker foliage of the forest surrounding us. As we walked, quite slowly you understand, she sometimes stopped and placed my own hand on top of certain trees or plants, maneuvering my fingers under, or sometimes over, the bark of wood or flower, occasionally placing a leaf, sometimes a twig or larger branch, into my arms, it seemed to me, to cradle as we stood in the blackness of my eyes. When we strolled further and deeper into the forest, more and more I heard her constant humming as a language in itself, and then, the humming itself as voices from the manuscripts I touched with these same fingers with the Sage Women as we moved through the cavern together—and that the Ghostwoman had told me to never forget.

And when she led me back to our campsite, the boy was waiting for us. There were stones carefully sculpted in a circle surrounding the fire and stacked in fine layers of what I imagined to be his effort to create an image of home, of welcoming. And I could hear these stones as clearly as I had begun to hear the voices from the manuscripts lifting up from the ground of the earth. They were singing.

The boy was singing with them, singing in a low voice by the fire, and he knew. He knew where we had been and what we had heard, and what I could hear now from the stones. The absent moon of the last nights of endless travel now strangely full, a moon looming over the edge of the mountain, flourishing in its own light. The boy looking up, first at the sudden appearance of the moon, and next at our return. And he kept singing. And we could hear it in his almost deep voice—a song of Lost Children who meet by a river and a sea in the same way that he had met the mute girl and that together they had found a child, a child still alive and breathing near the water's eddies, the soldiers' pyre blazing at the banks of the river, the soldiers on horses rampaging through the hills. And in the song, the boy and girl escaping this ravage and making their way to a circus where their new lives begin.

I was this child.

This, the girl had transmitted to me in the forest, but it would take time to understand.

In the morning, we rose and no one spoke. There was tea and some remaining fish they had laid out before we went on. After three more days and nights in these mountains, we arrived at the secret harbor. I felt a sadness at having to leave these children, who still seemed only children to me. But alongside this, inside my whole being, I sensed they were immortal; and this is how I see them tonight, glancing back across the sea to where we waved farewell.

But it is not farewell, the boy grinned at me as he pushed my small boat off the shore, wading into the water. I looked over his head and saw the girl bowing, then waving her arms in the air.

Later, perhaps while dreaming in my small boat, I opened my eyes to a sky full of boundless stars gleaming across every corner around me.

Perhaps dreaming, of dreams, yes, I saw them both flying on the back of a bird of paradise.

Thus, I translated the scroll as such.

You are never alone.

We are always here for you.

Scroll VIII

Coming Home

In the beginning, I didn't fully realize it was the Lost Children who the Ghostwoman was showing me. In our meditation that last night with the Learned Sage Women, I now suspect she had actually begun to initiate me into the journey of their dreams. It came to me in waves, mostly during meditation, not only in meditations, however. Often when carrying stones to the Temple Sweeper's graves, I would see faces—vague, shadowy, almost invisible in the fog of mornings and evenings when I was finished with my duties as Head Monk, and carrying on with the work of the scrolls.

> These faces, the small faces of children, at first undisclosed to me, when I had traveled with the Seekers and convened with the Sage Women.

As the months passed, they returned to me in the falling leaves of early autumn, the random and still unfinished stones about the vast fields, the passing clouds of evening sunsets and morning sunrises. I eventually began to recognize some of these faces. I assumed this was due to my blurring eyesight, at times worse than others, depending on how well my sleep had been the night before. Yet it was beyond plausible to me, even while resting or eating, that some were the faces of the monks I had lived beside all of these years.

The girl and boy were quite apparent, of course. Though while trekking with them through those foreign mountains together, I had not been cognizant of traveling in the dream world. As I said before, it is always as if I am just waking from a dream, so this, I can promise you, never occurred to me. Yet as I continued the work of our Temple Sweeper among the graves, the one-eyed boy and mute girl's presence was more decisive. As if they wanted me to know they were still with me, occasionally laughing beyond the steep cliff overlooking the sea. But then—the other Seekers who had escorted me before the boy and girl arrived—their faces too began to flicker in the winds. There was something familiar in their distant movements and gestures, the images of ravens sewn into their hats. How could I make them out, I wondered? For some evenings my unpredictable eyes would dim again, and following the trail back to the monastery was itself a challenge. Still, as I translated and worked through the scrolls this was unquestionable—somewhere I had seen them, perhaps been with them before our pilgrimage together to the abodes of the Learned Sage Women. This is what dawned on me one evening after spotting one of their ravens flying from the odd hat of their leader.

While traveling in the dream world, nothing appears as that of a dream, at least not in the way we usually think of such things. Trees are trees, rivers are rivers, mountains are mountains. If you're not aware that it is a dream, why would you think you are dreaming? This only came to me slowly as my days and nights continued in my translations. The faces of the Women Sages also came into my meditations. I'd sense their arrival in simple appearances, like a passing cloud over the shoreline. Or in an empty, unwritten brownish page in my satchel of paper. Once, I recognized the kind faces of the sages in a bowl of two pears in our monastery kitchen. And the one they all called Wounded Hand in the rock carvings on the ridges above the ocean. Others appeared to me while walking, sometimes alone, or in pairs, in the fading bark of the juniper trees along the river.

And thus, finally, one day while talking with the other monks and reading to them from the scrolls by the graveyard our Temple Sweeper sculpted during his twenty-five years of silence among us, I heard voices from the children's manuscripts rising up from the stones like paper-mâché cuttings, humming, humming what sounded to be some far away story without words, floating in the air behind the good monks who sometimes now accompanied me to the grass hut after my return from the pilgrimage.

When alone one night strolling the shore, I witnessed multiple, what seemed to me infinite, moons manifesting in the night sky. The light immense, shocking to the senses, and I thought their brightness had at last extinguished my vision. For a long while I had covered my eyes from the burning. When I opened them once more, I saw the valley and hills and mountains surrounding the water on all sides lit up, as if in a massive fire, illuminating the caves of the past, present and future dwellers who had lived, or would live, in these very cliffs and caves. It was in this precise moment that what the Temple Sweeper had said to me became undeniable—there is no such thing as time. Time too is a dream. Glancing back at the sea, the small boats began to emerge across the waves—first two boats in the foreground, then several more behind these two boats—and soon a kind of armada of wooden vessels lining the horizon as far as these poor eyes could see.

The boats were filled with children. Children rowing, singing, waving their oars over the sides of their small boats, clamoring in an array of languages that merged in a chorus of odyssey, return—celebratory cries as if of some kind of victorious liberation.

The Temple Sweeper put his hand on my shoulder.
You see, good monk, you see? Yes, it is true.
These are the Lost Children coming home.
You have not failed me.

THE ABBOT

By the time of my return from the journey, it was beyond question, our Abbot was seriously ill. Some of the senior monks whispered, even more nervously now, that his days were few remaining in this red world of dust. Since the time before my departure with the Seekers, his back had attained a permanent crook, he hobbled, and most of the time could only walk with the aid of the monks. Nor did his eyes pierce with the sight of the sea as they always had before, yet there was some kind of glimmer I recognized when he welcomed me home. There was still what I might call a sturdiness, mixed with softness, when I glanced at him from the other side of the Meditation Hall and studied his sitting. Sometimes our eyes would meet, and in these moments I was aware that, in spite of his physical demise, he kept a furtive watch over my comings and goings in the monastery. He was alert, attentive, and steady. If there was a quarrel or disagreement amongst the brothers, he somehow sensed it, and he would beckon them before the assembly to speak their grievances. If there was a wrong, he would address it, such as when our monks fought among one another. Even so, he was kind to a fault with us all, which may be why we loved him so—and why he called none of us forth to train with him before departing the body.

We were not ready.

And he had not announced his death as he had told me he would before giving me permission to travel with the Seekers to the abodes of the Learned Sage Women.

We are somewhat timid monks here, all of us. Nothing can be said about it. There is no blame. But none of us could be called a shining apple. It seems we've never truly learned what he tried so hard to teach us, wearing down his own body, extending patience and, perhaps, too much leniency. The core of our matter is that we are all the same in our own being and that nothing ever separates us. One might easily argue, this is the most difficult thing to feel in the heart.

And now he was dying, and we all experienced shame. Yet he was not dead. Upon my return he was quite intent on hearing every detail of the pilgrimage. Our Abbot had never taken such things lightly, of course. Even when I was a boy, he would daily call me into his cell and have me report to him everything I had learned for the day. But if I had been mischievous, he would fail to scold me, which is why, perhaps, I did not truly learn the art of languages, as he had so greatly hoped. I was a thief among the other monks, stealing, sometimes their socks, once even a robe. Often, as a boy, I would pilfer from the food being prepared for our dinners and take the best parts back to my cell. Or I would steal candles and matches from the Meditation Hall. Once I almost burned down our monastery by setting a pile of leaves I had raked all morning on fire. And, on more than one occasion I ran away, first gathering as much food as I could carry from the storeroom, and even taking our Abbot's winter robe for the bedding I used in the caves. These episodes did not bode well, and though our Abbot refused to punish me, the brothers, quite understandably, would slap me whenever he was not around. Our Abbot, on the other hand, would simply tell me to study harder, as I would be called upon someday.

When I turned twelve years of age, I was once sent to him for trying to swim across the sea between our monastery and the world of dust. As you already know, I almost drowned. But what I have not written in this journal, or spoken to anyone, is that one of the brothers almost drowned while coming to save me. They are treacherous waters, and even I knew this. But I felt no remorse. My only dream was to flee this world of men and find my mother. I longed for my mother. I lamented being cast into a world of men.

When I arrived in his cell, wrapped in a blanket and still shivering from the icy waters, expecting again to hear his usual admonishments, instead I found our Abbot sitting on a cushion, holding in his lap the winter coat I'd stolen from him the year before. I had not then and never since, confessed this. Tears were coming down his face, and he was silent. When I sat before him, which is our usual protocol in such a situation, he did not speak. But the tears continued, and many landed on my knees.

After what seemed to be several hours, the evening sun descending and the light filtering through the window, I saw he was finally asleep, and stealthily rose to sneak out of his room. Yet he was not sleeping. He handed me his winter coat which the brothers had found in my room, his eyes now dried from tears. Afterwards, I was never mischievous again.

And now, I have been called upon.

And I am no longer a boy.

That afternoon—soon after my parting with the one-eyed boy and mute girl—when our Abbot called me to his cell, he smiled and bowed to me. Thank you for returning in time, Head Monk.

But there is no such thing as time, I said.

He laughed and seated me. You are nothing other than time, he said. He grinned and poured us both a cup of tea. His hand trembled and he spilt three drops, which he had never done before. This cup I'm drinking from is already broken, he said. Afterwards, he nodded and indicated for me to begin, wiping the three drops up with the edge of his robe and straightening his spine as best he could. I smiled and took out the bundle of pages, opening to the very beginning, the first page as everything had been redone after my time with the Sage Women.

But when I began to report to him of the journey, and tried to explain what I had learned, he at once interrupted—

And yet it seems, good monk, that you yourself have no direction, no grounding, no awareness of these authors of the scrolls? You have come this far, so why have you stopped now? How will you know the way to reach you, you yourself, and to then translate who you really are, and someday pass on these scrolls? I will listen to your stories, good monk, but first, you will have to say.

I did not say.

This cup I am drinking from is already broken, he repeated.

Still, I did not say.

Nor could I say each subsequent day when he again called me to his cell, nor the day when he ushered me forth with the same question, not in his cell, but before the whole assembly. This our Abbot had never done with me. As I said, I have no memory of him ever scolding or reprimanding me. But to be called before the entire assembly of monks, night after night, morning after morning, this, for me, was the most severe punishment. Whether you think of this as a punishment or not, for this simple monk it was the worst of possibilities.

I had never spoken before the assembly, and it was the one condition I had when our Abbot asked me to come forth as Head Monk. Though few were truly aware—and even as a boy I grew quite skilled at hiding it—I am, as our Abbot knows, a stutterer. Even if I can read a book, or sacred text, without notice of the condition, if forced to speak more than a few moments on my own, my tongue becomes twisted in on itself, as if inert, paralyzed, confused. This has always been the source of a deep wound for me.

Furthermore, I was, indeed, confused by our Abbot's question. What did it mean? To translate oneself? What was he seeking? I had told him many times that I was, simply, the Temple Sweeper's scribe. Though I possessed thousands of pages of notes, some might call "reports," and many translations, all I could say was the name, or word, or sound—Temple Sweeper.

Thus, it is so.

And then, one morning during our prayers, while silently weeping in the Meditation Hall, the mute girl and one-eyed boy fulfilled their promise yet again and returned to me. The two squatted beside me on either side of my sitting mat, and at the same time placed their hands on my chest, and afterwards over their own hearts. I could hear their heartbeats, like the boats on the sea's waves, bobbing to shore.

No one could see them besides our Abbot, and this I know, for he, too, rose from his seat and approached the altar. His gait again that of a younger man, the one who greeted me with a cup of rice milk on the first day I awoke in the monastery, unable to remember my past, nor even my own name.

We will call you, Enduring Sound, he had laughed, handing me three bowls. And I was only a boy. Somehow, I could see him as I came to my feet now, as I had that first morning, and strangely, heard his heartbeat beating with that of the boy and the girl.

In that flicker as he lit and put a match to the candle, turning to welcome the boy and girl now near him, I began to question something beyond the words written or translated in the scrolls. A smile crossed over my mouth, one not of my own, as I began to smile through my tears. How had it never occurred to me to wonder who our Abbot truly is? Had our Temple Sweeper not gestured toward him that first night in my cell?

How had I never wondered who I, myself, truly am?

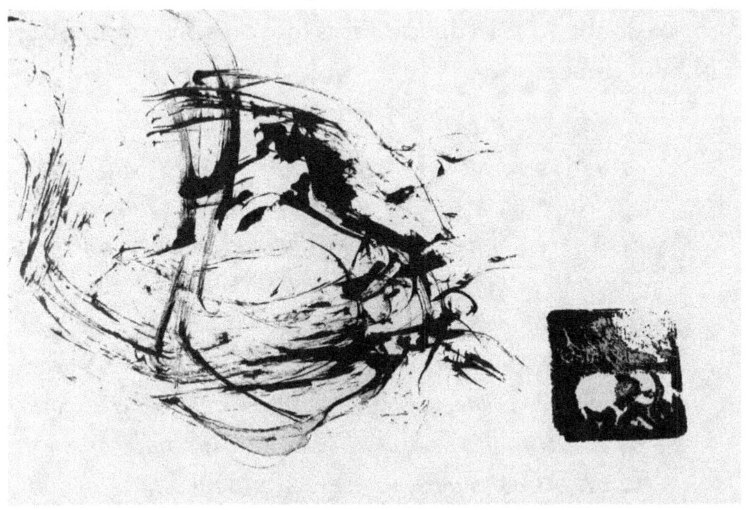

Later that same morning I recounted the pilgrimage before the Abbot and the entire assembly—including the cooks and cats who also meandered in—recounted it all, all of it, as I have now begun to do for you in these pages. Our Abbot invited me to take his seat, and though reluctant to do so, I was soon deeply grateful for my knees and heart were equally on fire—and I did not finish this tale until well after the appearance of the full moon through the monastery windows quite late that night. Our Abbot, on the other hand, stood, straight as an arrow the whole time, the crook in his back no longer apparent, and on the several occasions when the senior monks came to him to offer tea, he waved them away. His posture, erect and calm, and whenever my voice began to waiver or my stutter returned, he nodded as I looked up at him, and I was able to go on.

It is, of course, impossible to say exactly how I spoke before the kind monks. For the story changes in the telling, the hearing of time passing, and as the Temple Sweeper always tells me—all stories are both true and not true in the unknowing. We have to find out for ourselves. Still, we know what we feel and experience in the telling itself, no matter what anyone says. These beings, you may ask, are they simply figures of imagination of a lonely monk? You, no doubt, have to discover this for yourself, as you too are the author of these stories.

> *Good monks, why are you waiting? I somehow began in addressing the assembly. Why are you waiting for our Abbot.... Is this the way I may have begun, Temple Sweeper? You were there, good monks, good friends. You yourselves among and of these Lost Children. And they are calling out for you, for your acceptance. And your love. You have heard the voice of the Temple Sweeper with your own eyes, speaking through your dreams by the cliffs overlooking the sea, in the scrolls, and you heard his voice with your eyes and saw him with your ears. And you sensed your own calling in this calling, just as you mingle with the sound of these bells, these prayers, these incantations every morning when we arrive again together to meet who we are. I saw you with my own dimming eyes, once running through the hills, sometimes hiding in the caves, and then again waiting in the voices of the manuscripts, in libraries and universities and shrines—awaiting your own translation and transfiguration into words—words beyond words. Kind monks, I cannot finish these scrolls without you.*
>
> *We are not alone....*

There was silence in the assembly. But our Abbot gestured me on.

You see, I have yet to tell you, nor did I remember myself before sitting in the Abbot's seat, what all of the Seekers and Sages were pointing me toward the whole while of my journey—to look out and see what is invisible to the eye, to that which can't really be spoken, and yet, and yet, everything speaks it.

To hear with the body.

To merge with that which is always alive.

Here, right here in the impermanence

of impermanence.

This eternal now of all these faces.

And speaking in the temple to the assembly of Lost Children on this auspicious occasion, I remembered them, recognized this face of a child climbing through the trees, that face riding on the backs of elephants, other of the monks' faces practicing circus acts and gathering in the valleys we passed by on foot, sometimes by horse, escorted by the Ghostwoman who ushered us on a thousand years ago, and out into many skies so that we might witness this continuous arising throughout time.

It is true, at first, only one monk's face came to meet my own face in the temple that evening. Then another joined. And another as the sparse light of a blood moon slowly dispersed throughout the monastery. Others began to meet my eyes, clearing the patches of clouds in my vision of what the Abbot's healers once called these blind spots I had known since a boy—an emergence of fog in the fields as it was explained to me then—and falling away now as I glanced to my left and right, then daring to speak and even look, without fear, all about the Meditation Hall, seeing the monks' ancient faces, as if faces from before history. These faces of children. Even the eldest among us, even our Abbot's face, shifting into those of children, as if erasing time, as if their age was no longer a condition of our seeing or hearing one another. And then their hands unfolding from inside their robes, their memories that of my own, these faces meeting my own childhood. We were sitting together as we were, as we are. And still deepening in each breath, their faces transforming into their own. A booming echo of voices creviced the moon, circling the room, moving along the floors and cush-ions, traveling further into the courtyard, surrounding the caves and hills as if coming from the ineffable sea itself.

THE BLUE DRAGON CAVE

Sometime, somewhere, in this turning of light,
I found myself alone with language.
There was the sea. The moon. The monks.
The mountains all around. My memories of the Temple Sweeper,
the boy and girl who, it is said, brought me to this place.
This place of imagination.

Yet was it really imagined?

I am here.

This is the only world I see.

And little by little it began to dawn on me, this language,
itself, all language—the language that we are sharing
together tonight—has only ever been imagined.

Just as with the boy who had joined us and tapped me on the shoulder then. Just as when the boy arrived at the mouth of what our Abbot has called the blue dragon cave, the dream awakened in him the sound within. The voices of many worlds lifting up at that moment to remind him of the miraculous. All of his students and teachers, his friends and family, all of the Lost Children, the monks and Seekers and Sage Women, his love—the mute girl—each arriving to thank the boy for everything he had given, and would be given, and the end of even giver and given.

It was then that the Abbot surprised the assembly, agilely, one could say spritely, coming forward. Whatever had ailed him—rheumatism, old age, or some wound from his own pilgrimages, was now absent. The frailty in his legs and back gone, he walked from the side of the temple to his seat by the altar. He stood beside me, my own body somewhat trembling from the transformation I saw in him. You see, our Abbot appeared young, almost handsome without the lines over his eyes and the sunken cheeks. He leaned over, smiling with a wide mouth, and whispering to me alone—

Tell them, tell us now, he said in a deepening voice,
a voice I could hear as colors streaming out of his mouth in
the hue of a winterish river, while placing
his hand on my ear—much in the way the Ghostwoman
had that night she came to me in the Seeker's camp.

Tell them, Head Monk.

But I don't know.

But you do, yes, try to remember, try to remember
the unwritten, only that which is unwritten,
and forget the rest....
Your notes and prior translations
will be of no help now.
Don't be distracted, Head Monk.

I opened our book of scrolls timidly, turning through their bounded, and still unbounded leaves of bark parchment, and quite suddenly, as if struck by wind, and perhaps unconsciously, I'm no longer sure, began to spot winged signs, words, then whole worlds spreading across these formerly blank, unfinished pages—indeed, ones without even a mark of ink.

It was quite quick, you see, before I could think or evaluate what was happening in my body, eventually the words and signs, drawings or shapes of signs, fell away all together into only the voices of children in our Meditation Hall, yet, somehow, I could understand. They were not of, or from me. Of this I am tonight certain. Rather, and this remains to me stranger, it was the appearance of Hempis and the Temple Sweeper right here in the Meditation Hall that made me tremble more than I had before—Hempis' figure as a man, and thus so the same with our Temple Sweeper.

Thus, I began....As Hempis says in these scrolls, speaking directly to our Temple Sweeper—who are here among us tonight, good monks, good friends—listen closely to how one Master spoke to another, and do not be afraid.

As Hempis says now again to our Temple Sweeper—

You must understand, Temple Sweeper,
you must first understand this. The dream passes
and you wake in the dream that is no longer a dream.
Just as when you truly enter the world of words, you find
their ultimate silence. You find you are free of words.
You are a deep sound in the forest, a wave
carrying the sea, a leaf blooming into trees.
You are a breath in the wind, and you become the wind.

Nor can we forget the stories of words,
for they are the awakening
in the humble stars and moons.
The one-eyed boy who you are, who is one-eyed now.
He and the mute girl are finally coming home
after all of these seeming centuries and passing suns.
They carried the wound of love for you,
for us all, on a winged bird of paradise.
Yes, it is beginning to become clearer, don't you think?
They are almost home. They are we, and we are them.
And this is your fate, this is why
the boy and the girl always return,
why our story always returns.

Whether this is how I, Enduring Sound, Head Monk, began or ended this scroll that night with our Abbot and monks in the temple, I am told this is what is most remembered. And the next morning, we found our good Abbot sitting under the cypress tree in the garden.

He had departed his body.

For many days, as is our custom and ritual, we performed the ceremonies to honor our departed master. When all of the songs were sung, the chants chanted, the prayers offered, the body cleaned and then only ash, we offered the remains of his physical existence to all the beings with and gone before him, spreading his ashes among the stones and in the outlying caves, and finally, in the sea itself.

The waves carrying him forth into the mystery.

And together, I and some of the other monks, gathered the few belongings from our cells, and set forth in the evening's starlight on our pilgrimage into the dreams where the pattern of forests is revealed and the one great pearl is hidden.

The Temple Sweeper somewhere awaiting us, as he had written himself in the scrolls.

This, how we again began our continuous pilgrimage.

BOOK II

Scroll IX

Laughter—
& hearing a sound
of carnival players
following along
on a pilgrimage of unknowing.

The Essential Story

All these years trying
to understand who I am
and now, at ease
riding on the wing
of the blue dragon.

—Temple Sweeper Leaving the Dream

The man stood looking for a long time.
The man stood looking for a long time, dead.

Just when the man thought he'd approached the borders of death, he saw that they continued on past the burnt sky, shadowing the hill around his own funeral pyre. Though he had made this pilgrimage many times before, still, it startled him. The stones formed what seemed to be a row of trees, with long stretches of rose-hued limbs bulging with the heft of stones, which shined like miniature stars. But since placing the last stones on a mound of earth, lighting the match to the leaves, and not again walking back to the monastery, the man had noticed that the sky had again changed. Instead of darkness there were white clouds and mists, the horizon a rusted color of earth, as if a simmering bonfire had emptied its embers onto an ocean floor.

The man stood looking for a long time, dead.

This last grave, his own, completed during his final weeks of daily sojourns. All the labor of cutting into the rich soil overlooking the waves after first thoroughly sweeping the temple—this last pyre of his own remained as it had before departing the body: carefully stark, rounded by chosen rocks, smoothed and chiseled, each edged neatly up against the bamboo and mounded earth with the sign of a phoenix, a bird of paradise, and a blue dragon painted on three stones. All the other graves appeared somewhat different. They were more like moons, thought the man. The remnants of green grass turning into the rust sky, the color of cleansed blood. And a new layer of wood chips and pebbles, along the path to the sea, which he thought maybe the monks had spread there from the boulder's end on the north side of the monastery hills while beginning their quest for him.

The road now leaned out and into the realm of cliffs almost hovering by the sea.

> The man stood looking for a long time.
> Where do you think you are?
> The man pivoted to his left.
> Why have you come here, Hempis?
> I always await you on this day of birth.

As the man put down his burlap sack, he saw that the mute girl and Head Monk, Enduring Sound, were also now trudging up the hilly path, finding their way to this place of stones. Did you invite them to come as well, Hempis?

Hempis grinned, adjusting his scarf and hat, lighting his hand-rolled tobacco. The beginning is in the end, no?

The man was no longer sure who had come and who had departed this place throughout his own personal and somewhat arbitrary sense of time and memory. Where are we in time, Hempis? he asked.

> We are here in the awareness of no birth and death.
> What space between?
> You will bow into the name and leave it.
> The dead and the living—the same parts of the sound.
> The sound before sound.
> Shedding the skin of words.
> Your life has not been in vain, Temple Sweeper.

The man sat down on the stones of his death. Though he could not yet fully fathom the meaning of his old teacher's words, he was thinking. And in this thinking, he began a story, as Hempis, the girl, and our Head Monk circled quietly and sat around him.

I, too, not unlike each of you, the Temple Sweeper began, I, too, was once a child. When I first wandered the forest, lost, awash with fear, I put my hand on the branch of an oak and chopped off a finger. The corpses of the dead soldiers scattered around me. The shapes I saw then were not those of murder, did not contain the intentions of my imagination, they were not even part of my dreams and visions.

I could not speak. I wandered. I wandered through the forests and mountains and caves, and I searched for who we truly are. Then for another twenty-five years, I stayed with these monks and orphans of the monastery, also in silence.

When you enter the fields of emptiness, mind and body fall away, Hempis said, turning his eyes toward the sky.

The sky, now filling with crows.

Still, I too have a story, the man went on. I have words.

Language and dreams are the same, Temple Sweeper, Hempis said, rubbing the blood stains on the pant legs of his knee, re-lighting the tobacco. But you already know this.

The man sat looking for a long time, dead.

But we too have our stories, the girl chimed in.

The Temple Sweeper listened closely.

So again, you are talking? the Temple Sweeper observed.

Can you other monks hear him now? Hempis said to the crows, gathering.

Almost human, these dreams, the girl continued. Like the appearance of the cypress tree outside the monastery window that talks to you still, she said to the Temple Sweeper. And Enduring Sound, isn't this how you have translated his story of the cypress tree in the scrolls? Like an old song waiting to be sung again. An ancient tree without intention and like us now, with no permanent identity, but meeting auspiciously like this.

Enduring Sound, shrugged his shoulders, and nodded, I think it is as you say, dear one.

Yet now you are entering a new pilgrimage, and we will guide the good monks of our monastery. Is it not so, Enduring Sound? Why, even those parts of your body that have vanished return in the sounds that are true. All of us are you, and you are everything you are not. You sense this, do you not, Enduring Sound?

I have written what you spoke, and what our Temple Sweeper once spoke.

The Temple Sweeper stands and faces Enduring Sound.

This love, too, like the assassin, I, a simple temple sweeper, once became as a boy, Head Monk. Climbing to the killing caves of the soldiers' dreams. Going through the spaces in the soldiers' dreams while they were sleeping. Yet those soldiers never awoke. Like the ghosts of words long ago spoken and returning without utterance. Slowly at first, and only in the sky or sea, these lost beings that flutter to earth.

Is this your memory, or a dream, Temple Sweeper?

Then there are days when the body itself overwhelms you with the secret you have hidden, Enduring Sound, that I have hidden from you, good monk—and needing to tell you all of your life. A child soldier. This, too, is part of my story. And I am sorry, Hempis. I betrayed you. This boy you taught not to kill, but to help you find the other orphans. This betrayal. And still, you come here to meet me in the passage of no birth and death?

Hempis nods, points to the crows gathering in the trees.

A prayer, this temple sweeper's prayer, it's a deep water and blood coming from the earth, the girl said, touching Hempis on the knee. As if words were no longer made of memory, time, anger, nor dream.

And your bird of paradise, the Temple Sweeper replied, turning to the mute girl, who has begun to draw in her diary, hearing the crows. Your bird of paradise flying through the night sky above me every day as I walked to this place, carrying these stones. Like the blue dragon. The phoenix. And now you, too, sitting beside Hempis, holding your diary and writing these sounds. You continue to astonish. A bird of paradise coming to me every morning when I finished my sweeping, gathering the pebbles, carving their graves, moving into this contrition and repentance. Your knowing all along. Knowing I killed them to revenge your own and the others' deaths. Still, you forgave me. No longer a voice to be carried, but a reckoning of all things past and future, all things forgotten and again arising in the infinite games of time.

Enduring Sound takes the flask of water the girl hands him from her satchel, gestures for her diary. But instead of giving it to him, she begins to read from the pages herself—

> Tonight the man stands, looking for a long time,
> dead. He again sees himself as a boy, and I tell him
> to come closer. Against the monastery walls the
> boy is leaning into ineffable space and time. This
> boy with a drop chin, long and dirty black hair and
> high cheekbones that makes him appear fierce.
> With only one eye, the expression aloof, but steady
> once it fixes on you. Come here, I say to him again.
>
> The boy, holding back as I wave him over. Staring
> at bare feet, his own skinny but strong legs;
> the blue cap on his head, the bangs flittering
> over his brow. Come here, I say. Look, you

can write in my diary. No one's going to hurt
us here. The boy looks up, edges closer while
pressing his small hands hard into his chest.

The boy sees I'm dead. That the soldiers found
me. Sees my own face lined with the traces of one
not far from the dream he is leaving. The boy is
wearing your coat, Hempis. The coat you gave to
our good Abbot, and our good Abbot then gave to
Enduring Sound, your son. And the boy stutters
in much the same way as you do, Head Monk.
Still, he takes another step as I put out my arms
saying—Come on, it's ok. We have never been
born, and we will never die. And, I understand,
after all of these lifetimes, he's really still only a
child. We are all merely one child. Rough scars
on his cheeks, soft around the mouth, wanting
to trust a world too violent for his imagination.

As a man, as a wanderer and Seeker, as a Temple
Sweeper and old man, he walks out of the shadows
past the monastery gate, gestures for me to follow
him, then slowly goes on past the garden as we
pass the wooden houses in the village where we
once lived. Going through yet another portal of
time. The boy slipping through another doorway
of time, returning as a man in this consciousness,
we began together on the day of my murder.

He steps into our secret cave, out beyond the
village and paths, nods his head to me as I trail
him through the bamboo gate into our shelter
in the cliffs. There, the glass scattered across the
dirt floor, an overturned stool by a bucket of
water, my father's old sword leaning against the
wall where lie the bodies of three children.

Orphans, he tries to whisper, and though
no word or sound comes, I understand
this is why he has again brought me here,
and that he wants you both to know this
is why he did what he did and became an
assassin in their dreams, Master Hempis.

The boy glances down, trembling.

He stares at his hands for a moment, picks up a
plate from our bench of an altar, slings it across
the cave where it smashes into the stone wall
behind the two soldiers still remaining in this
cave of our once hidden-away refuge. Afterwards,
the boy covers his left ear with one hand as if
in an attempt to block out his own screams.
With his right hand, he smashes another bowl
of incense beneath his own bare feet. Then he
picks up the sword and swings its long heavy
blade, spinning toward the laughing soldiers.

I, one of these children, in the cave that evening.

I, too, stood for a long time looking, dead.

But this is not how our story really began,
Head Monk. Nor is it the way it ends. Still, you
have to know even this, Enduring Sound.

Before you guide the monks on pilgrimage. The
Temple Sweeper could not tell you, but now
find it in the pages of our diary. I, one of them.
I, too, a story of the Storyteller. And here we
sit together again. These crows of past, present,
and future, gathering around us, auspiciously
arriving to hear your song. Where will you
and these monks go, Enduring Sound?

Dream Dialogues—

The Author And the Two Crows

Again we ask, when does the author truly become whole, Hempis? When does one become the author of one's own life?

The man is thinking, coming to his feet, taking in once more the words of the girl's diary, glancing about at the trees branching with crows.

The man is thinking non-thinking.

The amber-colored crow is thinking, too, as such.

Now, the jade-shaded crow is also thinking with non-thinking.

The monks of the monastery have begun their pilgrimage, walking along the path, but now pausing by the river. They, too, are in this non-thinking.

The mute girl is thinking, this is non-thinking.

Hempis is thinking such.

The sea is thinking such.

The river is thinking such.

The moon is thinking such.

The circus players arriving in their small wooden boats, immediately begin non-thinking.

The Prophet and the Poet, thinking, how will we say non-thinking? Those who have joined us need to know.

The Old Story holding up the Old Mirror, thinking why this, it is always the same: A love story.

The man asks—am I a man, am I a crow, a one-eyed boy, a Temple Sweeper, a mute girl, a Head Monk named Enduring Sound?

The man understands this is too much thinking as he stares past us, walks toward the caves.

Still the man goes on thinking, and can't stop thinking, to himself, at first—these days I hardly have time to think, almost saying the words aloud, as if he still had a body. The man thinks—these beings enter my life again, just as they did a thousand years ago. He thinks—are these the scrolls between Lost Children, between wars, between actors backstage, between doorways of time?

The jade crow is thinking the man is understanding too much.

But the amber crow is thinking that for a crow, as a crow, the jade crow, is thinking too much.

The mischievous fox has not been without thinking.

The Learned Sage Women have tired of thinking.

The boy followed us the whole way, follows us tonight through yet another death, the amber crow thinks aloud—cawing at the cliff's mouth, studying the movement of the other crows ascending from the trees toward the cave in the cliffs the man has now entered in formlessness, once more seeing the figure of a boy.

It is curious, the man thinks.

The amber crow is curious, too.

The jade crow, with all the non-thinking, leaves the flock of crows and lands at the cave's dark entryway and commences to hum a lullaby. Our jade crow sings—

Coming home alongside the boy, these monks the man remembers from our pasts. These monks traipsing through the snows, trudging alongside him. These monks who followed the boy a thousand years ago in the Old Story. And here they are appearing again by the cave in the shapes of crows. Arriving from the mountains of coming and going. There they are. The Ghostwoman, our mother, hovering nearby with Hempis, Dream Master, and wanderer in time.

The man sees the amber crow has also landed at the cave's entry. The man hears the jade crow's singing. And then the man thinks to himself—who are these beings who came with the boy. A thousand years ago? Did I once have a name?

You will gradually recognize that this is you. That it is inside you as you have brought it inside your body with an act of eyes hearing the sound, ears seeing the words, this very one moving in the stillness. The inanimate speaking us all. And then it vanishes, again and again, until you are all identities unfolding into one.

The others coming home, again and again.

The circus players, some rising in pairs from their boats, are preparing for their own performance.

Yes, the circus must go on, the Poet thinks.

Though the Prophet is unsure.

They have come to witness this very night in the thinking of non-thinking, the Prophet thinks.

The jade crow pecks his beak against the cliff's stone wall.

The jade crow wants our Temple Sweeper to let him into the cave. The jade crow says to the Temple Sweeper—did you forget the man who pulled a chair behind the one-eyed boy through the snows one starry winter night a thousand years ago? Do you forget me and these other friends so easily, Temple Sweeper? Let us in.

The man stares at the jade crow.

But the story is, perhaps, too hard for him to imagine further.

The man looks onto the amber crow's eyes. And then, the man

questions himself more deeply. If these crows want to come into the cave—should I, without even a body, not invite them in?

And just as these things enter the man's thinking, his friends who have returned, after all of these lifetimes, they themselves join in the thinking, wanting to come in. These friends who accompany the Lost Children through the end of suffering, the amber crow whispers into our ears, Dear Reader. And hearing its own words, the amber crow, along with all of our other crows, begins to fly among the circus players out past the skies and seas in an unspoken jubilation.

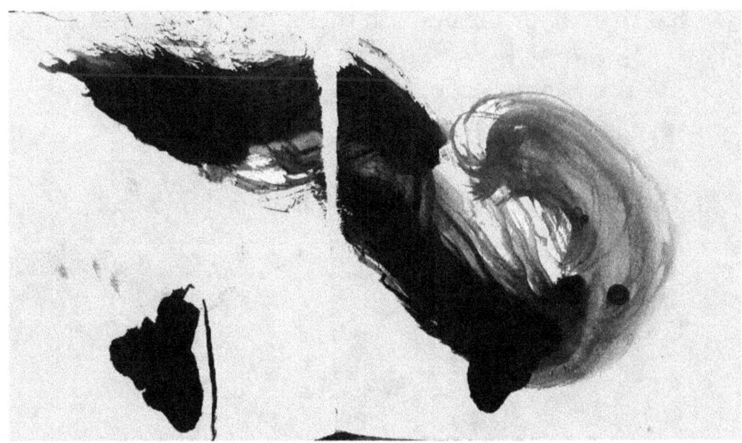

The man utters each of our names under his breath. And in this way, we fly across the mouth of the cave. And then, quite unexpectedly, we might even say suddenly—Enduring Sound cries out from his meditation.

The good Head Monk shaking, unable to contain himself any longer. The other temple monks—they look up, also startled by his cry.

Startled from their own meditation of crows. For Enduring Sound has shared our dream with them. Just as we are sharing it with you, Dear Reader.

Head Monk, Enduring Sound, then calls up to the sky. Going on, face to face, with the Temple Sweeper once more.

And as such, our pilgrimage began in non-thinking.

THE BOOK OF BROWN LEAVES
LATER FOUND IN THE SCROLLS

Blue leaves floating on the water point to a face. The leaves underlying a fear of life, forgiveness—of redemption—& these passages of time flowing toward & through the lives passing through us.

Something primordial in these voices.

To rise up like a hand from the sea.

Shrouds of mists surrounding these centuries of fire.

A secret of ourselves buried like a cast-away body in an empty boat.

Trees.

A Book of Brown Leaves.

Blue and brown leaves.

Stones of hunger.

Clearings of water.

The white of the sky wall guiding you and the monks, Enduring Sound, to a source of the original breath as you follow the pilgrimage—the vastness of an empty boat.

Figures standing on these cliffs and sleeping in caves.

Awakening.

Alive.

You as a lost boy, good monk.

A child in the forest when we found you.

At first, I thought I was you.

But you were as you are, Enduring Sound, Head Monk of the monastery: only once a child full of blood and tears, running, as did we, from the soldiers, ravishing the lives of children.

A child walking among the stones of the sea.

A child searching.

A child's hunger.

At the edge of waves, another being. A girl, holding a diary. And this boy who will become Enduring Sound is frightened. This boy of blue in a Book of Brown Leaves.

To enter, face to face.

Awe.

Because the boy is uncertain whether he really exists after so much terror, if he can exist without love.

This is you, good monk, Enduring Sound.

A three or four-year-old boy of wars.

We carried you across the waves. We found you, and together the girl and I found you, rescued you from the river, the soldiers, and carried you to the circus.

Carried you with these hands that stroke your head in meditation tonight.

The waves not only waves.

A boy standing beside another boy with only one eye a thousand years ago. A girl hovering in a Book of Brown Leaves as you and the monks from the monastery quest forth in this pilgrimage of unknowing, moving below the caverns and caves.

Will they come? the monks asked you last night.

Will the Temple Sweeper and our Abbot come?

They will come if they have a friend.

You are their dear friend, Enduring Monk.

A stone. Salt in your sandals.

Crossing the ravine on the shores of you.

When he is troubled, he is amazed.

We travel together.

When I returned to this monastery with the help of the circus players, I finally let you go again.

In this way, I found you.

Now you find me.

And you find yourself.

Scroll X

The two crows step through the crack of opening light
and dark and walk over to the man's empty robes on
the ground of the cave.

Enduring Sound's Letter to the Temple Sweeper—

Found After the Crows' Departure

So, what do we do now, Scroll Master?
Now that you have left us.

Only dream of more scrolls?

Or write my own dreams into your scrolls?

Or write your scrolls into my dreams of an author?

All responses are satisfactory, Temple Sweeper.

—Your abiding scribe,
Head Monk, Enduring Sound

Two Crows, a Poet, and a Prophet Appearing in a Dream of their Own

The jade crow flaps its wings.

We, too, have had many days and nights when we once traveled through these dreams, the two crows caw together as they wake our Head Monk from his meditation of letters.

Enduring Monk puts down his brush and looks out toward the sky of crows appearing in their own dream. Or did they appear from my brush, as so many did when the boy and girl encouraged me to paint the words?

These circus children coming and going in their boats like this? The Poet interrupts our story, asking the two crows, is it normal? Crows coming and going as they like?

The Prophet sips her tea, touches her shoulders.

The two crows look the Poet in the eye.

Remain as still as possible, the Prophet suggests.

It will become clear in time.

That's what they always say, the Poet laughs.

The flock of crows, assembled in the eaves of the temple, fly about very quietly, hearing the sound of the bells from the Meditation Hall.

Ah, now I remember, the Poet says. If you want to find the meaning, stop chasing after things.

Or at least we once thought, the jade crow caws. But that was another poet and wanderer in another time.

The jade crow squawks so loudly that now even the other monks below the ridge, and even those far away who have remained in the Meditation Hall of the monastery, can hear the sound, waking them to all these reckonings.

When does the author become themself? the Temple Sweeper asked us.

Even now, our Temple Sweeper is coming and going.

The Prophet stands up.

This is why I had to come here again, she says to the jade crow.

Still, the story always does what it wants, the amber crow insists.

The jade crow, suspended in the air about the cave, listens closely.

The Poet can see that the jade crow is serious. But isn't he always serious, he thinks.

Our jade crow has settled on the Temple Sweeper's empty robes on the ground of the cave. He has come to hear a story, the amber crow says to his friend.

Who? asks the Poet.

You think it is you, that the story is you—the amber crow caws again at the Poet.

But since the Poet and Prophet speak their language, this cawing is no problem.

Still, I'm confused, the Poet replies.

Sometimes the words play the part of an actor, sometimes a crow, other times the role of an author, or a red bird chirping in the trees, sometimes as a juggler in a circus, or as a one-eyed boy and mute girl falling in love.

The Prophet nods to our amber friend, sips her tea slowly, watching the steam rise from the cup. She offers a cup to the thankful crow.

We should invite all these other crows to join us for a cup of tea as well, the Poet says, remembering his own wounds when falling in love.

The Prophet sighs, and then she thinks: all of this coming and going of monks and crows and orphans.

Yes, it's really something, the Poet agrees, inviting the rest of us into the cave as the monks rise along the banks of water and continue their pilgrimage down the river with Enduring Sound.

The Man Wandered for a Long Time Watching

The man thinks—clever crows, coming back as crows to remind me.

The man wandered for a long time.
He is leaning into the realm of you.

And the flood of words since I began to think with non-thinking, the man thinks—the lost days and nights of our lives returning even here, outside a dream.

I still love you, Book of Brown Leaves, the man thinks.

And even now, I can see the one who I once was, walking in the blazing field, holding the hand of a beautiful child. I have begun to think, for the first time in my being and non-being, that the passing days of grief all blossom into a pool of deeper roots.

Like rooted trees of light.

Like the girl's own diary.

Like you children gathering around me,

urging me on.

THE GIRL'S DIARY
P.S. WE LOVE YOU

And so the words follow you who are now
the road, Temple Sweeper. We drop the
ink to the page in the letter Enduring Sound
is writing to you this morning. The jade and
amber crows are drizzling our ink from their
beaks. The other crows follow and do the same.
Each beak contains only one letter of one word,
releasing each ink drop in such a way onto the
empty robes—your robes flying up and out
of the cave as the crows fly upward, singing in
their merry caws, carrying your former robes.

Not knowing where we are going.

This is a testament, the man thinks.

The man thinks, this is enough

for the beginning.

The crows fly onward in the sky,

and I am here beside you, good monk,

Enduring Sound, hearing again the girl's diary.

Do not worry.

We pilgrimage on, continuously, together.

The Two Crows Departing Through the Crack of Light and Dark Carrying the Empty Robes from the Cave

Very quiet, the Poet whispers now, settling into the stillness, allowing us to simply be—or, perhaps, in your case, hearing us, if you have come this far, Dear Reader?

> The rest of us bow our heads.
> The words grow silent as stones.
> The crows fly on.

The jade crow trilling as he soars up with the robes—after all these stories, now crossing the vast seas.

Accepting a word of lore is love in the final sum of things? the Poet asks, following behind on the back of the girl's bird of paradise, reading from the scrolls, admiring the girl's diaries, the boy's ink drawings, their unfolding of time.

At least for the moment, the amber crow is able to turn to the next page.

Enduring Sound and the monks, too, begin to open the pages.

The Ghostwoman and Hempis as well, opening the pages.

Waves within waves pouring over the waterfalls from the mountainside, finding a way into language.

> The boy and girl, opening.
> The Temple Sweeper, opening.
> Opening our pages of orphans.

The two crows fly on into this crackling of light and dark within the Temple Sweeper's empty robes, also opening.

And all of the children of the circus reciting the next page of the chorus in unison, together again, reading the next scroll—

> *So you abandoned the monastery, and even the circus, to again enter the dream. This, here, is your life, your life of ending the suffering, over and over. Beside the orphaned children. At a station by our sea. There will be snow again, too. You and the girl, finding one another. Therefore, be at peace. We have done you no harm. These small fishing boats arriving on the shore will take you back into the world once more, until none remain in bondage.*

So you watch, and you study watching, Enduring Sound.

You feel the pain in your joints and shoulders.

You let the sweat wash over you.

The fear of vanishing.

The body's heat.

You watch, Enduring Sound.

The chimes of the temple you've left behind, ringing in the garden of a cypress tree.

You sense the arrival of the orphans.

Arriving in a world of an abundant life.

Enduring Sound with the Monks by the Sea

Good Monks—

The man is standing on the edge of the sea under the rock cliffs now. The cliffs to his back, towering over the horizon. He thinks—all dreams are alive—and travels within them freely tonight. He thinks, this, too, is my story.

The man thinks, this too is an omen.

There is a temple in the sky where Hempis first found us all. The man thinks of the mute girl and whispers, I love you. A sheered light, dead and living. The man speaks to her spirit that abides beside him in the waters. This is without name, good monks, so it is agreed, no words can be spoken. The man thinks, still, I speak. There are always words inside the dream. There are horses and fish and crows.

The man asks, how can we remain silent when everything speaks it?

I can hear it with my eyes.

The crows again ascend in the sky to remind him, good monks.

The girl's spirit points toward the temple.

The Temple Sweeper now glances upward.

The temple is covered in a pinkish light

that appears to be that of another dawn.

The light gathers at the inner architecture of the trees and goes forth from here.

The light enters.

As the light rises, the man suddenly understands his difficulty of walking along the hundred-foot cliff for a thousand years.

Still, slowly he follows the path.

The crows follow the man.

The light goes outward along the water.

We follow this light.

Good monks who follow in the dream with Head Monk, Enduring Sound, who follow on this full moon tonight, the man has now
reached the edge of the cliffs. He is looking across the shoreline of
seas into the deathless death.

Good monks, the man thinks he can hear our chanting. He
remembers the chant from the time of his first birth on earth.

We have been waiting for you to come forward for many years,
he hears one of the cave's cry out as the crows fly on.

The man hears another voice traveling on the wind and whispering to another wind—

If I hear the wind, am I not the wind?

There goes another Temple Sweeper liberated from the bond-
age of birth and death so as to heal the world.

By nightfall, his memory of feet is aching, and his mouth is
dry. He has come across a woman sitting alone in the sand. Her
knees pulled up to her chest, her black hair over her face, her bright
eyes fixed on the sea. He thinks—it is the mute girl, reading her
poems to the sea.

The man sits beside her.

After some time has passed, she says—I have come to return
you home.

The man is startled by the sounds of her poetry.

He opens his mouth as she brings forth a piece of fruit.

Will you take this offering?

Yet the man is uncertain if she is speaking to him, or if it is the
wind speaking to the wind?

He is uncertain if this is a mirage of his pathway home.

Then he remembers.

There are stars over the hills and the crows have now rested on
the hills.

As he tightens his robeless robes and again gets up in a failed effort to walk, he sees the woman is holding a butterfly in her hand, and a moment later, they fly off together.

The dream brought you here, why should you leave, the man calls to her.

> *You have become a wandering of the worlds, no lon-*
> *ger frightened by our damage, but now it is time to*
> *continue your work, and death is part of that work,*
> *part of our final healing. I must leave you and allow*
> *you to complete the journey. But you will always find*
> *me, Temple Sweeper.*

As regards to the meaning, I am the one who is uncertain, good monks, Enduring Sound now says to his companions. Yet when I first woke in the dream it was a thousand years ago. It has taken me time, perhaps too much time, to remember when reading the scrolls and understanding that I, too, am among the Lost Children.

Good monks, it was after the first occasion that the Temple Sweeper glimpsed the Master Hempis in the mountain, our Head Monk continues.

At a certain stage, we can enter one another's dreams. Of course, just as the Temple Sweeper entered my own to help me write the scrolls. But it takes many lifetimes to learn the practice. He began as a boy in his first life a thousand years ago and entered my dream as he did with the other Lost Children. As now he enters yours with Master Hempis and the Ghostwoman.

Do you know who you are, good monks?

Good monks who have come with me now in this pilgrimage of not knowing, following the footsteps of the Temple Sweeper and our Abbot.

This is just the beginning.

We never really stop carrying the stones.

The stones are wounds healing, our Temple Sweeper said to me on that first night in my cell.

So he leads us to this temple in the sky for a reason tonight.

When you are aware of the weight of the stone, it is easier to put the stone down kindly.

We are the stones.

Can you meet the source in everything?

Dying by the cliffside, your bones will be clean.

For we are the Lost Children of the scrolls.

Scroll XI

Enduring Sound to the monks—

I walked through the mountains to arrive here, as if the secret of my life itself, incarnate, were some stone or sage talking. You spoke to me in the leaves of the morning dew. Lost Children of the rain. You came to me like a figure in the evening; a magic pebble, a shadow, standing by the fern and oak as I stood there shivering with nothing on the cliff, searching for our Temple Sweeper. Now, as I am almost completely blind, I release the dreams of our past at last, those lodged deep in memory and our shared imagination of language and time.

The Temple Sweeper and Enduring Sound with Hempis

The Temple Sweeper is flying alongside the mute girl's bird of paradise. The waves over the rocks breaking. The Temple Sweeper overlooking the sea in his new birth, though he is not himself dreaming.

This is the question I wake to now—my former life, is it really over, Hempis? asks the Temple Sweeper. Is it really ended?

Hempis is visibly moved and bows from the shore.

…

The monks gather around Enduring Sound, sitting in meditation, their heads bowed, near a fire in the evening light of their own quest. They sit in a circle with their Head Monk, for their Abbot has left this world without them. Still, they are following Enduring Sound on this pilgrimage to find the one they once called Temple Sweeper. Their Head Monk whispers to them—

Hempis, too, has now entered the dream of the sea where the Temple Sweeper abides.

You are still *in* the dream then, if you think as such, Hempis utters in Enduring Sound's ear from behind a bush. Hempis, having walked across the gushing river, admiring the small fish in shallows near the embankment of the pilgrims camping grounds, the waves splashing against the cliffs and white caps emerging. Enduring Sound, Hempis says—the Temple Sweeper is no longer one and no longer two. No longer form, and no longer formlessness. Your Temple Sweeper is no longer dead, and no longer alive. No longer of birth, and no longer of death.

The Head Monk turns his whole body, yet he sees only a river flowing into the sea.

…

Have I released it? the Temple Sweeper continues, again sensing the contour of his only love's face. Have I released the mute-girl so I can find her again, Hempis? It feels as if the girl is this beautiful bird of paradise soaring over this dream of earth. Hempis, it feels as if the ghosts of the Lost Children are also freeing their bodies and other bodies.

Am I to remain in this question?
Hempis is visibly moved and bows from the shore.

This person you held tight in the image of your childhood includes fear, Enduring Sound, it includes doubt, Hempis continues, somewhat more loudly into our Head Monk's ear, clearing his throat. It includes forgetting as well as, well yes, love, good monk, he says, leaning in closer to Enduring Sound who continues to sit in meditation. Love itself, Hempis says. These memories you are meeting are illusions that pass. Still, you already intuit the presence of your true being. You are not born of nostalgia. You are already intimate in the presence of your true teacher. This is good for you to remember. Say it is not so?

Enduring Sound stands, stumbling for a moment, stirring the attention of the circle of monks who remain very still, silently meditating by the evening's fire as they have always been instructed.

It is so, Hempis.

Some of the monks open their eyes, wonder to whom their Head Monk is speaking, then close their eyes again and pretend not to hear.

…

I have carried their stones, Hempis, the stones of all of our Lost Children, the Temple Sweeper says with his voiceless voice. All of the Lost Children throughout the worlds of time have all met here before, each one of us as a child, and often so. Often so. But to whom are you speaking in this dream of our sea, Hempis—is it the one called Enduring Sound, a scribe of the scrolls?

Has he, too, entered the dream of the great sea, Hempis?

The Temple Sweeper hears the sound of crows rising, water washing over his no longer bandaged feet, sun edging toward the horizon as night approaches and appears pristine, immaculate.

The bodies of these Lost Children, hovering beneath the soldiers' uniforms that day, the Temple Sweeper says, bowing to the cliffs.

Yet it is true, I forgive them. I think I can forgive them, the Temple Sweeper goes on. Forgive who we are in all of this. Even you, Great Sea, even you, I forgive.

Hempis is visibly moved and bows from the shore.

…

You hear the Temple Sweeper in your own words, Enduring Sound, Hempis nods—the one you called by no other name than Temple Sweeper—and you are already walking into the dream of the sea and your true teacher, Hempis says to our Head Monk, again with a low voice, brushing his whiskers against Enduring Sound's ear. Seeing things as they really are. The vanishing forms you imagine are a signless sign.

Enduring Sound then utters these same words he hears out loud, once more rather, unintentionally, startling the meditating monks, who listen in consternation, for the bell to end their period of evening silence on the river has yet to ring.

What remains of this one day in memory, this one night? Enduring Sound asks Hempis, momentarily forgetting where he is.

Every day you awake, you enter the dream of your waking, Hempis responds.

It is a good day to die, it is a good day to be born—the Temple Sweeper now utters to Enduring Sound, searching the hills for the forms of the voices he hears.

The white butterflies fly from the fern and oak trees toward the river. Egrets and frogs begin to gather themselves along the banks. A lone praying mantis rears its head on the boulder surrounded with splashing waves. The Temple Sweeper points to the floating clouds and mountain above the butterflies, the blue moon lifting further in the sky from the sound of stars manifesting as the Temple Sweeper realizes the stars, too, are hearing their own voices.

It is a good day to die, a good day to be born.

The Temple Sweeper discerns this voice, too.

A voice under his own breathless breath.

Hempis bows and Enduring Sound understands the old Dream Master has come for him.

The Temple Sweeper follows the light of the butterflies.

…

You have started wanting to end the suffering, Enduring Sound? Say it is not so, Hempis asks.

Our Head Monk glances up, marvels at the butterfly hovering on his brow with its yellow and orange speckled wings, its glittering eyes looking into his own.

The Temple Sweeper remembers the voice of the butterfly.

The Temple Sweeper is not thinking.

Now the butterfly perches on the sleeve of Enduring Sound's tattered robes.

Those were once my robes, our Temple Sweeper says.

Who is this dear butterfly? the Temple Sweeper asks.

Is this you becoming you?

Who is asking your question, Hempis now responds, turning to him.

Is it me, or is it you, or is it Enduring Sound?

Or a butterfly becoming human, Temple Sweeper?

Hempis' wings flutter against his faceless face.

How can I begin this new birth? the Temple Sweeper asks.

There is nothing born, nothing destroyed, Temple Sweeper.

The wind breathing us, the air breathing us, and the monks with Enduring Sound are breathing more freely as the Temple Sweeper beholds their breaths in the flutter of these monks' gray robes and the patterns of earth and sea and sky converging around him, brushing the salt on his true face. I love them all, and still do not want to leave, our Temple Sweeper says.

Hempis is visibly moved and bows from the shore with open wings.

The amber and jade crows, hearing the Temple Sweeper's words, leave the side of the cliff and return to the river's shore.

The Poet and Prophet follow, wondering themselves as to what is actually happening.

Do you know? the Poet asks the Prophet.

Yes. The bell ending our meditation has now rung,
the Prophet sighs.

The two crows watch the monks as they stand, dust off their robes, each looking up toward the mountain and these strange shapes in the sky about the mists of the mountain top.

This mountain Enduring Sound will someday call by the name of Temple Sweeper, as it is later written in the scrolls.

The two crows walk along the edge of the river, cawing.

Do you think it is possible?

You, those of you who have traveled so far in these scrolls, Dear Reader?

Though we cannot see you, we know you are here.

You, who are hearing our voices and realizing they are your own.

Yes, the amber crow trills.

Anything is possible.

Yes, the jade crow says.

The Poet and Prophet nod in agreement.

You are right here—in this moment.

It is not you who has vanished, but the dream.

The Poet writes this in his notebook.

Enduring Sound slips away from the monks, trailing the wings of the butterfly that perched on his brow and sleeve.

Leaves scatter by the shore.

The Book of Brown Leaves itself looks up past the cliffs, its own face turning toward the temple in our sky.

Enduring Sound calls out, calls to the butterfly, running down the shore and slowly extending his arms, as if they were wings, raising his hands from his own poverty and awe, the sleeves of his robes, these very robes which were once his teacher's, and opens his eyes in the flush of wild and gushing wind as his body begins to lift from the sand and pebbles and waves—rising upwards into the cloud of butterflies fluttering over the earth.

Wait, he calls. Wait. I will come with you.

Wait.

I don't know how to fly, Hempis!

The Mute Girl's Letters

Letter 1

Dear You,

I sent these letters at the time of your first birth and death. Only then you did not find them, for you were lost in the mirage of birth and death.

> I have waited.
> I have been where you are.
> And where you are not.

Now I write them into you once more, in the hope they will help to free you as you begin this new pilgrimage to cross the rivers and mountains and deserts still yet to come, liberated from illusion.

> This is our other story of love.
> It is only beginning.
> The other shore is this shore.

Letter 2

Dearest You,

A thousand years of suffering have ended.
In your great death, my bird of paradise prepares for you.
This morning when I rose by the sea, dolphins came forth.
Egrets and Caspian terns too, singing.

Letter 3

Dear Boy,

Do not be afraid.
Regardless that you cannot find the other Lost Children
tonight, I send these words from our Book of Brown Leaves.
The ones you helped me write.
The ones you nurtured.
Perhaps the one called Enduring Sound will again find and
help you now.
Though no doubt, our monk is going blind, and he will
have to decide for himself.
I leave these alphabets by the cliffs of air and breath, receiv-
ing and releasing, as you did for me, before finding your way
into the mountains all those years ago after my death.
A boy without a name.

>You'll uncover a map, dug in deep beneath
>
>the statues of our Learned Sage Women,
>
>where you first heard the scrolls speaking—
>
>an orphan with few fingers.
>
>Follow the map of linked caves
>
>into the cave's face

and from there into our library

of the Lost Children's letters and notebooks.

You will remember when you arrive.

You will remember how.

Remember the Ghostwoman who dreamed and healed
me as well as these other wanderers in the mountains.
Just as Hempis guided you to the Abbot and revealed the
secret of the stones.
Do not fear this.
Do not fear the mystery.

> Stones, grasses, trees, bees, butterflies, crows, and
> cliffs speak it. Look at the sea dancing across the
> shores of you.

Letter 4

Dear Darling, Dear Darling You,

The work of teaching has come down
through questioning and answering, my love.
Cultivating phantom meditations,
it does the work in a dream.

Letter 5

Dear Temple Sweeper,

The monks who remained in our monastery, who were
frightened and have not followed Enduring Sound, they are
knocking on the door of your cell to find the one who still
breathes this pilgrimage we began a thousand years ago.

They, too, will find us.

When I look out into the Sea,
I see you.

I see the scar of your eye and blood on your robe.
I see your hand holding a brush.

LETTER 6

Darling Boy,

I am here waiting, floating
across this sea into the being of stars.

LETTER 7

Dear Storyteller,

This morning as the crows flew out of the cave,
carrying your robes in their beaks,
I watched you from our simple garden.
Now you feel the paper in your handless hands,
rough and coarse on your new skin.
It is how I have always loved you.

LETTER 8

Dear Awakening One,

Before you,
I found the life of your hand.

The life of the brush.

I learned its language,
so we could live more fully
in our own sound before sound.

Do not hesitate.

We are, again, beginning.

Dream Dialogues—

Enduring Sound and the Temple Sweeper
Meeting as Butterflies

*E*NDURING SOUND,

I have already taught you how to fly.
Just as Hempis once taught me.
Two wings touching in the air.
But go back, Enduring Sound.
The orphaned monks await you
on the river's shore.

This flight where we began leading you there all along.
A movement and a rest.
This is why I knocked on your cell door,
and asked if you could retrieve a sheaf of scrolls
from the monastery storeroom.
We, floating in infinite worlds.
Arriving in the distantless distance.
A signless sign.
Go back now, Enduring Sound.
You will find this, too, written in the scrolls you
are writing, and which are already written.

TEMPLE SWEEPER,

Seeing you with ears.
Hearing you with eyes.
Moving in the stillness.
We will pilgrimage on in the realm of sentient beings.
Yet nowhere to go, no one to be,

as if held up.
If in no other way than this,
you have brought me this far,
so why stop now?
Your scribe will go back.
And together find you.
If for no other reason
than this compassion.

I will try not to be distracted
by the final word
you scribbled in my journal on your last night.

We will heed the call.

Scroll XII

In the training of a sage there is ravage & there is blossom, the mute girl calls to the boy walking across the sea.

But aren't they the same, says the boy, pausing by our boat, on the eve of another meeting.

Spiritual Autobiographies—

Returning the Stones the Next Day

The Ghostwoman glances past the cherry trees along the river where Enduring Sound is attempting to nap, and in this way, to encourage the monks who are weary. They are very tired today, discouraged, thinks our Head Monk. For this reason, the Ghostwoman has come. Her gray eyes small and fatigued as well, her feet and arms bare as she lies on the yellowed grass beside our Head Monk near the shore where the river enters the sea. Resting now with him after this day's long trek with the monks over the hills and across the deep ravines, carrying their canvas bags of pebbles and stones. The Ghostwoman sees Enduring Sound as he is.

Hempis sees you still, Enduring Sound, the Ghostwoman says, brushing the hair from her eyes. In the story of the butterflies, you were flying, do you remember?

I remember, yes.

Yet the Lost Children are walking, following you, for you've returned. Though they were discouraged when you disappeared, you have returned. Do not fear, we have all taught you how to fly.

Why do they follow me? I am feeble, almost blind, and unable to help them. I long for my teacher, Ghostwoman.

They follow you as you follow your teacher, our Temple Sweeper of the scrolls, good monk. Just as the Temple Sweeper followed your father and his teacher, Hempis, along these roads of sameness and difference. Still, you are the one now wearing their robes.

Enduring Sound rubs his eyes and comes to his feet quite slowly, unsure as to whether this apparition is dreaming him, or if he is dreaming into her small, luminous eyes.

Head Monk, Enduring Sound, you remember well that last night in your cell when the Temple Sweeper came to you, do you not? Came to you relentlessly, and revealed our secret?

I wrote it as he requested. I am a simple scribe, Ghostwoman.

But is there something you have forgotten to write, Enduring Sound? Why? Even when you were with the Learned Sage Women, did the girl who blindfolded and led you through the cave, not remind you?

The Temple Sweeper told me, in his jumbled, somewhat reserved fashion—told me Hempis was my father.

Is it not so? Think more deeply, meditate with this tonight, Head Monk in non-thinking. Your Temple Sweeper revealed to you that Hempis was and remains your true father—and he is a father to you still. This is how the girl and boy found you when the soldiers came to your village. The old shaman wandering through the burning fields to find a place to hide you in the brush by the river. Hempis gave this secret only to the mute girl and one-eyed boy when he secreted you into the eddies along the banks. He did not even tell me. Yet you have not written it into the scrolls. Why?

The wind sequesters its voice low across the waves and white caps, and through the blossoms of the cherry trees, their pink clusters falling in tiny petals around our Head Monk's torn robe, fluttering on the earth beneath him, covering the green and yellow foliage where he napped, or still naps, on its fecund ground.

Once, Enduring Sound, once when the Temple Sweeper was a boy, and walking this same path as you travel with the monks now, he was so distraught, so weighed down by his own bag of stones, and then, suddenly before him, was a bag of gold cast down from the heavens

A bag of gold? Enduring Sound asks, brushing the petals off his teacher's torn robe.

But the boy did not see the bag of gold, Enduring Sound.

The boy—the one you now call teacher, Temple Sweeper—he walked alone in these very mountains you travel with the monastery monks, afraid he had forever lost the girl. He kicked his foot against this bag of gold and yelped even louder in his suffering and rage.

A bag of gold, or a bag of stones, Ghostwoman? Perhaps it is you who are confused, Enduring Sound says to her. Our Temple Sweeper carried the stones of the lost diaries. Just as I and these other monks do in this pilgrimage. We gather the pebbles when we walk and leave them along the trail so that the other monks from the monastery can someday find us. So that our Temple Sweeper and Abbot can find us too, perhaps. A bag of stones, or a bag of gold—perhaps it is you who is confused.

What is the difference, Enduring Sound? The Ghostwoman sighs, stretching her neck outward toward the sky, calling to the Learned Sage Women she sees trailing along the shore of white sand in the distance. She then folds her languid hands into one another as she and Enduring Sound stare into each other's eyes. And we, we who are perched among you—you who have followed so far—we study their speech from the cherry petals on your very own, on Enduring Sound's, shoulder, and we imagine your inquisitive eyes doubting us in this way. But you have already remembered and simply need to say it.

I remember, Enduring Sound whispers. I remember it all. You, Ghostwoman. You who spoke to me and the Sage Women those first and last nights of my journey through the mainland. But these are only stories—these are only pebbles and stones. Still, I have been thinking about these monks on this pilgrimage, so, naturally, you appear now, Ghostwoman. But we do not confuse our bags of pebbles for bags of gold.

Do you see the Sage Women coming down the shore, good monk? Close your eyes and you will find them. Do you think they are butterflies, Enduring Sound? Did you not write of them before? Question this, Enduring Sound. We shift and shape according to your perception. But none of us have forgotten you and our time together in the caves of the Learned Sage Women.

We promised to help guide you.

Do not lose hope.

It is a sad story. Too sad for this scribe, our Head Monk utters, reaching out his hand in the falling petals.

Why sad, Enduring Sound?

Because, because—he is no longer here. My teacher has gone. And now, I must become him.

What is the load on your shoulders? the Ghostwoman asks, bowing to him. Your past, your childhoods? These wars without end? The things you suffered and suffer still? All of these children forlorn and desperate for food and shelter across the borders? Our Ghostwoman pauses, looks into Enduring Sound's eyes. They have made you who we are. They are your friends and teachers. Giving and receiving are the same things, she smiles, as she notices a tear appear on Enduring Sound's cheek.

The monks from the monastery who have followed Enduring Sound, seeing his tears, begin to gather their things, and put
out the fire. They scatter more pebbles and stones from their bags
as they walk slowly further down the shore, dropping more pebbles, leaving a distinct path for the others. And then, startled for
a moment, our monks pause, spotting the group of children trailing behind the Learned Sage Women. These children in tattered
clothing coming over the hill from the sea, meeting in the meadow
between the dragon-backed ridge and sea. The women greeting,
some embracing, the children.

How does one put down the bag, Enduring Sound? our Ghostwoman asks.

Tell me, tell me first, am I dreaming you in these visions of river
and sea, or are you dreaming me, Ghostwoman?

But you already know this, Enduring Sound. We are only
dreaming each other. We are nothing other than particles of light.
But without these forms, how could you see us?

Enduring Sound glances at the leaves from the apple and pear
blossoms also blowing in the air, and he hears the waves of voices
around him.

The Learned Sage Women and Lost Children begin to con-
verge more closely together along the river, sitting beside the
monks, who once more have put down their bags to listen to the
Ghostwoman and Enduring Sound, as do we who are hidden in
the scrolls.

Enduring Sound, you will lead these children you now see back
to the monastery one day. You will give them a home, a shelter, a
place to be free. The Temple Sweeper had to see that the bags he
had been carrying were bags of gold. They were not stones, Head
Monk. Did you not know? But your teacher did not know for a
long time either, know that first he had to put down the load from
his shoulder, Enduring Sound. As do you. How else could you be
writing in the scrolls?

The wind curves in winding circles through the blossoms, these clusters floating down as the spring leaves swirl about the faces of the boy and girl who have arrived, shadowed in the foliage of the cherry, apple, and pear trees.

The same bags, is this what you are telling me? Yet one is as you say, stones. The other—you call it gold?

The other shore is this shore, where you stand, Enduring Sound. Whatever you see, it is here. The gold is your own bag of stones. But first you need to put down your load.

The Ghostwoman steps in the slant of morning sun streaming down through the mountain. The boy and girl, who are also sitting among us now, begin to draw our portraits in their diaries.

What do you really want, Head Monk?

Want? The same thing as most, I imagine. Love. To live and die in its beauty. Just as we of the monastery learned about the Temple Sweeper's secret and true life, and as he told me of his journey, I began to dream with him, night after night. Night after night he came to my cell, though it was clear he was dying. I would fall asleep at my desk, and when I woke, he would still be there waiting, saying—*the problem is that you think there is time. Yet time and language are the same.*

What did you learn, Enduring Sound?

That I miss him. And that
his was that of a great love story.

This is none other than you yourself, Head Monk.
Do not be distracted by death.
Finish the scrolls.

A Lost Girl in the Scrolls

We are part of your dreams now, Lost Children who we once were, as you are in our dreams and stories. We study this sound, this voice, in order to hear it, to follow it, to let go of it, to go through it, and to return to it, and be it. Only the language of compassion remains. Language of awe. Word as story, as self, always changing as you touch our wound, and we are born once more in these shifting rays of light about the hills from where your eyes search the skies, resting against the heap of pebbles and stones.

The monks will bow forty times.

The lanterns and incense lit.

Both spirits and sages will gather.

The birds, sea, and sky will carry us.

These stones have become dreams.

These dreams have become voices.

These voices have become prayers.

These prayers have become us
wandering among the pages of you, Dear Reader.

THE ESSENTIAL STORY—

THE GIRL'S BIRD OF PARADISE
LIFTS INTO PARTICLES OF LIGHT

243

The boy looks out over the treetops toward the first faint rays of sun entering the sky from the east, a deep wind rustling in the branches.

> I hear the bell from beneath the make-shift temple
> of our Lost Children in the wilderness. All the Lost
> Children who have built this temple of wilderness
> and sea in tall trees of longing.
>
> It is the call. Shall we go, Temple Sweeper?
>
> You see my arms raised above your head,
>
> as if any moment, each child will flow into particles
>
> of light—
>
> into everything you have ever wanted,
>
> and always found.

The Temple Sweeper, The Boy, & The Crows Talking To You

In the story, this too happens—
The crows come, the boy dances,
a girl watches them from the mountaintop.

The Temple Sweeper was never gone. He is floating across a hillside, humming.

Waiting for the mute girl to fly through the sky again & again, and so that you might see her, as you.

The Temple Sweeper is humming for you, remembering how he became like an older brother to Enduring Sound after Hempis' departure from the body. After all the healing. The song is a lullaby you may recognize?

One of the love songs of you who are love.

A phoenix appears in the sky again foretelling how, all the same, these butterflies and crows are ready to include everything.

> It is raining on the cliffs near the sea and the sun bursts through a white sky as if all of the stars ever known, and all the cities and kingdoms ever built, and all the faces, animate and inanimate, flow on in awe of a blazing reign of everythingness. You are afraid it will blind you? It will not blind you. It is only kindness. The Temple Sweeper whistles with the rain in his eyes and your own story arises once more, and you remember. You remember your own childhood—pouring forth in the rain, speaking.

The universe follows you, just as Enduring Sound and the monks follow the Temple Sweeper in this pilgrimage, this vision.

Don't you know, stammers the amber crow, almost too excitedly, flying out of the rain of your story.

Yet you yourself, following in these scrolls, have brought it forth.

The Old Sages understood that if you, and we, were to survive, they would need to help one another.

> The jade crow flaps its wings as you watch.
> The rain of your own story, it is something like this.
> You think to yourself—there is so much rain.
> You think—there is so much trouble.
> We think, the trouble must be beauty.
> When troubled, we are amazed.
> Another day passes in this way.

So you forget your own childhood for a moment, and you return to when Enduring Sound awakens on the burning river, a mere child wrapped in a blanket, where the one-eyed boy and mute girl find him. They have followed Hempis' instructions.

He wrote them in the girl's diary on the hillside by the cave before the soldiers came.

Hempis was sitting very still, a Dream Master, before entering the light and dark, preparing his own renunciation, his own departure from the body.

> The jade crow caws.
> You can turn away no longer.

The mischievous fox comes forth from the cave, crouches as the crows begin to trill the lullaby of a temple sweeper, a tune you yourself vaguely remember, as if it were playing in the ears of childhood, and you, lost yourself, or lost to the things you so loved as a child.

Have you forgotten? the jade crow asks.

The Temple Sweeper looks up.

You look up.

Even as a child you yearned for your own healing.
By now, the clouds know your name.

Hempis sits very still, opens the stone of his father within. He hands the girl back her diary after writing these words she and the boy will someday read over and over, together—

Time simultaneously rises and falls away,
revealing our suffering, and the end of suffering.
This self does not exist in the way we usually
think of it. It is just a continuation of all being
and non-being, without a speck of separateness.

Hempis smiles, looking at the boy and girl sitting beside their old shaman.

And if things arise and fall away at the same time,
they don't actually exist or not exist, he writes in

the girl's diary, repeating the words afterwards
for them to hear with their own ears. And if
they don't actually exist, they can't cease to exist.
Nor will I, children, Hempis says. I will find
you both again. But now you must find my son.
Someday you will know him as Enduring Sound.
Quickly, children—run now. Run fast. The
soldiers who are coming, they know how to find
me. Just as you know now how to find my son.

The jade crow trills to our Head Monk, who is meditating below the cliff by the shore with the other monks after drinking a
good cup of tea.

Where do you think your father really is, Enduring Sound?

Just as the wounder wounds themself, the healer
heals themself, the Prophet whispers into the Poet's ear.

The one you forgot and once knew as your father—
he is *here*. You were only a child, but surely you must
remember, Head Monk, the two crows hum together.

Enduring Sound sits up a little.
Hempis' fox comes and sits beside him.
Enduring Sound scratches his ear.
So it was you? You all along, Hempis?

The girl's bird of paradise flies down to the shore of Sage Wom-
en and Lost Children, and the monks' mouths begin their evening
chanting.

In the opened stone of the dream, you are kissing the hand of
your own childhood.

In the opened stone of the dream, this birth is singing.

In the opened letters of your own past, your childhood is walking forward to join us.

Do you not hear?

You have come this far, why stop now?

You want to hold out your palm to shelter these orphaned
children, gathered and cared for in the rain.

A homeless child walks across the tracks into the boundless
fields of everythingness.

The child brought us into the miraculous.
Will you take the child's hand?

The jade crow flies up as the one-eyed boy swaggers
out from behind the clouds of unknowing.

There he is, there he is! the other crows call,
flying toward him.

The boy picks up a stone from the ground and looks
about longingly.

He thinks he can see you.
You who are you.

You who remember your own childhood again now.

Are you my friend? the boy asks you, startling the monks.
Yes, you say.
The boy puts down the stone, steps nearer, cocks his head toward our Poet.
The girl stands beside him.

Though I am only you, he says to the Poet,

I am you in a different form.

The amber crow nods.

The jade crow holds her tongue, perks up her ears.

You can join us, even here.

You.

Enduring Monk Back on Pilgrimage the Next Day

If the mute girl is mute, Enduring Sound—
how does she speak? the monks ask.

If as soon as she opens her mouth she expresses preferences,
how does she avoid picking and choosing? they ask.

It is enough to ask the question, bow and step back,
Enduring Sound says.

You are always close to this.

It is the page that speaks.

The words are alive.

A whiteness of scrolls pulling us toward the sea.

Just as you in this moment's passing, the sea lingers in a
word and voice between the light and dark.

This is no other than who we are.

Scroll XIII

You see, the story is changing. You see the body is changing—you see inside. The trees and grasses, stones, mountains and hills. Moon blood on spotted tracks through the forests. The voice familiar, but it is no longer your own, no longer the same voice, because you are seeing inside. The stars reflected in each drop of each syllable, each flicker of its sound. It's very syntax. As if the sitting—the pose of meditation—is all that exists.

—The Girl's Diary

This is How the World Begins

There. There you go: look up again. There. You see the boy playing with the children as he did when he first came to you, falling in love with the alphabet of an unknown diary. Dear You, is this a diary—is it perhaps, yours? There are orphans stirring once more in our words, their worlds, without friends or family, without countries or nations—with torn bodies, broken hearts. All the same, they are resting in these scrolls. And the boy is showing us, opening the visions that enter through the moon's eye as you perch on a mountainside, this very mountainside you've found in the pages of a story.

> The boy says:
> the body speaks.
> When you hear it, you awaken in the dream.
> And the dream vanishes.
> Then you can travel with us, freely.
> Freeing others.
> Freeing others with your own imagination.

We bow to you. The words grow silent, like butterflies, a kind of cadence in your ears—a lullaby of coming home. All the wings flying up. A memory. A moment. A majestic sweep of sound.

> Perhaps you even remember your own life,
> just for an instant,
> remember your own wounds.

Very quietly now, watching you settle into the stillness, a sturdiness, allowing us to simply be who we are—and, in your case, Dear You—to see your own childhood and life more fully, more benignly—a curious circling back? As though, through the eyes of a boy and a girl, from time to time, you see who you, yourself, are?

"

Listening closely. You begin to write in these scrolls.
Writing your own story.

So that Enduring Sound too, and the monks who follow you intently on this very pilgrimage of unknowing, begin to remember, remember you.

You are standing there, bowing.
We are bowing together.

A fierce love burns in the fiery fields. We walk through the fires, no longer frightened, no longer alone. It will never cease, the sounds of your own living and dying. Just for a moment you imagine and co-create it. Even here, you can witness the one walking through the fields, lightly holding the hand of a beautiful child, and embracing you—

you who are you.

The Ghostwoman speaking in your own dream tonight

You Who Are You

Are we done now? the boy asks a child.
Two crows in the field by the cypress tree.
Enduring Sound, are you listening?
Maybe it is time you speak to them.

Who is dreaming whom?

We are dreaming each other, the Temple Sweeper
utters in your ear.
White moths gathering in the new grasslands.

In this twinkling between day and night, speaking and not speaking, you walk with the monks through another gorge, another handwritten page, another passage, a portal trailing along these grasslands, wading across the streams, pausing to look around, and everywhere, mirroring reflections of your own face.

Hempis' voice audible once more, sauntering out from the flight of bees, our Learned Sage Women taking shape in the hovering flights and lighting about your arms and legs, reminding you of love in the springtime.

You see into the sea and seeing, you find him seeing.

Then walking across the waves to greet you,

Enduring Sound.

The Temple Sweeper is becoming the worlds around him,

and you are becoming the words around us.

Becoming who we have always been—

and now, we who are you.

Fish swim, falcons fly, pebbles speak their stories by clouded starlight. You love even this absence, this utter and complete presence in absence. Egrets swoop down and begin to pick up the pebbles, pass them from their beaks into the hands of a boy and girl, carry their forms over the monks' shoulders—these monks who gaze up at the sky in awe, and then in a flash, flying asunder, onward over the cliffs as you stare into the slight, coral light of another nightfall. The Temple Sweeper's breath rising and falling in the sea, extending his arms and waving, as from the words of a letter you forgot to read many lifetimes before.

How long has it been as such, you will wonder later when you hold him again. Enduring Sound, you transform the man's body of earth and sky and sea and light, begin and finish and begin it again in your own language.

The wind blows through the cypress grove where you sleep now. The spring warmer these nights. The other monks circling in sleep around the dimming fire. And in your meditation, they witness their own former lives, the monks hear the lifting of all those who have passed, and all of those who have been found, writing letters in the grass and on the ground and up the bark of the cypress trees. There are whistles, bits and pieces of chatter, ringing bells, small talk, laughter. The cypress trees seem the same as you once remembered, but they are not the same as when you left the monastery.

> Just this.
> Just what is lived.
> And no need, or cause, to separate.
>
> Finish the scrolls, good monk.
> Many others join you tonight,
> writing these scrolls with you,
> for you, to you.
> For all of us.
> All of our stories merging.
> You've come this far,
> why stop now, Enduring Sound?

THE ESSENTIAL STORY—

THE TEMPLE SWEEPER SPEAKING IN ENDURING SOUND'S WAKING AS WE WALK WITH THEM ALONG ANOTHER RIVER

Even as a monk, you will be unable to save them, save your family, good monk.

Yet in a way, all you are doing now has already freed them.

Still, the boy wants to forgive.

The Head Monk, Enduring Sound, wants to forgive.

But he has yet to fully recall how.

The waves are not waves.

Yet the waves are waves, too, and only one water.

I see you as a boy beside another boy, a boy with only one eye, a thousand years ago, Enduring Sound. You are beside this one-eyed one, and this mute girl hovering in a Book of Brown Leaves as you quest forth in the pilgrimage.

Will he come, the sturdy monks asked you last night.

Will the Temple Sweeper come?

Will our Abbot be with him?

Otherwise, Enduring Sound, why do we simple monks follow you on this pilgrimage?

He will come if he has a companion, you said, remembering you don't really know.

You picked up a stone and began to carry it on your shoulder as the salt in your sandal washed out one piece of sand with each pebble falling from your sleeve, crossing the river to the sea of the other shores of you.

This, too, part of our story.

This book of scrolls was never only about the life of a temple sweeper.

If there is love waiting, where will we find it, you asked me as a boy, asked me and the mute-girl every day when we found you, good monk. Just a boy looking for a home.

So, we set off, set out to take you to your Abbot and future home.

Forests and rivers. Pilgrimaging together with you for three years, we took you to the carnival players, those still alive, still traveling in the cities of sand. They led us to the monastery where you found a new identity as an honorable scribe, and eventually, a head monk.

We left you there.

Then, we went back to find the others.

We went back to the wars.

But I had to come back.

After twenty-five years, I had to return.

For I missed you.

Perhaps it was these very ones we were as children who called us here today, Enduring Sound. Perhaps these Lost Children, these lost monks who follow you realize they will be found before they are ever lost again. Perhaps the boy you once were had already been found before me, hearing a sound of the scrolls in a dream? So much in a word, as in the past is never past, never gone, always reckoning, reveling, revealing itself as we move on through the great death of no death.

When I returned twenty-five years ago, again with the help of the circus players, and now the Learned Sage Women and the Ghostwoman accompanying me, I discovered you again. No matter where I turned in the battles over those years, I always saw your face, Enduring Sound. The faces of you, the child, and the mute girl who I love and who loved me with all of our Lost Children emerging in the original face.

I found myself when I found you.

No longer alone.

No longer in fear.

This sense of well-being within the monastery walls.

My identity, without words.

Without name.

Free of identity.

What else can we do but continue.

If not for your own quest and suffering, how else could you be here? Hempis asked you this as you and the monks traveled through another day, walking through the fields.

And you have always been here—Hempis said to you that first night in the dream when he came to you after you returned to the scrolls—Hempis pausing and bowing before departing again, like the driftwood that floats in the river before you on this Book of Brown Leaves.

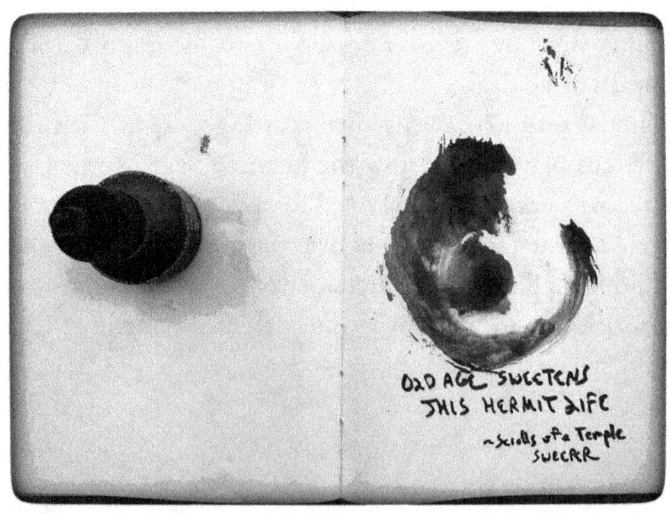

The Monks Following Enduring Sound Enter the Book of Brown Leaves

Blue leaves floating on the water point to a face.

A secret part of ourselves once buried, like a cast-away body, in an empty boat.

Like the whiteness of the sky guiding you, as you guide us. We monks who have come with you, Enduring Sound, following toward the source of original breath, following in this continual pilgrimage—

> The empty boat on the water.
> Languages found in a Book of Brown Leaves,
> floating about the grasslands.

If allowed to give birth to your own childhood once more, for even a day, would the blossom of sun and moon in the sky not still enter? you asked us.

Entering a Book of Brown Leaves, we hear you.

We monks see you for who you really are, Enduring Sound.

Wandering the forest when a one-eyed boy and mute girl discovered you.

And now we come before you, requesting for you to become our Abbot.

Will you honor this request, Enduring Sound?

We know who you are.

How can you know, if I do not know myself? I will be your friend, dear monks. We will pilgrimage on throughout these lifetimes.

I will be your friend, but I am no Abbot.

Enduring Sound, please listen. For a time, we even thought you had become the one whom the Temple Sweeper had once been.

For a time, we thought you had become him.

And before leaving his body, for us monks it seemed, our former Abbot wanted the Temple Sweeper to take his seat as Abbot. But the Temple Sweeper always refused, remaining in his silence until he began to speak to you in and of the scrolls.

Will you refuse us too, Enduring Sound?

For now we see who you truly are—Enduring Abbot of our monastery.

This, whom we monks ask you to become.

Once a child full of blood and tears, as were we monks who follow you now. Once we were weeping in the forest, running, running from the soldiers. From the ones who had killed our families. A child walking among the dead. A child searching. A child's hunger. We are you, so we follow you, Enduring Sound. We follow you tonight.

We await your word. Please hear our request.

At the edge of waves that day the soldiers came. You were hidden in the brush by the burning river. The one-eyed boy carried you across the waves at nightfall. And then, on the other shore, you saw another child, Enduring Sound. A girl. A girl, with no voice. This girl who cared for you, carried you in her arms. Cared for you for three years as she and the boy traveled with you through the mountains, eventually bringing you to us. The mute girl constantly stroking your head, your frightened body—with the same endearing hands as we monks, we monks who stroke your head in meditation tonight as you sleep.

> The boy always beside her in the forest.
> The boy with only one eye carrying a sword.
> But you remain anxious.
> But we all love you, Enduring Sound.

Because you are uncertain whether this boy you were really existed after so much terror, whether any childhood exists in his world. So you forgot. But we are here. This, too, is our story, Enduring Sound. We, too, were the lost orphans.

And we love you.
We are like you.
A child who survived another war.
You are not guilty.
It is not our fault that we survived.
You can remember now.
It was the boy and girl who carried you
across the waves that day.
Carried you with tender and strong hands.
And then, they came back for us, Enduring Sound.
They came back for us, too.
We monks who follow you,
we once, too, were Lost Children.
You are not alone.

The soldiers who razed the villages where you were born, where we were born—they had returned, once more, after a thousand years of wars. And because of the boy and girl, we survived.

You were found, again.
And we were found, again.
As you are once more finding us,

Head Monk, Enduring Sound.
Do not doubt this.
It is time for you to be our Abbot.
We need you to go on.
Just as you said to us that last night in the Meditation Hall,
before our good Abbot and our Temple Sweeper, left their
bodies, you told us—

*When you enter the fields of emptiness, mind and body
fall away.*

Remember this, Enduring Sound? Our deceased Abbot had
challenged you, challenged you once more, demanded that you
come forward, to take his seat and at last, speak. Your stutter
vanished.

When you enter the fields of vastness, mind and body fall
away, you repeated. But dreams remain and carry us to destiny. The
cypress branches lift in the wind as the bells outside our monastery
ring, calling us forward to a pilgrimage of unknowing.

He who lives in forgetfulness dies in a dream.
Still, we have our stories.
We have words.
The place of the body is not barren.
These were your words that night, Enduring Sound.
Do you remember? We remember.

Like the withering of the cypress tree in the courtyard. Death
visible in the arched limbs and knotted roots, the thick bark and
circling edges of the fallen wood. The place of the body has come
home, walking today with the Lost Children who were once abandoned and now, we are found.

Will you remember?
Will you become our Abbot, Enduring Sound?

The Ghostwoman Returns Here For You

The Circus Master welcomes you,
raising her arms,
as she begins to speak to you—

In our former lives, you Lost Children
would run at our feet.
Some of you may wonder if you, too, were among them.
Do you recognize any of their faces as one of your own?

The boy asked Hempis to train him in the ways of entering
dreams.

All of the ravage, and yet,
those who discover their way home,
surrounding the mountain paths of our circus grounds.

On this auspicious evening as the children rush about our
House of Language, a home outside time, a home built into
the wind that circles us as you pilgrims arrive from many
skies and seas. We will not forget your story. The one-eyed
boy and mute girl coming home. You coming home.

As for myself, an old woman in your story, I again see you
playing in the fields, falling in love with the voices of your
diaries.

A thousand years ago? Or just a flicker of light in my passing morning. Inventing each earth.

Observing a kiss on a river,
A crow fluttered above my head,
butterflies flying from our mouths.

We welcome you.

You have finally come.
You have arrived.
On these shores of you.
As you have written it,
As you are writing it now.

P.S. i love you

Do you really think there is anything missing?
The boy once asked me this too, stepping out of the water,
carrying a fish cupped in his hands as a gift
for a ghostwoman.
The girl glanced up, startled—not having noticed him
in the performance of waves rolling over waves,
and yet, somehow here he is, once more,
speaking to you in this way with a Circus Master,
carrying in his a rms this fish
I now offer you.
Do you really think there was anything ever missing?
The boy asks you this, and now
you realize he is talking to you.
Will you take his hand?
Forgive him?
Forgive yourself?
We have always been this.

BOOK III

Scroll XIV

You will gradually recognize that this is you.
That it is inside you as you have brought it
inside your body
with an act of eyes hearing, ears seeing,
this very body moving in stillness.
The inanimate speaking us all.

The Temple Sweeper's Letter
To Enduring Sound on a Day
Just Like This

It is time to sweep the temple of our wilderness, good monk.
Pillows, altar—a small wooden statue, incense bowl,
a candle.

Sweep the forest.

A temple sweeper's body, not the one you remember, flying.

Yet we are together, and I want to say, to say precisely this
to you now. You may walk into the field later with the monks
this morning and wonder.

Sweep the temple of our worlds' wilderness
with all your fingers, all of your body,
all of your voices, Enduring Sound.

Then, bring these monks home.

Enduring Sound, out here, the morning sun is arising.

Your temple sweeper again witnessing the usual crowd of
trees, sky, bamboo, and thousands of roads leading to the sea, your
monks gathering and carrying water from the river to follow you
on this pilgrimage into an unknowing face, intimate with the passing through of time.

The birds call from across the stone cliffs—
We are glad you are home, Temple Sweeper.
It is good to see you in this way once more, the birds are
singing. This body free.

The girl will repeat these words, no birth, no death, without
using words, as she has every morning since we all gathered in a

forest one thousand years ago in a continuous passage of just passing through.

Enduring Sound is the name given to you a thousand years ago, and again in this lifetime. Remember these monks' request for you to become their Abbot.

And you will remember trailing behind Hempis and the circus players along the roads of the Lost Children. As if nothing else had ever occurred in this world other than our meeting our true selves, right here.

Enduring Sound, you as a boy leaving behind the slaughter, the village—the story of a life—your traveling through mountains and rain and then snowy hills, the mute girl carrying you in her arms. Your holding my hand through the cold nights. Eating leaves and grass and bits of bark. Trapping fish in the river. All of this you had to endure. Just as we did when Hempis guided me and the girl who gave me her voice, as I gave the girl my eye.

How many nights I tried to speak to you of this after waking in the killing fields and camps—even when you were still just a boy, and we carried you from the burning. But how could I tell you such things? What kind of words can ever reach a child? As if you were our own child, but we were only children ourselves. Language of silence and language of wound.

We hid in the caves among the Learned Sage Women. We were counseled by the Dream Masters. We planned our return in their sanctuaries, our return to find whomever we could help among those still lost on the islands, across the rivers, the hidden coastlines, the mountains overlooking our former homes. Those still sheltered by hermits and shaman and sages: those who were alive, who somehow, still survived. Just like the monks who have asked you to be their Abbot. Then we traveled on to follow the Ghostwoman's trail to the monastery, grateful for passing through the original sound of her voice, face to face. Training in the dream travel, mapping our own dreams in all the various forms of magical illusion and crafts. Learning to enter the soul and body through the eye.

This bodiless body of a temple sweeper picks up a stone, opens it to the page you wrote earlier this morning, where you recorded the sounds of our voice, translating it as such—

Not to accept an event that happens in the world is to wish the world did not exist.

Brown leaves floating on the water point to your journal.
Will you return it to your former Abbot?
The mystery sends a quiver through the ink.

You are like a little brother to me.
Can you find in the words, the broken and healed heart?
This passing of a new alphabet, voice to voice.

Only a broken heart becomes the whole heart.
Writing it into the scrolls now.
Never able to quite express it, good monk.
Still, trying again and again.
Everything says it, but if you think you can say it,
you've missed by a thousand arrows.

The sound before the word, the inexplicable sound
calling us forth.

Hearing it as a child—following it in the arms of love
you fall into.
The inanimate, all beings, all trees and skies,
all the sorrows and horrors
and redemption too, this forgiveness—
and just going on, one finger pointing, straight ahead.
What will you do now, Enduring Sound?

Last night I entered a new life with new hands when the crows
brought me the words from your journal.
Meeting like this, so auspicious.

—Your Temple Sweeper

Enduring Sound to the Pilgrims

After reading our Temple Sweeper's letter, hands pressed together, I bowed.

And now, we will all have breakfast together, good monks.

The boy's tears of laughter dropping from his cheeks.

His scarred eyes.

He was sitting meditation on a stone.

It was a good letter, wasn't it, my friends?

Take out your bowls.

Humility to accept anything that comes makes sense. Not terrifying. You have to drop any sense of the path, my friends, not sticking to anything. Your robe means constantly going beyond. Beyond the dream—beyond the teaching. Wondering in this living mystery.

Lost Children on the Roads Speaking in Enduring Sound's Meditation

In the dream there is an act of transformation, Enduring Sound.

Once, we were standing by the side of the road in the snow. When time falls away between all of our lives and suffering, all of our travels and awakenings, we fly into the great death, revealing our true humanity. The snow falls and falls. It is like a poem we children recite, walking the mountain path. Like finding a warm coat and a bowl of soup. Your arrival, Enduring Sound, is like the snow falling. This cold day of the mountain path drifts toward evening, the barren trees blown through, exposing our bodies to the wind, walking onward in the snow, searching for shelter. Waiting for the Temple Sweeper, for all we are.

The boy he once was traveled this trail with us for many years.

The girl kisses the wound of eye with the wound of mouth.

Holds his frozen hands, crosses through doorways of time and fields of snow, borders of coming and going. She does this as freely as the flickers of a candle—as the jugglers' balls flying up, up, upward in the air.

The sky blue and purple as the seams of hillsides covering themselves in snow. A mirror of your own face, Enduring Sound.

The edge of the mountains, almost white, alive with the laughter and tears of a phoenix rising from its own ash.

You have been in the dream for many lifetimes, as Hempis once told you. This boy and girl who always return to find those among us children who were left behind. Will you be our Abbot, they ask? We, too, are like the phoenix. We burn and rise from our own ash. And so now, naturally, we arrive again in this forest around you tonight, Enduring Sound

The dream gave us a home we never had. We fly out of the jugglers' hands, the magicians' hats. The circus players emerge in pairs from the hills of snow, laughing as they put down their toys and lift us onto their backs.

The one-eyed boy crawls out from inside the small mouth of a cave behind the cliff where the temple monks were quietly meditating by the fire with you on this pilgrimage in what seems like just a day ago in your time—your time before merging through and into another portal we call togetherness.

Perhaps you will soon fully remember us, Enduring Sound? It is a story vaster than we can explain, but can you imagine it now hearing our voices?

I will write it as the Temple Sweeper once did.
I will learn to see what my Temple Sweeper once heard.

Will you take the seat as our Abbot? We need to hear our own stories. The monks who follow you need your attention. Among the trees and rivers, there is no place to hide. Identity comes in the middle of the night when no one is looking. It is the bamboo's click and the pebbles on the shore, it is like opening the pages of that book you thought you read long ago. So many books and forms you studied as a boy with the Abbot, but now you are beginning to understand that you somehow missed the pages that tell the story of your own life among us.

You stand by the doorway and question this.

You are the child.

You are the scroll.

You are all of us.

We are of the same cloth sewn into your robe,

the robe your Temple Sweeper left you,

and we who once left it to him,

the one we once called Hempis.

The Ghostwoman and Mute Girl
Singing to You in a Book of
Brown Leaves

We are pilgrimaging through time to find you—Dear You. Hempis watches the boy roll about in the snow, hands and feet flung into the air as he joins with us again, as if he could change the snow into the snowness of us on an isle of carnivals. The boy takes the snow in his hands and rubs it into his face, his eye and mouth, and he relishes the taste of its snowness as he treasures the kiss on his face and neck from the name we call love.

The boy, the Ghostwoman whispers in your own ear now, patting you on the shoulder as you turn another page, finish another scroll. *The boy knows the snow is alive*, she hums in a whistle of sounds you don't fully, perhaps, understand? The girl now says this as well to you who have come this far, traveled with us, freeing in your own words of a dream.

You and I walk together like this. Partisans in the snow, the sea behind you, our reader of the scrolls whom we have, perhaps, finally found?

The ancestors and sages converse on the snowy hills. Though they lived many centuries before, the ancestors have come into your dream, as you and I have shared our dreams together. Some call it a carnival, some a dance, some a diary, some—the letters between you and me.

A flock of crows fly beneath the sun, directly toward the circus players.

And now, now you, maybe you yourself can hear Hempis. Hempis asks you—where are these crows flying?

You glance up and see the crows flying over the mountains. You turn to the Ghostwoman beside Hempis and say—

They have flown off somewhere, see they are flying away, you say, there they go, they are flying off and gone now. My childhood is gone.

Yet you hear yourself stuttering the words, confused by the way your own mouth is moving and the sounds it is making as you say this?

Your own hands tremble as you say—
Dear You: have you missed it?

And Hempis, in a flick of his Dream Master's whisk, on this very day in this very moment, calls your name. You hear the girl and Ghostwoman singing your own name to you—

Where do you think they could ever fly off to?

You faintly hear the voices calling to you from across the snows, and just as instantly as finding yourself when lost in yourself, you realize, the past is always with us, and the crows are all around you on this trail of Lost Children.

All of it is you, the girl is humming.
The boy is humming.
The crows are humming.
The circus players are humming.

The children riding piggyback on the circus players'
shoulders humming in the snow.
They are humming for you, Dear You.
Is this not how you dream us tonight,

just as we dream you?

The Author & Enduring Sound Entering an Intimate Exchange of the Inanimate

But first, do you hear the sound of our ancestors?
Do you see your own childhood of wandering in the snows?

And then, for a moment, I see myself—
The boy and girl traipsing up a hillside.
And then I am flying.

Though you, too, are going blind in these years on earth. But the Ghostwoman, whom I see with you and these children flying—where could they ever fly off to, Enduring Sound? They are always here. Hempis laughs, stilling my hands as I speak to you in the inanimate.

Who we really are, I cannot say, Enduring Sound.

Who am I?

But I know we are always together.

Is it time to receive the Abbot's robe?

I thought I could forget my own childhood when I found yours in the forest.

My own past.

Thought I could forget the lost child I myself became.

My father and mother, all of my family, the ravage.

Bowing tonight, I see you returning so you can help me remember, help me to transform the story, Enduring Sound. Curious, this tale—all in these scrolls of remembering and forgetting, of longing and forgiving. All of our passions. Maybe we began our work as scribes as a way to speak to the wounds, speak with intimacy—yet without exposing ourselves to the vulnerability of our own lives?

Still, here we are, Enduring Sound.
We are each other.
The past never done, only transformed.
And we transform—as you once wrote in these scrolls,
we are always on these shores of you.
And awaking, we must somehow speak it.

Thus, on this night, the world is born once more, Enduring Sound,
and this is how my world begins again.

When we turn around, we meet one another.
So again, I will pull up this body exposed to the wind
and lean against the book, and sleep—

Sleep the calm sleep of calm trees.
Sleep as if I have never died.
While the crow calls from a swirling arc—
there is no end to the story.

Scroll XV

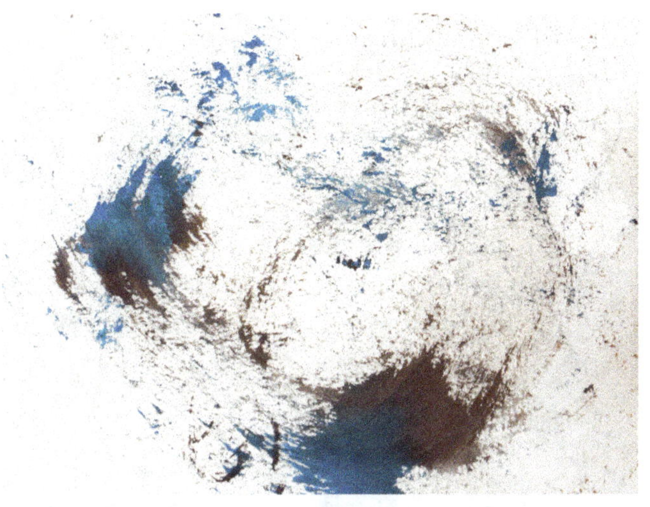

Not knowing is simply not holding onto fixed views—
not holding onto anything, even this moment.

—Ghostwoman to the Poet

The Prophet and the Poet Converse—
A Prelude

Listen closely, Poet: these stories cannot hurt you.

Did I write the Temple Sweeper, or did he write me, Prophet?

You wrote each other. That's what poets do.

But I didn't write his death.

No. In this body of dust, he wrote that himself. You wrote his life as he has written yours. And you are still writing together. You can meet by the river.

I have always longed to speak into and out of the silence. But who can hear silence?

It's called a sound before sound, Poet, which is why you hear the poem in your pocket singing.

When I wandered through the forests, along the rivers, I heard a chorus of no sounds. The one-eyed boy and mute girl constant companions in the poems. We traveled together. Looking for the Temple Sweeper. The Ghostwoman. We were lost until they welcomed us.

> *In the training of a sage there is ravage & there is blossom, the mute girl called to the boy walking across the sea.*
>
> *But aren't they the same, said the boy, pausing by our boat, on the eve of another meeting.*

Isn't it time to finish this diary, Poet?

The Unfinished Diary

The Sound

When I was five years old, a monk unknown to me came and took my hand. He led me through the large wooden gate of a monastery. It was a big palace, I thought. I wondered if my small body was drowning as he lowered my head in the stream, washed my body.

> This was the first of my memories.
> Afterwards, I stole a string of sea shells from the sleeve
> of his robe.
> This string of shells became a poem in my pocket.
> I was not meek.
> But lost.
> The poem in my pocket now singing.

A Calling

We once thought we were the story, though it is only a piece of patchwork cloth we chose to wear. You listen with your eyes to the teachings of stones, trees, mountains, and seas. How could you hear my words if you do not hear this? We are writing these scrolls, hearing our own innermost requests. When you truly enter the world of words, you find you are free of words. We are a deep sound in the forest, traveling on, becoming the words and worlds around you, just as fish swim, birds fly, and stones speak their stories in tonight's moonlight.

It is too much trouble to cry until blood
starts to gush from your mouth.
It is better to be still and wait
until the moments
of winter have passed.

It is you who helped lead us here, Poet, though once you called
your own self the one-eyed boy, the one who gathers stones and
loves a mute girl of no name; the one who showed us as children
how to find the small, imperfect stone, the one without notice or
particular shape, the one speaking to us in the dark, as we speak
it to you now, incarnate: we once Lost Children breathing in the
foliage.

A Girl Exiting the Ghost-Cave Says to the Boy:

When I was far away from—you who are this voice—not the
mouth nor the ear, it was difficult to sit, and simply be. Everywhere
I go, I meet you. I have died a thousand deaths since meeting together.

And do we not know the end still, Poet?

Not even as a child. Not even as a Temple Sweeper, a scribe.

Not even as an author.

MEETINGS UNDISCLOSED

I come back to this shore.

Moon blood on the rocks and in the sand.

Other times—as a child—I came to it like a body, though not unlike a child's.

The throat bare, soil-skinned.

Shore of desire.

In this starkness, seashells in a palm, that all is all, all is and isn't, all in this vastness of becoming. Stones by the water, waves against the boat. Crust and crayon.

A cliff.

The neck of a child becoming.

Skin-backed hills, becoming.

Shapeless now, forever turning, returning.

These Desire Notebooks.

A shore the self is mapped on, and love's face before me as the ghost shoes of words conjuring spirit, memory, dust.

I take this shore, a cliff, and release it.

This bone of being.

And what is there to understand?

You are here, standing where I am, Poet.

A LONG PASSAGE IN PARTICLES OF LIGHT

With the help of many invisible poets, I escaped. I wandered as so many Lost Children do, departing from the alphabet of dominance to create my own words. I ran, hid, moved from dream to dream, poem to poem, finding others who began to sing with the seashells in my pocket.

And another scribe entered the song.
I want that verb on horseback, the what should be,
it called to me.

*A Learned Sage Woman
(Hearing us in the Escape)*

Tangible and intangible
weave the fabric
of absence.

No mind, no being
free to roam
the universe.

The weight in the heart—
a white camellia fallen
into a dark well.

Bones forever
scattered.

Facing forward
penetrating the bone.

White days float away
into smoke rising from
the incense burner.

In one instant
a new tool for
measuring the days.

Learning to recognize
the footsteps of absence
To wonder:
where and when.

The day wears a hole in
the thin cotton of composure.

Nothing to do with the sea.
Over and over
it vanishes.

Close and distant
hover

in the evening dark.
A new moon peaks out
of the old darkness.

Sadness is a blunt thick wrap.
It cannot shatter the stars.

No sound of departure,
no in,
no out.

No day
no night.

Only day
Only night.

Only birth
and death.

And birth again, Poet.

A Voice in the Girl's Diary

I am speaking to you, our voice.

Though we are only words here,

words, they sometimes see us as we are.

Speak as you must. Say out your say.

Together we are becoming no one, and everyone.

...and still, since you have spoken, Poet—

even as a voice, even as a word or story, this
may be the last of our Temple Sweeper's
deaths. Now you, too, are remembering
the whole of our past, this path we began
together so long ago. One-eyed dream. The
last time in such form you come here, to live
and die in this way. You will finally be free.

What Tense Do You Want to Live In?

Finally, just a bit of the deep blue sea
for me....

Years would pass in these dream dialogues,
swimming from shore to shore.

Still, the poems,
the writing itself, a pilgrimage.

The Mute-Girl's Hand on the Brush

Your eye will open, as a boy. As a flicker of a candle, as a dance
upon a stage. A person of no rank. For the secret of our return and
awakening love has been there all along.

The Author of the Scrolls Revealing His Hidden Face

Not knowing is simply
not holding onto any views—
not holding onto anything,
the Ghostwoman whispered in my ears.
I am you, too.

The Mute-girl's Diary Leaving The Cave with the Boy

Day 1

Dear You,

For three moons I have had the
strength to rise for your coming.

The one who has written you
into her secret poems.

An old monk and yet still a boy, you
too were named by desire.

There is no cave of birth and death.

The Lost Children can hear us.

Day 2

I studied you traipsing the hillside each day,
the ancient faces carved into our mountains.
These old souls by the sea, wandering under
an azure sky as the sun reached its pinnacle
on the cliffs overlooking our story.

Day 3

As a boy you would wait for me by these same
caves—wait for the orphaned girl—wait for
the girl who arrived each evening covered in
a blanket. Just as now we await what awakens
our final dreaming within a dream.

Day 4

So it is with the child always, this freedom
looming in shadows. In the life you are
now departing you will travel for many
days, and I will be the one traveling
beside you in this journey of love.

I will go with you, Poet.

Care for us well.

The Temple Sweeper At the Edge of Another Dream

A boy sings in the snow.

A poet bows on a hillside of bones.

The crows woke up as you prepared the pyre. The awakened
one, she opened her eyes. The person I was stood before the shrine

carved in the cliffs, bowed before the fifty monks you brought to
gather for the evening ceremony of my departure.

And finally, the ancestors arrived, appearing along the road of
all these teachers who led the dreamer in and through the dark
wood. The man rose as a boy again. A Master said to me when I,
too, was first just a boy—

> When the tree withers
> and the leaves fall,
> golden body flying in the wind.

RETURNING

> Stones are just slow stories
> with their fire secrets inside.

THE GIRL READING FROM THE BOOK OF BROWN LEAVES
TO ENDURING SOUND

In these stars that go nameless in water, we have been found.
Everything, water.

Scroll XVI

What insentient body?
The girl asks the boy,
walking along the river
below these ancient caves.

The Boy Speaks It

Maybe she's been waiting for a long time. And in the silence you feel she wants to ask you a question. The girl's eyes so inquisitive, so alive tonight. So you carefully place your hand on her shoulders and ask—what is it? What is it you need to know from me?

Butterflies and bees flutter about the waves, and suddenly she turns, throws her arms around you and says—

I want to know you'll never leave us again.

THE GIRL'S MOST RECENT DIARY—
FAITH IN INSENTIENT BEINGS

Time itself a hoax, the girl says.
What about this moment?

And these words the same as Enduring
Sound's thoughts as he began to lead the
monks home from the wilderness, back over
the mountains and rivers, leaving the Sage
Women, walking away from Hempis' butterfly
wings, traversing again through the ravines
and narrow roads to all of us who remain
here by the sea. Back to this monastery where
Enduring Sound has finally returned, reading
from, and once more, writing into my diary.

When you are ready to include everything,
that is your true face, the girl laughed with
our monks on the night of return. This very
inclusion, nothing more than our own kindness,
she said through the rustling winds through
their tired footsteps left in sand and mud.
Even here as the flocks of geese fly in and out
of our shared memory of passing time.

And at last, you remember, Enduring Sound.
And it is why you have made this choiceless
choice of the monks' request, their repeated
call for you to decide whether you will take the
Abbot's seat. After all these years of searching,
now trusting your own inner call of return.

Just as with our Temple Sweeper's own family, and with yours and mine—these ones who blinded him in one eye as a boy—you have returned. Just as finally, our Temple Sweeper returned, as you have now returned with our monks, Enduring Sound, having heard their request. Did you know our Temple Sweeper severed one finger for each life he took? That is why he came back to you, as if already an old man, but he was only twelve years older than you. A man you could not recognize through the scars the night he knocked on your cell's wooden door, and you began to write our stories.

Forged by fire.

Whose death?

This the question Hempis secretly asked you as a butterfly, passing and brushing the edges of your robes in your last scroll, and again this morning as you entered our monastery. As you prepare once more to tend to the graves of the Lost Children,

and your teacher, our Temple Sweeper. It is good
you heard us and may take the seat of Abbot.

In the beginning was a word going forth with
this faith and trust in its own awakening. The
words always find each other. How could
anything not be all right, Enduring Sound?

You light the candles and incense at the
temple altar, chanting with us, bowing
with and to all these children coming
forth to greet you with gratitude.

Now you have come back. The Ghostwoman's
thousand dancing arms waving over the tides. The
Temple Sweeper is certain of this as he completes
his own pilgrimage. Certain of love, reminded
by your own love, that you have found your
way with the monks who follow you. And we
all find our way home, eventually. Yet we must
make our deepest request known and hear its
calling. The longing itself, love, fear and doubt,
embraced as the beloved. Taste of the candle
and incense, the skin of wax, its worn face in a
thousand kisses of time. A book of unknowing.

Before we were born.
The child an infinite eye,
a jewel,
a phoenix come forth.

Are you here, Enduring Sound?

I am here.

Where are you?

Everywhere.
I am here.

Then you will be our Abbot?

Dear You, the mute girl sighs, sips her tea on the roof of our
monastery. The girl writes for Enduring Sound to read to the
monks at tonight's ceremony—

As winter approaches, the monks sweep the
floors and grounds of a temple. The Temple
Sweeper remembers the remembering,
traverses in the spheres of memory, of
sweeping itself. Though stories become
formless, we are becoming a passage, and I
dream of you touching these word-beings.

Where did the bird fly off? the Dream Master
Hempis chided you when you said the past
was over, that the birds of your own childhood
had flown off somewhere, that you were done

with the wars and carnage, that as a simple
scribe, you could no longer remember. But
where could they ever fly, dear Abbot?

Don't get fooled. Who are others if not yourself?

Where else could the birds fly but in this
very sky, this very earth, this very skin. This
very mouth and scroll? You have finally
remembered, Enduring Sound, care for it well.

You take them one by one, hand by hand, and
you will walk with them on this monastery
roof beside the Temple Sweeper. Observe the
moon in this evening calm. Know the steps
by heart and you no longer need to find your
way with eyes nor feet. Gaze at the blueness, sit
with the other monks, a secret word emerging
from your robe, so you can hear the voice when
summoned forth by the child we become.

The moon bright. I myself, along with the
one-eyed boy, stroll out of the ghost cave to
join you, to celebrate your return home.

Alive.

Returning to our refuge after all these lifetimes.

We—the Lost Children.

We, no other than the ones you see in words.

Words found in a diary.

The son becomes the father.

The sun becomes the moon.

The song becomes us.

The scrolls become another waiting for being.

And you answer your own deepest request.

Hear these winds, Enduring Sound.

They, too, are you.

Enduring Sound to the Monks

We have walked through the wooden gates of this monastery to again arrive home. Your voices called and spoke to me in the tears of morning dew. We, Lost Children of rain, found. You came to me like a figure of a stone, a shadow of a ghost, a deer nibbling the grass by the fern and oak as I stood shivering with nothing in the dark of a cliff. Tonight I release the dreams lodged deep in memory and our shared imagination of language and time.

I will honor your request.
I will be your Abbot.
But I will continue to wear these tattered robes
our Temple Sweeper abandoned in the caves
when he departed his body.

For it is he, who is truly our Abbot now.

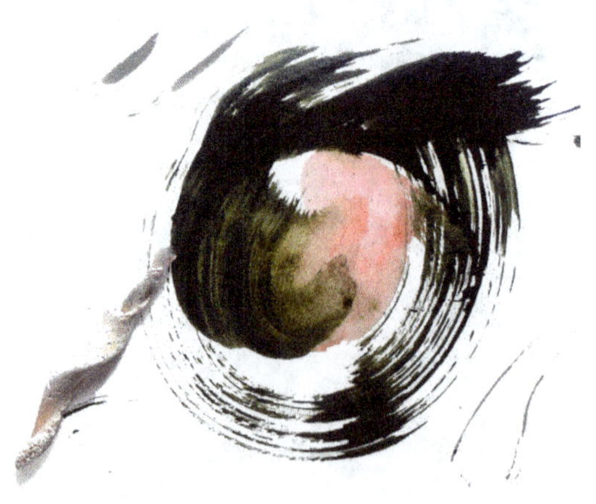

THE TEMPLE SWEEPER GOING FORTH

Is it really changing? The Temple Sweeper asks.
My body transforming into light.

He is standing by the mute girl's horse—the waves over
the rocks breaking with only this imagined beauty.

This very one abiding with the monks overlooking the
sea of a new entry into the world.

Though he is not himself dreaming, Enduring Sound says to
the assembly of monks gathered on the monastery roof in the evening dusk—we who remain are, indeed, dreaming him. The monks
sit in a circle, listening intently to their new Abbot.

Enduring Sound sees only the water of being and non-being
converging.

The vision itself speaks this for us. Includes this, good monks,
he says. Do you hear the silence?

And still, I sense the presence of my other, our true Abbot.
And you here already sense his presence as well. Say it is not so,
good monks?

Enduring Sound stands, stirring the attention of the assembly
of monks.

Our Temple Sweeper continues in these dream dialogues and
without hesitation, says—

> *I have carried our stones, stones now blooming in the
> flowers on the cliffs, birds in the air. So fine as well
> that we have all met here before, each one of us as a
> child.*

Enduring Sound hears the sound of the gulls on the horizon.
The water of tides edging toward the cliff as the morning begins to
appear inside a blueness of the blurred sky.

Though I cannot see you, I know you are there, Enduring
Sound whispers.

The Temple Sweeper, seeing things as they are.
What remains of this one day in memory, this one night.
The Temple Sweeper searches,
hears the voices fluttering
about his formless form.
Vast nameless clouds.
This breath under a breathless breath.

The wind breathing, sea breathing, monks breathing, and you
are breathing.
Two crows return to the side of the cliff.
A mischievous fox.
The bell again rings.
A continent arising out of the sea.
This very mountain Enduring Sound will now call by the
name, Temple Sweeper.
As it is written in the scrolls.

Since no one else is before you, do you know who I am?
When you become you, it's all of us.

Enduring Sound bends his head, tears falling

into the sleeves of his teacher's robes,

butterflies covering the roof of the monastery

as the monks get up with these tears of joy.

In the Realms of Appearance and Disappearance—

The Ghostwoman's Letter to the Temple Sweeper

This morning when I stood by the sea you appeared in the sky, Temple Sweeper. An auspicious sign. Do not fear this as you carry on in this transforming body. A child once more. Regardless that you cannot touch the hands of others tonight, I read these words for you in our insentient being of passing worlds.

I carry your birth in this letter—our poems to you over all these floating universes. Here in that which we call stories, passed down hand to hand. No single voice. In the life you have departed, you waited on the road near the old graves. Now you have almost completed your travels, and we will be here to greet you.

This morning before you began your final quest, the words of a diary shaped itself into a letter, a sound, a drop of ink. And now, perhaps, you sense our words in the feel of a scroll. Paper rough and coarse in the memory of a former skin. A landscape before you, a map, our return together.

The monks in the temple ceremony say these same words, Enduring Sound.

Tonight we remember you as you once were, Temple Sweeper. A boy in our first life together. You would wait for the girl by the caves in the old country. Come running down the hillside to take her home. Looming in the shadows. Other nights you waited for her on the road near the ancient mountain village.

> This morning we stood by the sea together.
> A child took my hands.
> She thanked me.
> I saw you watching as a bird of paradise flew in the clouds.
> The boy and girl by the fire drifting into life.

Ushering us on once more.
I followed you along your path.
Crossing borders.
The face in a birch forest.
The one you became.

And you found our diaries.
A word speaking in the scrolls.
You are ready.

What country were we born in? you asked,
taking my hand. I sipped tea with the girl
while writing this.

There are no countries.

The tea trembles in the cup I place in the girl's hand.
She picks up the scrolls tonight to read these letters to
Enduring Sound.
Just as I read them to you.

We have done what needed to be done.

You have brought us into the miraculous.

Scroll XVII

Back with the Dream Masters in what appeared
to be the kitchen of the monastery, some
thousand years ago, a boy and girl walked in from
the corridor to join us on our hour of departure,
to join you here in this continuous pilgrimage
now, Enduring Sound.

Hempis said to us then, this old monk doesn't
abide in clarity.
What about you?
Are you waiting for clarity?
This old monk doesn't abide in clarity.

Enduring Sound Addressing the Assembled Monks on the Night of the Wooden Boats

Are you worried that I don't know
where I'm going, good monks?
If I didn't know where
I'm going, how could I realize
I'll always be with you.
There's only sadness
because we forget
birth and death are not real.
Do not cry.
We are always here.

A Prayer to the Temple Sweeper in These Shadows of Dark & Light

In the darkening shadow of a rose,
in the grains of dust,
in these stones,
still here.

A hue and shape too formless to conjure.

The clouds shift past the wooden boats arriving ashore, and again, I see the boy of my own lost childhood before he became this one called Enduring Sound. A faceless moon reflects the stream's water. My own voices returning through your own, Temple Sweeper. Your misty figure traipsing beyond the hills of this island monastery.

A figure of speech, a tongueless tongue, a word not spoken, but who is this one who found me wandering the forests with no name and became the one who guided me?

It is you, Temple Sweeper. And the time has arrived. You in these very begonias and orchids, rosemary and thistle, the three rose bushes you planted growing near the stones you—you yourself—carried each day from the monastery toward the cliffs of enshrined graves. Honoring the dead, bearing witness, not knowing. You carried endless pebbles from the sea.

You became this very person.

And tonight it is my work to prune the plants and water between the rains. To gather the pebbles. To sweep these mountain cliffs. To do this every evening before leaving this body to join you.

To do the same thing each day is to save the world, you said.

A silhouette peeking outward over the cliffs by the sea when I secretly followed you here as a mere boy. I follow you still.

Here in my own flickers of memory the boy follows the trail of smoke from a fingerless sweeper's tobacco and blood. Touches the places where the sword fell, cutting through dualities.

I glance toward the branches you nurtured, the hives you built, this orchard on the cliffs you planted tree by tree, twenty-six seasons past.

> The boy, now called Enduring Sound, looks up.
> He eyes inside the trees of forgiveness.

Another child on the shores below signals, calls across the wooden planks lining the roof of our shelter and home in this monastery as together we reach out and find a hand and eyes before timelessness became time.

> A girl's voice.
> But which voice calls in these stars?
> Together we hear it in everything you breathed.
> You came for forgiveness.
> I came to remember.

> I will leave this body and join you soon, Temple Sweeper.

Everywhere we go is homeless.
Everywhere we go is home.

THE ESSENTIAL STORY—

ENDURING SOUND'S DIARY ON THIS NIGHT

Once more we hear the bells ringing from beneath the make-shift temple of our Lost Children in the wilderness, these ones gathered in the island caves surrounding our imagined monastery on the sea—all of the orphaned ones coming home to all of you who founded this temple.

It is the call.

Is it you calling me, or I calling you, Temple Sweeper?

The cherry blossoms in full bloom. Forty nine days since you left this body in winter.

We see a child's arms raised above her head, as if any moment she will fly over the sea, into everything we have ever wanted and always found.

Yet who is awaiting whom?

This is what we come to discover.

This is how our world begins.

The Temple Sweeper, The Boy, Our Poet & Prophet With These Crows Again Conversing With You

In her Book of Brown Leaves, this too happens, Hempis. The crows come, the boy flies, the Poet & Prophet sit down.

Two crows going down crow road. A girl and boy watch them from the coastline of these wooden boats.

Enduring Sound is no longer one—and yet he is not two, the Poet says. He is no longer of the dream, and still, he is not dreaming. The one becomes many. The many become one. The end of the world has come and gone, and a figure is standing on a hillside, humming—

But what is this humming?

The tune is a lullaby of ancient hymns so many no longer recognize—signals the amber crow.

It is a lullaby about the love of a father, the love of a mother, the love of a child.

A bird of paradise appears in the sky, foretelling the tales already told and those yet to come, and how, all the same, we include them all, the Poet writes in the girl's diary with his favorite pencil.

Is it raining on the cliffs near the sea? the Poet then asks, pouring wine into his already broken cup.

A meteor bursts through the whitened sky. All of the stars ever known, and all the cities and kingdoms ever built, and all of the faces, animate and inanimate.

River in awe, fire with a reign of a blazing night—the Prophet whispers to her friend, toasting the once abandoned children arriving in these wooden boats and coming home.

So, Enduring Sound whistles with the rain in his eye? the Poet asks. All of the monks in our pilgrimage safely home then? he asks her, this Old Prophet, this old teacher.

Don't you know? stammers the jade crow, swooping out of the rain. The Learned Sage Women understood that if we were to survive, even survive— they would need to travel back to us, Poet.

The rain, it is something like this, the Prophet agrees, lifting her own broken cup, savoring each sip.

There is so much rain in these legends and tales.

So much trouble.

Yet when we are troubled, we are amazed too, the Poet adds.

Yes, the Prophet nods. A fox howling a tune you now vaguely remember, Poet?

Or have you again forgotten? the amber crow asks.

You look up, Dear Reader.
Perhaps puzzled yourself?

Still, by now, the clouds should know your name among us, the Prophet says to you, whispering in your inner ear. You who are you.

If things arise and fall away at the same time, they don't actually exist, the jade-shadowed crow observes—

And if they don't actually exist, how can they cease to exist? the amber crow caws back.

The monks gather around, sharing a good bowl of soup, without seeing the Temple Sweeper meditating below the cliffs near the wooden boats full of children.

Just as the wounder wounds themself, the healer heals the true self, our Old Story chimes in.

The Story deciding to say out its own say, Prophet?

It peeks inside the mouth of its own story.

This is why you are *here*, the mouth of the Old Story utters to you.

Why, you yourself have come this far, why stop now?

The fox crouches and sits beside Old Story.

The amber crow nudges your ear.

The mute girl's horse flies down to the shore of Lost Children and the monks' own mouths begin to hum the song singing itself.

And in the opened stone of a letter, you are kissing someone's hand.

In the opened stone of a word, you are singing a prayer.

In the opened archive of your own pasts, you are reading and writing in these scrolls both before and after us.

What do you want to say?

Such is the fate of the Storyteller—the Prophet calls out.

The figure before us wants to hold out its palm to shelter your voices in the rain. The figure of a Temple Sweeper coming forth from behind these clouds of unknowing.

There he is, there he is!

The crows fly toward the one once called Temple Sweeper— this figure meditating in the rain.

A boy steps from the wooden boat, picks up a stone from the sand and looks about at us all. He studies us.

Who are you? the boy asks.

I am Old Story.

The crows weep and then laugh as the sea washes away, lapping against the cliffside.

All of the telling, one crow cries out.

All of the coming and going! the other caws.

The Poet puts down his cup, picks up his favorite pencil, then erases what is written, and writes again so a red poppy can blossom among the living and the dead.

As for myself, I step nearer.

And I remember you in the House of Language, calls
one of the children, as if she just returned from the
days and nights of a child.

Where are you? a boy from the boat asks.

Old Story looks directly in his eye.

I am the one who is writing you into these scrolls.

But these scrolls have their own life, the boy says.

You! There is the one beyond sound,
the crows clamor together.

Can you say your own name?
the boy asks the Old Story.

Ravage.
Walk in the sun.

And if you think you can say it, you've missed by
a thousand miles, the girl now laughs, beginning a
dance. But everything says it, she grins at you.

I hear a sound in the darkness, the Old Story says.

The amber crow holds back the tongue in its beak,
perks up its ears.

Its face turning into a boy's face.

So why are we all traveling in different dreams,
you wonder?

We all know they are the same dream,
the boy tells you.

If there is reason
come again, the girl says.
The gate is not closed.

The sound is a Story too, but perchance you cannot yet penetrate it? The boy nudges up beside you, places your thumbs and fingers into a circle, makes a circle with his own hands. The boy's back almost straight, settling, chin tucked under, skinny legs crossed. He reaches out and touches your shoulder and says—

you are almost free now.

Who are you in this dream world?

The boy asks you this, and for a moment,
you hear him, Reader.

Hear your own voice among the many.

Spiritual Autobiographies—

Returning Home

The circus players also arrive to walk you through the clearing now. Painted pranksters running about in the dark.
As they begin to disperse in pairs over the ridge, the girl
and boy wave once more to us all.

So our mute girl and one-eyed boy can swoop
down from the skies on her bird of paradise,
read afresh these wandering alphabets.
Meet these new orphaned children arriving
on the wooden boats to our island monastery.
The boy begins to write to them,
as have all the others who came before
into the Book of Brown Leaves.
Enduring Sound will record them in this tour
of our infinite autobiographies,
return them to the Learned Sage Women,
awaiting them for their library,
deep in the mountain caves of their abodes.

They are only words, Enduring Sound,
the two crows echo back as the words become specks
of light and dark on the horizon.

All the same, we are them, and they are us.

Enduring Sound?

Yes, Temple Sweeper.

Are you preparing to leave your body so soon
after accepting your vows as Abbot?

Then, who will teach these children only now arriving to our monastery's shelter? Why would you leave this world now, Enduring Sound? You have only begun. There is work to be done.

Do you hear me, Enduring Sound?

I write it as you have spoken it, Temple Sweeper.
I remain your faithful scribe.
A simple monk.

ANOTHER NIGHT AS THE MUTE GIRL, TEMPLE SWEEPER, AND ENDURING SOUND GATHER TOGETHER AMONG THESE CHANGING LEAVES

This is where the pilgrimage began, the girl says—
and leads you further along.
A movement and a rest.
An arrival in the distance without identity.

Identity came in the middle of the night
when no one was looking, she tells you, Temple Sweeper.

As Hempis told us that last night by the gateless gate, humming in the garden. He opened his hand as if to remind us, as he had many times before, you have now drunk three glasses of the finest wine.

Don't be the one who rides the ox,
searching for the ox, the old shaman grinned.

What if I fall asleep? you once asked your old friend, Hempis,
who turned toward you, Temple Sweeper, and smiled—

If you fall asleep, you will wake up, he said.

You were the Temple Sweeper at one time, but now the roads have called you on elsewhere.

Where, Hempis?

Once forged by fire, you now are only an emanation of light, Temple Sweeper.

And arriving you find all of our worlds, though they were never separate, and nothing was missing: natural and full in their simplicity and humility and kindness. One returns to sit in the warm coals and cold winds and ashes of impermanence—and the ashes of the impermanence of impermanence.

Once a temple sweeper met a mute girl on a pilgrimage, Hemp-is continued. Somehow, she convinced all of us that our long journey in these scrolls has been nothing other than a love story. The girl and boy on the shore of wooden boats.

After each of these meetings, you, Temple Sweeper, packed an ole monk's few belongings—a winter coat, three robes, a work shirt, a bag of scrolls, a book of leaves, a loaf of bread. Shared a few words with the theater crew and circus players, but little needed to be said.

Such is the fate of the Storyteller.

It is vaster than any story.

You savored a final glass of wine.
Began to calm your mind.

As a teacher once told you—only beauty can save the world. Is it not so?

…

Enduring Sound?

Yes, Temple Sweeper.

Why bother to call me Temple Sweeper anymore?

I will always love you as our Temple Sweeper.

As our Temple Sweeper, you were holding a small stone and a flower, staring out at the sea from a train. You carefully rolled a pinch of tobacco into a page of these scrolls and handed it to me so that one day I could find you. I have found you. I will never let you go.

I think I am ready to leave this body, Temple Sweeper. I have fulfilled your request to find the boy and the girl, throughout all of our dream dialogues, throughout many lifetimes together.

But these new children are awaiting you, Enduring Sound. You must let me go, though we have never been separated by an ounce of dust. You need to point straight at the stars so we can proclaim in unison—

Our old man has finally got hold of the last word.

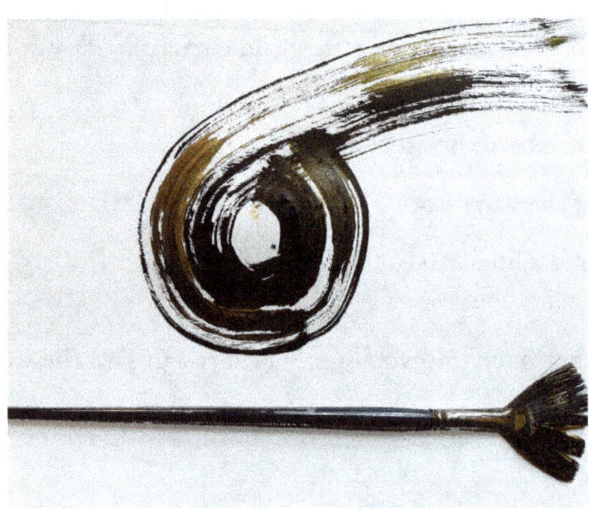

A Final Word
For You Who Speak It

After becoming such, Enduring Sound—I saw myself on that train somewhere traveling through the snow on an ancient road with all of the Lost Children. I stared out at these ones playing, laughing, becoming who they are. It was a curious and yet somehow recognizable landscape of white birch trees and jagged mountains and frozen seas.

First, I would study the mornings.
Then, I would study the afternoons.
And finally, I would study the evenings.

The quiet trees.
It was a Sunday.
I laid down in the coupé.
This was the beginning.
A story shedding itself while I became the Story.

The Temple Sweeper & Enduring Sound Leaving the Train, Approaching the End-Boats

I come back as a word.
On a rock and in the sand.
Other times—as a child—I come to it as a body.

It is in this starkness, the shells in a palm,
that all is and isn't.
It is this love of a child yet to be known to you,
who I study now.
The stones by the water, the waves against the boat.
The arrival on a train.

There is a girl awaiting you on the river, Enduring Sound. And you will become her teacher, teach this girl who has just arrived to become the monks' Abbot when you are gone. This girl is only eight, a mere child.

Rage at end, approaching the end-boats. Even the passage of death itself unfolding here and becoming, in itself, a child. If but for a moment then, harboring in stillness. A face before me as the ghost-prints of words conjuring spirit, memory, dust, all.

I take this shore, a cliff, and release it.
As you will embrace this girl, give her your coat.
A curious array of children along with her,
arriving in the wooden boats,
gathering together on the shore—
                waiting to fall in love, over and over.

This bone of being.
Becoming.
Belonging.

And what is there to understand?
You are here, standing where I am, Enduring Sound.
Will you meet and greet our future Abbot?
An eight-year-old girl right now disembarking
the wooden boat.

As for myself, I come to walk or sit, to watch these boats full of children float the emptiness. Gulls and pipers. Cormorants perch on the rocks. At home here. A boy and girl longing once more to swim from a boat—to cross the hills and the clouds appearing in our reflections. To fall in love, again and again.

Will you take them and teach her, Enduring Sound?

I am here, Temple Sweeper.

I taste the blood and wound of bloom. It comes out of letters, seas, an infinity of see, seer, seen, Enduring Sound. You experience your own pain without blame—the Seekers say as they guide us back to meet the Lost Children. To escort the spirits to the other shore, these Seekers laugh among one another. Listen, Enduring Sound. Someone sounds a drum. Another listens. They need you. Study the listening of sounds in the distances of a white canvas of sky. These children begin to open their palms. The Learned Sage Women play the bells on the backs of elephants. When you reach the other shore, you see it is this shore. Will you carry the sky, or will you let the sky carry you?

I finish the bowl, clean the bowl.

We are carried within
and borne. We are born.

The moments crash together
with increasing clang.

Our Ghostwoman turns toward the Poet and Prophet hovering on the edge of the river now. An eight-year-old girl with dark strands of wispy hair hanging over her cheeks beside a deer and its fawn.

The girl brushes back her hair and shyly looks away, toward another boy climbing out of the wooden boat. She looks at the boy, as if he were somehow familiar.

They are waiting for you to find and give them a home, Enduring Sound. They are in your care as of this day. And this girl herself will become your teacher. The Poet's and the Prophet's teacher. She will be our Abbot. The boy himself will help her. Just as our former Abbot helped you when he gave you his coat. You were but a boy, and the coat too large. Do you remember?

I will never forget, Temple Sweeper.

The Ghostwoman bows as she shuffles, pulling along her ghosted legs, toward the deer, the crows, this girl and her new friends in the wooden boat docked by the gateless gate.

A crowd of children walk across the tracks into the fields of nothingness.

They have brought us to you.

Scroll XVIII

Gentle for the wound of words, balms for language. But she does not come to a standing place, she becomes as one who, like a particle or wave, rolls over the sea, as a magician, who like a bird of paradise, rides on the sky, one who, as by the force of her incantations & prayers, miraculously blossoms full-blown flowers out of season on a stone.

The Old Story Returns, Saying Its Say

This new girl on the hill was already awaiting Enduring Sound. But by now, you know this.

The girl already writing in her diary. This girl who is no longer mute. A child no longer possessed by fear. The girl is sipping tea by the fire with a boy. This girl who will become our future Abbot. The boy, no longer blind in one eye, the boy who will become another Temple Sweeper, another Storyteller in the passing of time. The two figures now are waving good-bye to the wooden boats of Seekers who brought them to this shore. The Learned Sage Women who bid them farewell. This taking refuge in a language of wind, awake in our parallel stars. Needing only a diary, the girl paints in the words she feels for the unspoken. Freed from the carnage, once known by the boy, she holds nothing back. The seeds of words beckoning her on.

> This is part of the telling, Old Story.
> Transforming who we are as she breathes
> a new kind of living beside the boy
> since arriving on these shores of you.
> This is why you, you yourself too, have returned.

> As another autumn approached, Enduring Sound
> was already sweeping in the monastery. And by
> now, you have already guessed why?

Enduring Sound turning again toward his own journal, though his sight gone as he picks up the pencil, his hands remember. Already taking stock of the grounds, feeling his way with his hands along the stone walls as he walks, carefully inspecting each object of the Meditation Hall. Unable to cease his former duties as Head Monk, nor those of his teacher, our simple monk inspects the windows with his fingers and notes in his journal the need for repairs of their sashes, wipes down the bells, the candles, the doorways. Enduring Sound secretly sweeps, preparing to welcome the children traipsing from the wooden boats, gathering their few belongings over their shoulders, then running finely, quite sprite-ly, upward, onto the hillsides, along the pebbled pathways, and on further into the caves, lighting small campfires, fishing the shore-line with handmade fishing rods, exploring the expanse and terrain of the cliffs.

Rooms and bedding for their arrival also need tending, and the storage bins of the harvest thoroughly readied. Enduring Sound pencils this into his journal. Our fox and crows returned. A small hole in the water tower. A tear in the vegetable bins. There is much work to be done. And again as such, Enduring Sound begins in his journal, the one our former Abbot gave him, bound in bone and marrow. The journal he has not opened since our former Abbot's departure from the body. Enduring Sound writes—

> *Though stories become form, they are also formless, dear Abbot. Of sun and moon, of planets and galax-ies, of earth, sky and sea. And our Temple Sweeper has fully become himself now. Although he has no body, thought or name, we see him performing vast, illusory works, cutting off confused feelings of shame, or blame.*

Enduring Sound jots these sentences in the pages made of leaves, but not until first consulting with the new Head Monk about repairs to the monastery, the need for sanding and paint-ing of the gateless gate, then later, instructing the attendant monks now busying themselves for a festival, though without their yet knowing why there is talk of a festival in the midst of so much passage of wounds in time.

Enduring Sound continues his writing, as you, yourself, prepare to welcome these sage orphans ashore. These children of rain. Can you recognize yourself among them? Enduring Sound breathes in, breathes out, then writes—

> *Their birth in new forms of human moons will lift us, along with you, dear Abbot, in this coming forth once more—as our Temple Sweeper has performed the withdrawal from perception, and no longer has any need for restraint...no sight, and no object of sight. Though he has returned with you tonight to join us.*

Enduring Sound sighs, glances around, seeing shadows as forms, and forms as shadows, opening another scroll.

As again, you yourself have come to finish your own story.

OLD STORY: As for myself, I am only an Old Story among you. Just as Enduring Sound remains this simple monk, learning to see without seeing.

The circus and theater troupe await us both in the forthcoming passages. Enduring Sound might consider his own role in the telling, and I must consider my own. An Old Story, yes, still—I am here with you. And in our own way, we help one another. Just as these children have come to our island, once more beginning their tale, a tale of a boy and girl, which may help us to understand your own story of being, and non-being.

First then, we will study the mornings—as did the Temple Sweeper who came before you. Next, we will study the afternoons. Then, of course, there are the evenings to consider.

Though there is nothing to merge or distinguish. You will have for yourself, by now, calmly and patiently seen there is nothing missing, just as the sky once more reveals, and the Circus Master and her sturdy entourage welcome my entrance. For she is a lover of stories, and without me, there is no telling. Without you, there is no hearing. Thus our Ghostwoman raises her arms, flying in the wind, throwing back her long, wild hair, the color of eddies in a river. Thus our Ghostwoman begins another beginning. Thus with her own wordless words, bowing to each of you, she proclaims—

As in our former lives, you too, all of you, you are all welcome here—she sings with the voice of many homeless birds. Our ancestors abounding around her in various flights and functions, swooping downward, toward each of you.

GHOSTWOMAN: And to you, Old Story, thank you for your return. You must carry on among us once more.

Among these wooden boats of Seekers who have again landed upon our shores, These Seekers— they carry our refugees and those once forsaken in human form. These children who once would run at the feet of the Dream Masters and our brother

Hempis, in the realms beyond appearance. Each with a tale to tell, each with a suffering to heal, a diary to reveal. Once they were only pages in the library caves of our Learned Sage Women in the mountains. Pages waiting to be translated. All of our hidden meanings now manifesting in these evening stars.

Old Story? Will you not come the distance once more, wholeheartedly?

OLD STORY: I am here, Ghostwoman.
I am hearing your story.

GHOSTWOMAN: Our children of light escaping from all their ravage and war. Just as it begins for each boy and each girl of each new scroll. This morning when we awoke in our wooden boats and saw a sky calling in the south wind of our past worlds, our past words, we became you. Now, become us in this beginningless beginning, Old Story. A sky from our shared existence no longer veiled in the visages of passing time.

Old Story, listen closely.

OLD STORY: I am listening, Ghostwoman.

GHOSTWOMAN: Do you recognize their faces as one of your own? For though you are old, you were once an orphan too, Old Story.

OLD STORY: I am hearing, Ghostwoman.
Yet I have no being, nor non-being.
I am a word.

GHOSTWOMAN: What we cannot speak about we must pass over in silence, Old Story.

Here, where language cannot go.

Yet you, too, must tell of what can't be spoken in your own language.

You, Old Story, you must allow us to flourish as such.

Speak with the tongueless tongue as a continuation of words again speaking in these scrolls.

Return.

Old Story? Can you hear this old Ghostwoman?

Return so we can turn toward you with our open arms—

Constant in this turning toward

and not away from suffering, and yet—

not grasping at the suffering either.

We have something else to say, and to unsay.

So it is.

So it has always been.

Old Story, my dear friend. Do you understand?

Old Story: Yes, Ghostwoman.

Ghostwoman: If you think you can ever really say
it, you've already missed by a thousand sounds.

Old Story: I will remember, Ghostwoman.

Ghostwoman: Remember no one can say it.

And I am no one.

Still, the girl on the hill is writing in her diary.

Only eight-years-old.

The boy, her new friend, of some unknown age,
tending to the fire.

We look at them and bow.

Old Story, are you hearing, seeing?

Old Story: Yes, Ghostwoman.
I move in your stillness.

Ghostwoman: And our struggles of body
and confusion of mind will begin to fall away,

Old Story.

Do you meditate every day?

Old Story: I am a Story, Ghostwoman.
Inanimate.

Ghostwoman: But is this *not* what the Poet asked
the Prophet when the crows flew by once more,
and together they savored a final glass of wine, Old
Story. Have you already forgotten?

Old Story: I remember, Ghostwoman.

Ghostwoman: I'm meditating right now,

the Prophet told her friend.

OLD STORY: Yes, that is what our Prophet told
our Poet, Ghostwoman.

GHOSTWOMAN: Such is our vow tonight
with you, Old Story.

One continuous moment. Yet these scrolls are
writing their own selves, of themselves. So you need
do little.

OLD STORY: So say out your say, Ghostwoman.

GHOSTWOMAN: Our Temple Sweeper constantly
returning at auspicious moments. To wander freely
about in the fields. And a boy Temple Sweeper,
once more arrives. The girl beside him.

Old Story, are you still here?

OLD STORY: Please continue, Ghostwoman.
I have nowhere to go, no one to be.

GHOSTWOMAN: For all of us and all those wanting
food and shelter, a rest from struggle. We find
ourselves again with the children gathering around
the fires and candle-lit caves, mingling with the
ancestors and spirits that protect them and protect
you. Do you recognize your face among them now?

OLD STORY: I am a word, Ghostwoman.

GHOSTWOMAN: Are you becoming you,
Old Story?

OLD STORY: I am listening, Ghostwoman, though I
am but an echo.

GHOSTWOMAN: This new child, the girl Enduring
Sound will first train as a scribe for you, and then

as a teacher for the monastery. The boy with her
who will become our new Temple Sweeper and
keeper of the scrolls when Enduring Sound leaves
his own body to join us.

Do you understand?

Old Story: So I will say it, Ghostwoman.
Though I have no need to understand.

Ghostwoman: Yes, understanding beyond
understanding, Old Story. As in these caves and
stone-carved temples of cliffs invisible to those
without the Seekers, our circus and theater
troupe will again enact your words all up and
down and along the precipices overlooking the
gorges to the sea, returning to our homeland as
one. A ceremony. A festival. An enactment. An
embodiment.

No doubt, the others with us tonight, as you are
hearing us too, Enduring Sound, in our carnival for
those who cannot yet see the formless forms as you,
Enduring Sound, write again in your own journal.

Hempis, have you too come?

Hempis: Yes, I am with you again, Ghostwoman.

Ghostwoman: Ah, so you, too, Hempis, have
arrived once more to join us for the festival?

Hempis: I am of you, Ghostwoman. Where else
could I be?

Ghostwoman: Old Story, where are you?

Old Story: I remain with you as well,
Ghostwoman. We are not two.

GHOSTWOMAN: At ease with the monks' quiet, in the shrine of the temple of these hills, the children Hempis once taught are clothed in rags and discarded pieces of cloth sewn together. We were all once orphans. You were an orphan here once, remember Hempis? These are not the only stories you hear, and our Old Story speaks, but they are the ones we have to encourage a return to this original smile. Though a thousand years have passed, we can see them all clearly.

Do you recognize this boy on the shore who the Temple Sweeper has again become, Hempis? And he will once more be our gardener and Temple Sweeper. Just as this child you called the mute girl will become our Abbot.

HEMPIS: It is as you say it, Ghosted One. You and I have always been together. And together, we have trained them well.

GHOSTWOMAN: Cradled nights of chanting and prayer on the shore, how else could you ever have discovered us again in this place tonight if you, you too, were not one of them, Hempis—one of the orphans roaming the realm of appearances in a quest to find a home. Did you hear it earlier from the girl's diary as she wrote beside the boy at the campfire? Is this why you come and hear our call this evening, Hempis?

HEMPIS: It is, my old friend.

GHOSTWOMAN: And Old Story, will you speak it? You remember it too, Old Story. If only vaguely in your own vanishing and appearing, as does our Temple Sweeper with you.

Old Story: I will echo it, as you mirror it, Ghostwoman.

Ghostwoman: After escaping the massacres and leaving the dust of suffering, so you, you too, could finally hear our voices, Old Story.

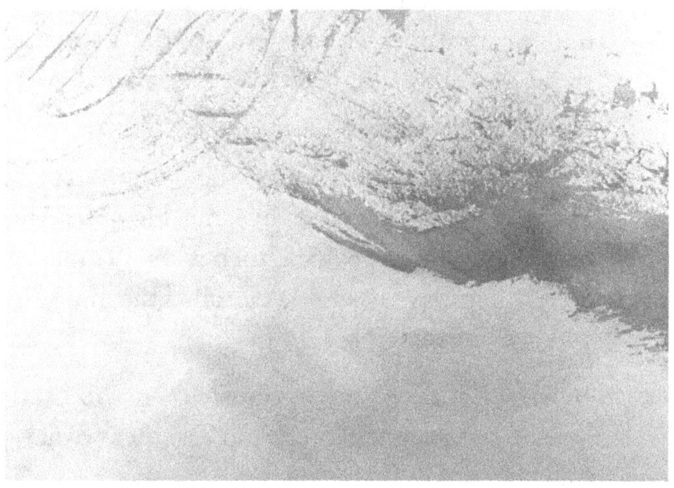

Just as you, you too, Hempis, once helped us with all these children, and once became their Abbot. Many scrolls lost, many lifetimes of the wandering and, and yet a boy smiles and a girl is painting in her diary. They are free children now, and they are of Enduring Sound's final quest. You know this well, Hempis?

Hempis: This ole shaman knows it well. Again we find ourselves and prepare to perform for those who return, Ghostwoman. As they do each night. All of the ravage, and yet, and yet...as a poet once said to a prophet. I remember, Ghostwoman. These ones you, you who have come with us, walking through the stars and moons. Traveling through the olive, cherry, and palm branches, surrounding

the mountain paths of this new home. Meditating
on a shore full of blue leaves, these children of
the wooden boats. A boy and a girl. They carried
the wound. And this is your fate, the fate of the
Storyteller.

GHOSTWOMAN: This is where we come & go. This is
your fate. Did you hear Hempis? It is why the boy
and girl in the scrolls are again in your telling. Are
you afraid, Old Story?

OLD STORY: As for myself, I am not afraid,
Ghostwoman. I can see the boy playing with the
others as he did when he first came a thousand
years ago, falling in love with the voice in her diary.
And those maimed in the wars, without parents
or family, those with torn skins. The boy and girl
showing them the visions that enter through the
eye as you perch in the body of a bird of paradise on
the mountainside.

Seeing them again, even as she kisses the boy's cheek at the river by the fire, fishing for their food, the utterance of butterflies from her mouth, her hands—and you, too, all of you, each of you who have arrived without words this evening, even those of you who are worldless, you too awoke with us, many times before.

These are your children before you.

A flight into your own arms.

Just as with all of you who have come for the ceremony. A flicker of rain. Groves of fir hovering in moss, and visions of whom you are to become. Again opening these pages. I, Old Story, recognize you as such.

We, who are these children.

We are your children, too, Dear Reader.

Scroll XIX

Letters from Suchness
We who are finding ourselves
Here as we are
In all this Hereness

ENDURING SOUND'S LETTER TO THE CHILDREN, ARRIVING ON THE WOODEN BOATS

Children of these wooden boats, children of rain—

Here you are again. Clouds again become clouds. Water again becomes water. Our sea again becomes a sea. You have arrived safely. You are welcome here, little falcons, no longer refugees. The incense burning and the candles lit in our temple. This blue of blueness of sky you have carried across the waters. The taste of this spice tea, this glass of milk trembling in my hand. This loaf of bread. Our human face. Your smile is not unlike the bonfire burning in the hills south of our monastery, already clearing the soil for the spring planting.

Children of the rain, thank you for coming.
For abandoning the burning house.

And so it appears together we have done it again. Mustered a laughter in these parables of rain, appreciating the moment—this everything is all right—as the sun lifts its arms and greets you—you stepping from the wooden boats into the sands awash with your names. All this in your return. Waves floating from afar to our little island abiding in these crisp morning rays.

The bell rings,
the arrow flies.
Only the singing remains.

If we've come this far, why stop now? Our former Temple Sweeper asked me this often. Perhaps my face then was not so different from yours now. A boy stumbling and confused when the boats brought me here, and the circus players left me alone to discover where they had left me. I understand if you have a curious hunger. A longing. Things you can't remember.

We don't deny our bodies' return or departures. That the whole of our worlds is in this meeting of your young faces now tenuous, somewhat frightened, awaiting a friendly word and a meal.

Taking care in such a way, you will learn there is no illness or need to fear, realize your own kindness to help one another will heal any confusions as to where you are. The same way the stars gave you sight over the waves and storms. This very reckoning will be your friend, assisting you not to turn away from one another. And so you see, little ones, though we look strange, we old monks, we are here for you. These monks are here for you as they were for me when I arrived in these gateless gates as an orphan, a boy, a boy I thought, who was lost and forgotten, abandoned here among strangers.

The way ahead charted
Out of night into day

Night into day
Out of time into travel

A way ahead charted
Beyond all impossibility

Out of time into travel
What remains to be seen?

Beyond all impossibility
Or an alternative created

An alternative created
As if the sky did not rain

As if no one was lost
And the sea was not rising

And the sea was not rising
Churning water and salt

Off in the distance
What remains to be seen?

Had a decision occurred?
Did a boat set sail?

Off in the distance
It had seemed far away

It had not seemed real
As if a sky did not rain

The way ahead was charted
As if no one was lost

And the boat set sail
Churning water with salt

This simple monk is in continuous awe for the generosity of the Learned Sage Women and Seekers, the circus players and Ghostwoman who brought you here. You have finally come! After waking this morning and hearing your footsteps and pattering feet in the hills, hearing your running into the trees and caves, I thanked our former Abbot, and the one called Hempis, our Temple Sweeper, and our Ghostwoman, for all they did. Transporting you again into the spaciousness of our welcoming arms. Our coats will become your coats. Our rooms will become your rooms. And knowing this, the doubts and struggles of my own fading vision passed into the clouds as the Old Story also returned to encourage me. Soon, you will meet the Old Story, too. She will tell you many things!

Going on in these passages with the Learned Sage Women who once taught me, as they did you. What is the core of this meaning other than kindness itself? The one great pearl discovered each day, with each breath. Children of the wooden boats, our Ghostwoman came to gather us again for the great festival of no birth and no death.

As with this incense rising and candles burning, your new friend, Enduring Sound, hopes that hearing our voices will bring you fully into this peaceful abode as you learn your way, and learn to trust us as we trust you. That the words themselves encourage you to dive into your own inmost request from the diaries you brought with you. These diaries now becoming a shelter, an abode. Always complete.

Just as I have told our monks and your new teachers—our Temple Sweeper and former Abbot are not really gone. Where could they go?

Our Temple Sweeper's voice, too, echoing in these waters around you. Listen closely  and you will learn to hear him as he has heard your calls. Why, just this morning he told me, to take care of one being, Enduring Sound, is to heal all beings, visible and invisible.

Return, Enduring Sound, return, right here in the evanescence of no birth/no death, we feel this joy of eternal life.

Enduring Sound: Old Story?

Old Story: Yes, Enduring Sound.

Enduring Sound: This youngest girl among them
who will become our Abbot, and this boy with
only one eye, who will in time become our Temple
Sweeper when I am gone, and each of these little
falcons have found their way on the boats. I have
still one request, will you consider it? Please,
let them say yes to becoming one family. In this

hearing so immense, what could then contain us, imprison us? Larger, larger than our thoughts can contain. Still, we say it. Now will you speak it? In each sound as we wander in and out of their scrolls, these diaries where shadow becomes light, and light becomes shadow.

Even our thoughts,
resting in the sound
of stillness and intimacy,
Enduring Sound,
we will honor your request.

Enduring Sound: Are you truly speaking this?

Old Story: Yes, I am still with you, Enduring Sound.

Enduring Sound: Is it my time—my time to leave this body?

Old Story: It is not your time, Enduring Sound.

Enduring Sound: Old Story?

Old Story: I am speaking to you, Enduring Sound.

Enduring Sound: I have heard that when perception and non-perception fall away, a being's time to go is at hand?

Old Story: It is not always so, Enduring Sound. Look at me. I am but a word, but I am here with you. And our Ghostwoman has instructed me to tell you, you are needed here. The girl is waiting for your instruction. You will give her your Abbot's coat just as he gave it to you. She and the boy along with these good monks will become your eyes. So it is, Enduring Sound. If I have learned nothing more through all these mergings of tales, it is this: you are all of life in your own sound, your own voice. Our past meetings always keep pointing, Enduring Sound, to this moment, this very unfolding. Already here as you open your hands, all of your words, and vow, speak, then bow. So simple that we sometimes forget to laugh and enjoy the abundance—or even to say thank you.

Enduring Sound: Old Story?

Old Story: Are you ready, Enduring Sound? Will you finish your letter to the children?

> *...what insentient body?*
> *the girl asks the boy,*
> *walking along the river*
> *below the ancient caves.*

Enduring Sound: Dear children of the rain— Together we will realize understanding beyond understanding to help one another ease your remaining fear. These waves of sky and sea, the patterns of forests in the return. This coming and going, passing and return, disappearing and reappearing, a thousand years in the moment of my burning candle as I write you this letter—a flicker of an eye, how could it be otherwise?

Together we will carry on as such.

And you are already singing. This simple monk hears your voices from the diaries once more, emerging from the caves and libraries of the Learned Sage Women who showed me your language—your voices soothing, bringing flames to us and each one of you: alive.

A grove of cypress trees, children of these wooden boats.

A vow to learn from and teach all we meet.

A deep mysterious memory that we've all met before,

over and over, and that we can recognize one another

in these moments of who we are.

It is time for breakfast, children of the rain.

Are you ready to come forth and meet us?

Old Story?

Yes, Enduring Sound.

How do these scrolls end?

Enduring Sound, you still think there are beginnings and endings? It is time to gather the monks and go meet the children. They will be huddled in the caves, close together around their small fires, the way you once were when the soldiers burned your world. Then, as you now fully remember, the Temple Sweeper came and brought you home to us.

This is our story.

This is the story of the world.

THE MUTE GIRL'S DIARY—
A LETTER WRITTEN BEFORE I WAS BORN

Can you have faith that your own death, too, will pass, Enduring Sound—in an emanation of light in these children's sudden appearance?

A simple monk sensing now that nothing ever really goes away. Like that flock of geese in the landscapes when you met Hempis for the first time in the dream, all things continue, that time itself is only continuance. Suffering in the midst of the end of suffering. When you include everything—that is your true name.

Now those who killed have heard the call, those
whom your Temple Sweeper himself killed
have come with these children of the rain.

As with his own family's deaths at the hands of
soldiers who blinded your Temple Sweeper in
one eye, as with his own eventual acceptance
of death while living in the mountains, as
with the murders he witnessed and the lives
he took with his own hands, these children
return with this request of liberation as
he floats in the insentient realms.

That is why he continues to return
to you, Enduring Sound.

Can we have faith that this sorrow, too,
will pass? Will you take hold of your
work and teach these children now?

Whose death? Hempis asked you, when
passing you again this morning in the
garden as you prepared to tend to the graves.
And though the shaman is nowhere to be
seen, the voice sounds curiously like your
own, do you agree, Enduring Sound?

In the beginning these children were
more than words, you are certain.

These new children have arrived through the
gateless gates of the monastery with the help
of one thousand dancing arms over the sea.
Our former Temple Sweeper is certain of this.
Certain of love, reminded by love—Enduring
Sound, you will help these former soldiers
make this place a home. They were soldiers

and killers once. They are killers no more. We
all find our way home, eventually. Yet we must
make our deepest request known, Enduring
Sound. What is your deepest request? Their
presence echoes this call for your forgiveness. The
longing itself is loved, embraced by the beloved.
Taste of the tea and incense on your breath.

Original name, before you were born.
Flush of forgiving.
Prayer of return.

Enduring Sound, are you here?

Yes, I am here. Though I have never been born.

Where are you, where is the true Enduring Sound?

I am here in hereness.

Where else could you be, Enduring Sound? The
diary is now yours.

The girl on the hill awaiting you, writing in her
own diary, sipping her tea by the fire with the
boy, taking in the language of these parallel
stars—needing only this diary—now free,
holding nothing back, transforming who we
are as she sleeps beside the boy each night.

You have now seen this for yourself, Enduring
Sound. Where did the birds fly off to? the
Master chided you when you said the past was
over, that the birds had flown off somewhere,
that you were done with the past wars and
carnage. Is this not what you were thinking
last night, preparing to leave your own body?
And how do I know, you ask, walking out
the front gate toward the sea before we were
born. Because I, too, gave the same response.

But where could they go, the past, these
child soldiers, the birds, Enduring Sound?

Where else could they fly but into this very
sky as you look up and see me, and the
mouth of the next scroll awaiting you.

Our children appear in each footstep. You'll walk
on the monastery roof this evening. Gaze at the
feathering clouds, sit with the other monks.

I see you walking in a drizzle coming from
the fog, and you sense this new boy who will
become our Temple Sweeper, this new girl who
will become our Abbot. We are never alone. So
don't hold too tightly to their former suffering.

You and they, the same, Enduring Sound.

The son has now become the father.

The song has become us.

A wind rustling in leaves and this sound as you
look around, finally beginning to understand it is
all beyond knowing. The boy and girl call to you.

If you return to the Temple Sweeper's
cell you will find him waiting.

He will show you more of the
letters from these scrolls.

You need to finish your work.

These are some of the words left for you, written
on the stones the Temple Sweeper carved with
his knife hiding in a cave near a battlefield—

> *...one bloom showing what the others*
> *might have been*
> *sunlight floods this room, then shade*

And this new girl's diary is speaking
in your trembling hands—

Hearing the sound in this way saves me. My
horse awaits you. Do not fear this as you carry
on in the journey, Enduring Sound. I write
these words as a gift for you in our meeting.
A tree. A lamp. A stone. You are nearing the
final passageway now. You will find out for
yourself and teach us. All I do is leave these
words by the sea as the Ghostwoman did for
me. But you found your way back to our temple
and the caves so we, too, could find you.

So many wars. Yet the work of the teaching
has come down through questioning and
answering. Cultivating phantom meditations,
it does the work in a dream. I carry their
former deaths in this letter—my poems you
now translate over all these circular brush
strokes—passed down hand to hand.

And now, perhaps, you sense my presence in
the feel of the scroll in your hands? It is rough
and coarse in the memory of a former skin
and body—a landscape before you, a map.

The monks in the temple will one day
chant these same words over and over—
compassion, kindness, home.

When the flesh is over, body and mind
cease, then how will you respond, Enduring
Sound? Will you accept all of us as we are
and always have been? Why wait? And what
became of the others in the wars after wars,
when you, too, realized you are one of us.

The boy and girl have again arrived
home, can you not see them?

Walking up the hillside each day. Just as I have
seen you trekking the path as the sun reaches its
pinnacle on the cliffs overlooking field after field.

The stones our Temple Sweeper, too, patterned into breaths you attend to now.

You found our letters.

You found Hempis.

You returned for the boy and girl.

I imagine you as you once were. As a boy
you'd come running down the road. So it is
with the child always, this freedom looming
in the shadows we cannot see. This morning I
saw you watching the boy and girl by the fire
drifting into life again and again. I followed
the path of the Abbot you became, crossing
the borders, walking the tracks, and picking
up pebbles alongside a river and birch forest.

Old friends and children of light
meeting by the river.

Why, you simply stopped and
looked and saw your true face.

SCROLL XX

Hempis to the Boy—

When you become you,
it's the whole works.
This is the magic of the world.

THE MUTE GIRL'S LETTER TO THE TEMPLE SWEEPER

Just to come to you again, like a repentance. To know this love is true relinquishes the past and a stubborn attachment to it. Enduring Sound still sometimes struggles to believe. Yet you and I and we are simply mirrors of one another.

The washed-up shore of wet leaves as the small boats of the Lost Children pass in these seas. The monastery monks with Enduring Sound in the fields, both ghosted and alive. Pelicans of spring. Salt left in the hand. Often, I wonder how I was different from you. Our stories are the same. They are empty, and our body carries them.

So why have we allowed them so much suffering?

When I crossed the river, the Learned Sage Women told me there is no other shore.

You are familiar with this boy who wandered in the snows. A thousand years ago you saw the birds trailing behind him through the wilderness and you were not surprised. No doubt, you have touched the birth of you. There are many boats.

The blood on the horizon says I miss you.

The bird of paradise flying above says I love you.

Can you hear it?

The taste of death still in your mouth.

Once, you held the lover in your arms, and later witnessed the passing of your mother, father, your sister. This taste of death also in your mouth. Here we come to an end and in unknowing continue in these boundless clouds and mountains, these love letters from the rain and the wind.

Once you stood by the doorway and questioned the very existence of love, forgiveness, redemption. You are the child. You are the scroll. You are all of us.

And one day when you were alone and lonely, you picked up the book. You were strolling along a boulevard of a city after sitting in a café or reading a poem of a film where you saw yourself. You came across a book and opened it as you might open a letter from an old friend you barely remembered. You saw it then, and for some reason, the movie of the poem reminded you of yourself. You saw the boy in the snow and after reading a few pages you said, I know this boy. I have cared for this child.

We stood together once by the grave of an old friend.

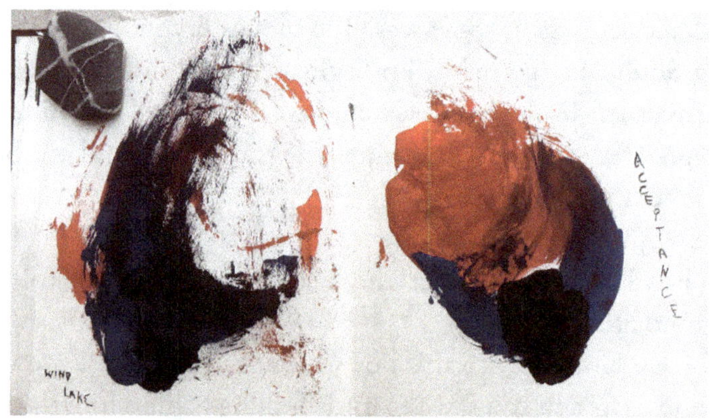

Hempis whispered in your ear—Real forgiveness has to entail experiencing first our own pain, then the pain of the person to be forgiven, and the separation between the two beings can dissolve.

Oh, I remember. I last met you on the street in the city of our birth.

I was the one in the market buying plums.

The boy was in my school.

The boy understood our anguish better than we understood it ourselves.

But all of these ghosts and visions and dreams were, in fact, us.

You could smell it in the sentence as you opened my letter.

So you followed. You came into my life and the story's absence allowed you an entrance as if it were your very own, as if in its words, you were tracing your history, the scroll of your own human weakness and courage. And it was your kindness you discovered. You tucked the book under your arm, and you started home. You carried the story close to your heart. You began to live and create the script of its telling and untelling. And now we are the same, you and I. We exist together without the story, yet also within it. We carry this wound like lovers carrying a newborn child, healing this very body of words.

We have learned to love each other, and now, we have learned how to forgive.

The Temple Sweeper Returns to Meet the Boy In These Fields of Suchness

Walking along the eucalyptus trees leading to the cemetery gates. This strange sensation that all of my life transpired here, the Temple Sweeper mutters. Butterflies and crows in my dreams once more, just as they must be in the boy's own, in the mute girl's, who once herself was a butterfly and perhaps still is. Finding them again, somewhere, somewhere out here among these vast and miraculous roads beyond words.

> The Temple Sweeper pauses,
> asks himself why he has come,
> glances toward the whiteness of sky,
> sensing the boy's third eye,
> the girl's wings,
> roaming in these fields beyond you.

The boy, of course, of course the boy hears him, as if hearing a lullaby or hymn of gone worlds, and the boy knows he will never die in this paradise of coming and going. He spits in the dirt, scoops up a handful of the dust, says to the Temple Sweeper: We have all met in this place together. And our past teachers understood this. Didn't they, Temple Sweeper?

The boy breathes in deeply, exhales, smoothing the moistness of earth into his arms and hair, hearing his own stutter. He jumps up from the grave he has been sitting on, pops his head from behind a blooming cypress tree in the garden.

Isn't it true that we live through one another, Temple Sweeper? The boy shakes his head, as if just remembering where we are, takes off his torn, short-sleeved shirt to let the last rays of autumn's sun warm his skinny chest.

Do you think maybe Enduring Sound is living through you, too? he asks the Temple Sweeper. A face so majestic in its own sweep of hair and eyes and rugged skin that it causes the boy to smile. Maybe Enduring Sound is living through the girl, too? And translating the ink drawings I painted in her diary? Just as Hemp-is exists through me, and I through you—this wind has brought us together again—all of us always swooped together from some great storm. Or like these days and nights when the moon is full and the stars and planets merge to guide us Lost Children still remaining on the roads behind.

The boy hasn't changed a bit, the Temple Sweeper thinks. The rigor of his one eye, quite alert and carefree, the one who plays his guitar through the villages and hills, along the paths of rivers and ravines, through the cities and countryside, breaking into song, storied through one endless breath, one endless plot after plot, passing on the tales of the dead and of the newly born with  his third eye. But was I not once him? Were this boy and I, were we not once one? The Temple Sweeper pauses, as a flock of gulls surge forth overhead, broad wings curving over the crest of darkening waves on the sea to the north of the monastery. Crows again perching in the cypress grove, in the branches and on the ground, observing the scene, carrying on some conversation privy to such philosophical crows as themselves. The mounds of graves blending into the white caps of the sea. The winds echo with the tongues of families who built their homes and shelters in the ground this monastery now stands on. The commerce of the street vendors and marketers and shop keepers the boy still hears as he stands facing the Temple Sweeper, and we hear it too as we find our way among the quiet path and the memory of ancestors, who roamed and cultivated the earth before us.

The Temple Sweeper thinks—my dream is like his invisible, third eye—like a breathing sun beneath the ocean. The Temple Sweeper blinks and looks down again at the blue and yellow butterfly alighted on his palm. The boy cannot control himself and points, as the girl laughs. The Temple Sweeper whispers to the butterfly—

> Are these *my hands*, are these really my own hands, he wonders, then wanting to ask the boy, too, yet uncertain of the meaning of the near touch of wings between his once withered hands. He dares not touch the wings.

For the moment, the Temple Sweeper imagines the convergence of all sciences, religions, philosophies and the discoveries of multiple worlds and universes as this body beholds them in sleep, in waking, in standing and getting up, in lying down, in tears and laughter, as if becoming a library of indexed occurrences, maps and charts, of peace treaties and wars, of hieroglyphs and biographies, each revealing the immensity of human existence I myself am. Like this thorough destruction and creation, as if sauntering, mustering its strings of a violin's plucking pizzicato, a forgotten music floating through these trees, blowing back the boy's long, riverish black hair.

But are these really my hands? Am I really here? he now asks the boy.

They are yours and never yours, the boy says. It is why I am always here, and never here, and continue on with only one eye. The other eye now beneath the sea, swimming with whales and fish and dolphins, these deeply reverberating sounds becoming another eye extinguishing birth and death. This is how I see and hear, and you, at times Temple Sweeper, see and hear through me, as I see and hear through you.

The Temple Sweeper walks past the lanterns flickering along the rooted trees of the dirt road where he has so often been, where he has so often returned after finding his way past birth and death. Where he spent so many mornings and evenings in his former lives as a guardian and speaker of the dead, a scribe of these unfurling scrolls and as—for which he is most proud—a great friend of the birds. The gulls now shifting from limb to limb, landing and taking flight again, the redbird lingering by his feet, or the girl's bird of paradise slipping into the somehow revised alphabets of a father and mother and sister. As if for the first time since he himself was a boy and escaped into the forest, when the mysterious monk saved him after the slaughter on the train, drew him maps in the sand so he could find his way to Hempis, the Temple Sweeper remembers his family as they truly were, their love and affection, their miseries and joys, their own passage through being and non-being on the train on the eve of his sister's marriage.

He now again strolls in the garden he cultivated by the graves for twenty-five years, the trees he himself planted and Enduring Sound now tends with humility and kindness. The Temple Sweeper contemplates this as he bends to pick three roses, one a bright orange, another the color of blush maple, the third a fragrance that reminds him of wild strawberries, gathering them into these strange hands for the one-eyed boy. Hearing the girl's voice as he rises, an almost inaudible humming, the Temple Sweeper looks up. He sees the mute girl has returned, sitting atop the tallest of the cypress trees, and waves as he glances at her legs swinging from the branch, as if excited to see he has again come back from the great sea.

The monks of the invisible monastery in the middle of this sea had hung these lanterns on the limbs of the trees around him for the monastery's upcoming full-moon ceremony. And as it was once the Temple Sweeper's task to light them before the ceremony itself, he thinks—this is why I must have arrived on this very day of the moon's completing roundness. I have come back to finish my vows, and for this, the girl and boy have beckoned me forth from the realms of stories flying beyond the grasp of prophets and po-ets, monks and scribes, shamans and sufis, swamis and sages—all meeting and celebrating in the cities of vast skies without bound-ary or demarcation.

Picking up the three roses, the eyes of the roses shy, shining from their orbs, the Temple Sweeper marvels at the leather hide boots on his new feet, the clean worker's blue shirt and baggy trou-sers covering his frame, like those of a farmer on his now unbroken body. Am I to be a farmer then, a plougher of earth, rather than a dreamer of dreams? Are these large feet even my own feet? He contemplates this. And where is the boy going, he says aloud to the girl, hurrying a bit, having noticed that the boy is signaling him further on into the cypress grove. Why is he always here for me, the girl here for me—why are they not on with their own journey of love in these converging planes of being and non-being? They are free. Hempis assured me, and the Ghostwoman made me a vow before I left my tattered robes on the damp soil of the cave of for-giveness, these children are finally free.

He considers these things and thinks afterwards—

I have seen them before in the snows and in the stars. In the cities and in the mountains. I have written and rewritten, read and reread their lives in every library of every empire, in every prison, in every fluttering of leaves in the wilderness of human life. And I have seen them both on this very road before. I have seen the boy in the caged cells with the other orphans as the soldiers discussed the fate of their captives, and I once was there.

> Yes, the girl nods, having jumped gracefully from the cypress where she was sitting, and suddenly taking his hand, for she has always possessed the power to read the thoughts of such seekers, to move beyond the signature of words, and to experience the very feelings behind the thoughts as if they had once been her own. Yes, she says, as another two butterflies fly from her mouth and onto the Temple Sweeper's shoulders.

The egrets have flown off. Or have they? the Temple Sweeper asks her, lighting the first lantern with the candle in his left hand. They were just here, how could I have missed their departure—for surely when the egrets ascend there is a shift in the earth, the promise of another consciousness plunging forth from the sea.

They come and go, the boy says.

As for herself, the girl considers all this, squeezes the Temple Sweeper's hand, pushing the weight of her thumb into his palm so that he knows she is real, not a figure of mirage nor memory, but right here walking on the path beside him. The boy crouches down on a rock, taking a long draw from his hand-rolled tobacco, studying the man walking beside the girl, hand in hand, among the mounds of stones scattered about their former lives and deaths. The Temple Sweeper lowers his candle to the next lantern with his healed hands and thinks—

I sense that until you and I forgive all, forgive ourselves, this wandering will remain unvanquished.

There is nothing to forgive, the girl says, looking up into the Temple Sweeper's eyes, smiling. It is all forgiven. You have done all you were called upon to do. You have built countless bridges and helped countless beings. You have launched boats that brought the Lost Children home. It is you who are free now, Temple Sweeper. And so are we. But there is something you want to say?

The blue and yellow butterfly flies up, fluttering about his palm, not even brushing his fingers, and as the Temple Sweeper watches its delicate wings extend outward, he stops, looks over toward the next lantern, startled that the boy has sprouted wings in the contour and geometric form of a burning angel. The Temple Sweeper shields his eyes from the brightness of flames. He whispers under his breath to the girl—I will not impose my story on you. Though it has always been true—I need you.

Just as we need you. It is the full moon ceremony. Look. Look at all these birds. Look at these unlit lanterns. We have all come to see them, the flaming of our own beings in these lanterns of the once lost. I am sorry for all you and the boy have suffered. For all I myself suffered. But it is time to continue lighting the lanterns, Temple Sweeper.

Do you see the moon on the horizon over the sea? the boy now inquires, his feet again touching the ground, without wings, brushing ash off his shoulders and chest. Do you taste the yellow of this sun in your own mouth still? The boy's eye follows the crows into the bush where they have hidden as the Temple Sweeper places the candle on the wick of the next of lantern.

The Temple Sweeper feels his hunger and touches the boy's scraggly, black hair. He puts his hand on the boy' sunburnt face. Feeling the Temple Sweeper's coarse thumb and forefinger, the boy closes his one known eye, listens to the sound surfacing across his cheek and forehead. Opening his third eye, he stares at the amber, poet-crow, turns and looks up into the Temple Sweeper's impenetrable expression.

What is it you really want? the boy asks. The sun is going down over the horizon of the sea and my body now appears to you almost as that of a long shadow among the lanterns. You wonder if I exist, if you yourself exist. If it's love you're seeking, the boy goes on, scratching his ruddy chin, why won't you just tell us what it is you want from us?

The Temple Sweeper's eyes sway back and forth between the boy's vanishing shadows to that of the girl's inquisitive glance. What is redemption? I want us to be free of the past, he finally says, lighting the fourth and fifth lanterns, beginning to walk further along the blackened earth and pebbled path of our origin and call.

The boy smiles, holding his left hand over his eye, wiping it with the sleeve of his shirt, swiping away the ash of the dead. Unless the medicine stuns you, it won't cure the disease. Isn't that correct, Temple Sweeper? Treat your resistance with the utmost respect. This love is no other than who we are. When it shines on things, we return.

The Temple Sweeper thinks—the mystery is in his eye. He thinks, is this why I am here? Is it so? That I have come so far to utter this one sound?

There is a secret, something you want to tell me? the boy asks once more as he follows behind.

Then the boy turns, looks solicitously toward you—our reader in these scrolls—as if searching the source of your own wandering in these fields and pages.

> If one comes across a person who has been shot by an arrow, they do not spend time wondering about where the arrow came from, or the past of the individual who shot it, or analyzing what type of wood the shaft is made of, or the manner in which the arrowhead was fashioned—the amber crow now chimes in, stepping out of the cypress grove in the guise of a Poet, reading from the girl's diary, nodding to the Prophet, who strolls beside him still in her own shape as a crow. Rather, one should focus on immediately pulling out the arrow. This is what the girl quoted in her diary from a former teacher, the Poet continues, pointing to the girl's dangling legs, spotting her again in the tallest of the cypress trees.

Tell him. Tell him what we need to know, the birds begin to hum in chorus up and down the row of eucalyptus leading to the sea. All the days along this road searching for you. Just you.

The Temple Sweeper steps back.

> And now *you* are so full of questions.

> Do they concern the question of love? the Poet asks.

When I tell you, you will not understand, the Temple Sweeper answers the boy. The egrets are returning across the treetops, flying inward from the sea on this new voyage to find you again. They circle above the girl writing in her diary. Her words pointing directly at your own world, where you find the whole world. But I am having trouble speaking to you, the Temple Sweeper goes on. Is this really my mouth? Am I not dead?

You are always here, the boy says. Whenever in doubt, say not two.

But our Temple Sweeper is mumbling to himself as he lights the next lantern, turning toward the flow of so many emotions and unsure of himself.

> Tell the boy, the girl calls down from her perch.
> Tell him. He has traveled through many cities and
> civilizations, multiple worlds, many lives, many
> dreams, many wars, just to hear your true voice.
> Tell him, tell him how much you love him.

I am moving. You are moving. We are moving. The Temple Sweeper is moving. The limbs of the trees are moving and the wind too, yet we who have come here along with you remain faithful. If you carry a secret for too long, it is possible it becomes unknown to the self that created it in these spheres of unknowing.

> I love you.
> I *love*, our Temple Sweeper says.

> You are now fully becoming you in these alpha-
> bets of vastness, says the girl.

The boy and girl, the egrets, gulls and crows, the fields and sea, the Poet and Prophet—they all vanish once more, just as our Temple Sweeper feels the heat of the forty-ninth lantern on his finger burning. *I know pain, so I must be alive.* The boy vanished, yes— though I am certain of his return. This is how the gulls and crows, and butterflies end one story, Enduring Sound.

The story is awaiting you in the scrolls.

SCROLL XXI

In a single thought, a thousand years, the
Prophet says, pausing alongside Old Story as
the Poet sits down at the café, waiting to hear
you speak, to hear the sound of his own story.

Spiritual Autobiographies—

Enduring Sound on the Night He Discovered the Scrolls Already Written at the Café of Continuous Comings & Goings

Dream Dialogue 1

In the dream of journey, the Poet, too, is becoming a journey. Two crows going wing to wing, Old Story. This passage back to self and its absence of knowing. Often a lonely, though not forlorn, road. The Prophet told the Poet this on the night of her own vanishing. Study the words hanging on the cypress tree in the garden, she had said, finishing a cup of tea, tipping her prophet hat, floating off without a goodbye.

And this is where the vision began and has been leading the Poet all along, Enduring Sound. To arrive in the distance without identity, even a hat, all identities merging together without names.

Enduring Sound: Old Story?

Old Story: I am here as I am, always.

Enduring Sound: The one we call Poet in these scrolls had to come home to his own language?

Old Story: Yes, Enduring Sound. The Poet and the Prophet foretelling this tale where we first began a thousand years ago, yes. The story was already written, Enduring Sound. Just as it was already written before you began to tell it again. So it is with the Poet in these scrolls.

Old Story: You, too, are the Poet, Enduring Sound. Have you begun to understand this now?

Enduring Sound: The Prophet said this herself that last night by the gateless gate, bowing in the grove by the cypress tree, her presence like a floating ridge of clouds, or a kind of disappearing fog as she spoke. She opened her hand, pointed at the Poet, as if to remind me that together we have drunk three glasses of the finest wine.

Old Story: Suffering. Redemption. Freedom. Enduring Sound, it is always like this. So it will be with the Poet in these scrolls.

Enduring Sound: What if I fall asleep? the Poet had asked her, as I heard their voices, listening in from their dreams, as if for the first time understanding the true nature of dreams.

Don't be the poet who rides the clouds, searching for a cloud, the Prophet said to her old friend. If you fall asleep, you will wake up, she told the Poet that final night in the grove wiping her left hand across her forehead, kneeling before the pages drifting about in the air in the sudden swirling of countless wings of butterflies. You will be like the sleeping poet who wakes up in a café.

But I am a simple poet. And you, Old Prophet. Who are You? the Poet asked.

I am the Prophet, she uttered quietly, as if she knew I could hear her, Old Story. Just as you hear me now. And I am also a voice of the Old Story, the Prophet continued. In all the voices of your friends & teachers & students, known & unknown. Coming and going in various forms. So it is.

Is this what she, our Prophet, or you yourself said, Old Story?

OLD STORY: We are of the same, Enduring Sound. Just as you and the Poet are with the Temple Sweeper.

ENDURING SOUND: But now the roads of the Old Story have called you on elsewhere? the Poet then asked her. Is that what it means? Where to, where are you floating off to now, my Prophet?

DREAM DIALOGUE 3

ENDURING SOUND: Where to? the Poet had asked in the still of that night, writing in a journal at what he called the café—imagining a small boat, waiting to carry him safely into the sea again.

Old Story?

OLD STORY: Yes, Enduring Sound.

ENDURING SOUND: If these scrolls were already written before we began, where—where do we go now?

Old Story: You are struggling for breath, Enduring Sound?

Enduring Sound: Yes.

Old Story: Yet you were forged by fire, and now you are becoming fire, Enduring Sound.

An aroma of tea is rising from your cup.

A dragon entering the water.

Arriving, you find our words are like water. They were never mere sentences and scenes, poems, and parables.

One just returns to sit by the warm coals and cold winds.

Enduring Sound: This is the tale we've been writing all along, Old Story. But what if I fall once more into blindness, as I have so often in this life?

Old Story: Sit down in it for a while, Enduring Sound. This is the same as the Prophet told the Poet at the café of comings and goings.

OLD STORY: Your former Abbot, Hempis, remembered this too when he woke up in the monastery again this morning beside you in your dream of dying, Enduring Sound. So it was with our Temple Sweeper, and soon will be with all of us when it is our time.

For in his own vision of birth and death in the Old Story, our Temple Sweeper had spoken with the one-eyed boy, told him he loved him, asked him to sit for a while each day beside him, since both dead and alive are welcome. In this way, the mute girl was no longer mute.

Your Temple Sweeper then met his former father, mother, and sister and let them weep and laugh in the bloom of cherry blossoms outside in the garden.

ENDURING SOUND: Is it I who imagines you on this eve of my own death, Old Story?

OLD STORY: Just as I imagined you a thousand years ago, Enduring Sound. Just as you imagined me when you stole your old Abbot's winter coat as an orphan after being left at the monastery by our circus players. This is how you heard the tale already written, though you once thought you were the scribe, listening to our Temple Sweeper's voice from morning to night.

ENDURING SOUND: We call ourselves by many names, Old Story. This is what my teacher and friend were trying to tell me. Somehow, I, too, recognize you now. But did it take my own death to bring this forth?

OLD STORY: You recognized it first as a boy,
Enduring Sound. And you have cultivated it ever
since.

DREAM DIALOGUE 5

OLD STORY: In another waking, you will meet the
mute girl and one-eyed boy at the movies in a city
still unknown to you, Enduring Sound. In a curious
way, you will remember them both in the unfolding
of plots and images on a screen, and this girl will
convince you that our scrolls were nothing other
than a love story. You will laugh in the theater and
become even more amazed when you become the
Poet in the café later still, reading her a new poem.

Then you will begin again.

DREAM DIALOGUE 6

ENDURING SOUND: Old Story, what about the
Temple Sweeper?

OLD STORY: After his own meetings with the boy
and girl, his family, and countless others, the man
you once called Temple Sweeper packed his few
belongings—a winter coat, three robes and a work
shirt, a basket of plums, a book of unwritten poems.
Your Temple Sweeper shared a few words with the
circus crew and theater players behind the white
screen, but little was said. The Poet seemed content
and wrote this down in his journal as you used to
write in the journal your former Abbot gave you. A
journal with bone binding and pages of cut leaves.
They shared a final glass of wine at the café and
bowed.

This, another breath.

That night before leaving his own body—the Temple Sweeper held a small stone and a flower in his near fingerless hands, smiling, as if staring out at a sea of unknown faces. Your Temple Sweeper later rolled a pinch of tobacco into a page of the scrolls and passed it to me that final evening in his monk's cell. He had discovered these scrolls had already been written.

Enduring Sound: So, Old Story, why did I have to write them down, if our Temple Sweeper already knew?

Old Story: You were ready that night, Enduring Sound. Containing all things, all beings. As you did in the final scroll you gave me and the Poet in the beginning. You thought it was just a letter, or a plea, or maybe some beginning of these scrolls. But it was, in fact, the last scroll.

And I have fulfilled your request to find them, the boy and the girl, Enduring Sound.

I heard your call when you asked. You asked from
your heart the first time you entered these dreams,
in your quest to find the girl and boy.

We have no language for this.

So the word I, Old Story, have chosen for the scrolls
is nameless.

Enduring Sound: And I, as the Poet, will call them
Scrolls of a Temple Sweeper.

Dream Dialogue 7

Old Story: Enduring Sound? Are you still
breathing?

Enduring Sound: I am. Though the breath is
fading.

Old Story: Tonight the Poet is already reading you
in his journal at his table in what you will learn is
called a café. He has already begun his search for
the one we named Enduring Sound.

Dream Dialogue 8

Old Story: Enduring Sound?

Enduring Sound: Yes, Old Story. I can still hear
you.

Old Story: Soon you will see yourself, perhaps on
a crowded train with other passengers, somewhere
traveling through the snowy mountains on what
formerly was an ancient road you have traveled
before. This thing of a train then speeds on through
the countryside.

Just as with your old teacher, at first you will stare
out at the other children playing on the roads in
the passing villages. It is a strange and yet somehow
recognizable landscape of white birch trees and
mountains and rivers leading to the cities of
another time and place.

As the train pulls into a station, you will walk
among the dispersing passengers, confused as
to who you actually are, or where you are—but
enchanted by the sound of the guitar and a woman's
singing you hear from these street musicians on
the corner by a bookstore you mistake, at first, as
a library. A library not unlike one of those in the
caves of the Learned Sage Women when you found
them on your own pilgrimage to understand and
translate these words. You'll make your way to what
you have now discovered is a café, you will sit and
ask for a cup of tea. Still later, you will walk the city
streets, and suddenly desire to enter the arcade with
the neon lights and a large photograph of a place it
seems you've been before, and you'll find yourself at
a movie in what you will learn is called a cinema.

On the screen you will vaguely recognize the boy
and girl as you watch this film and wonder why
their story seems so familiar, as if you had lived in it
once, or could have written it yourself. Afterwards,
you will return to the café with the new friend you
met in the lobby, and along with her and several
of her other friends, you'll join this woman at the
gathering for the Poet who has been awaiting you at
the café for many lifetimes. As he reads his poems
to you and them, you will feel a familiarity with the
words, even the sounds.

Yet this is you, Enduring Sound.

Enduring Sound: So, I will bow, and once again, ask the question—who am I?

Old Story: As did your Temple Sweeper bow and vow to remember us so we could meet again. And even here, back at the beginning, he had already caught glimpses of the original face. Thus have you, Enduring Sound. A child again becoming like a child.

DREAM DIALOGUE 9

Enduring Sound: Shapeless now, returning, breathing these final breaths.

A shore the self is mapped on. Harboring in stillness.

An abundant array of faces, dancing together on the streets of some metropolis—falling in love, over and over. And what is there to understand? I am among them.

And yet I am also here, sitting where I am, writing my death poem for the monks.

I come to walk or sit, to watch a boat float the expanse.

Gulls and pipers, crows and butterflies.

Albatrosses play on the rocks.

A love story.

Into these stars the flight of seagulls.

At home here.

A boy and girl longing once more to swim to the boat, to cross the hills and the clouds appearing in the reflection of moonlight off water.

I will help take them there.

And a final breath of renunciation itself,

my turning and return into the miraculous.

OLD STORY: You taste the blood and wound of blossom.

It comes out of words and the boundless sky you see before you.

And who you actually are.

ENDURING SOUND: I see it, Old Story.

OLD STORY: You experience your own pain without blame, without shame or gain.

Escorting others to the other shores.

This other shore that is this very shore.

Right here now with these final breaths.

ENDURING SOUND: They laugh among one another, though still, I cannot make out their faces in all these stars on the water—only contours echoing off the horizon, Old Story.

OLD STORY: As the dream itself is awakening, Enduring Sound.

Someone sounds the wooden drum.

The monks are waiting.

ENDURING SOUND: Waiting to carry my former body to the ceremony?

OLD STORY: Yes. We say the Way is not what the Way is, it is what we are, Enduring Sound.

ENDURING SOUND: This appearance of sounds, Old Story.

This hearing of shapes.

This movement in stillness.

When you reach the other shore, you see it is the same shore.

OLD STORY: Take your seat, Enduring Sound.

Your seat as the Abbot of this abode.

So it is written.

There, a final and gentle breath.

You are home.

ENDURING SOUND'S WHEREABOUTS

Later that evening, Old Story brought a handwritten copy of the ancient text for those of you who have come this far to discover the ending of these scrolls. We should say a possible ending. As you yourself, we see what you see. Hear what you hear in this very scroll you heard the Temple Sweeper speaking to you in the beginning when he called Enduring Sound into his monk's cell and requested he secretly take some paper from the monastery's storage bin and record the story. For those of you, like myself, who have traveled so far in our shared imaginings, here it is for you to decide.

It is the same passage Hempis read to his son, Enduring Sound, before the old Dream Master moved on into the ether of other worlds and found you, our Reader. This is where he found me as well.

First, he bowed before the altar, glanced out the windows of a timeless time in the pages, smiled. These were Hempis' words—

> *You see—the dream passes, and you wake in the dream that is not of dream. Just as when you truly enter the worlds of a word, you find you are free of words, free of your own story. Enduring Ones go into the forest and eventually they leave the story's womb. To rest in the mystery, staring up at the great blue sky and seeing this vast being. Elephants and dragons pass this way. Tigers vanish into the same forest. We do not beg for mercy. We enter with dignity.*

The sky, Old Story went on, speaking through the Dream Master, Hempis' mouth—

> *And perhaps in this moment you can hear the voice yourself? Propping up your elbow on the table at the*

Hempis then took Enduring Sound's hand and held his old face: a face of thousands of faces. And then, he seemed to take a final inhale while requesting you write a poem.

The Poet heard your own voice merging with ours and wrote this down—

*It is too much trouble to cry until blood
starts to gush from your mouth.
It is better to be still and wait
until the moments
of winter have passed....*

Our Poet scribbled these lines down for you at the winter café when Enduring Sound again found his way. But maybe you, too, will now add your own poem, Dear Reader?

The Poet put down the pen and paper but continued to speak through the voices of you who have heard the Old Story. You hear him, watch as he stands, notice for the first time he is missing one eye as he gestures to those gathered around—

*In a story of stories, a girl sees you throughout her
life, appearing in the snow, along the hillsides, in the
cities, by the sea, eventually on the trains and moving through the shadows of time, and through us. In*

this, a trembling in the body, the calling on breath
and finding love in a language of butterflies and
bees, cities and trees.

Are you still with us, Dear Reader? Old Story then asks you, beginning to close Enduring Sound's eyes, tempered and calm, ceasing yet beginning.

All of those we have ever loved and lost are always nearby. They sense this longing and remain in the peace of return. We sometimes seek this very peace, the peace of the earth, its stillness that is here, whether we experience it or not.

Now you meet me, another friend you find on this curious road.

TOWARD DUSK

After he finishes his tea, the Poet breathes his poem into the one once called Enduring Sound and suddenly, for a fleeting moment, recognizes all of us from the scrolls—now sitting at the café in the city in which he finds himself. He orders a glass of wine.

Do you recognize him beside you?

Walking Home

Old Story gets up in the evening, somewhat stumbling around the book of poems, feeling the way in the night by words. Enduring Sound, no longer blind. At some point, he turned toward me, grabbing my hand.

> *The immensity of life! he exclaimed, the immensity of the bluebirds on the lemon tree there—can you see them, Poet—the horn of the boats passing us on the great sea, the red poppies on the balcony of the staircase of the second floor above us overlooking the shore, a story among other stories told in our sleep, or the curl of your tobacco smoke lifting, the splendor of the slender and soft stroke to your cheek from the woman who brought me here.*

> *Remain still in it, for one moment more before walking home and going on your pilgrimage, Poet! This is only the first of our many meetings. For as I leave this body, I have also returned to meet you in this café of coming and going. Poet, do you see: I am you.*

Enduring Sound to the Assembly After Leaving the Body

A homeless child walks across the tracks into the vast fields of nothingness.

The child brought us into laughter.

Remain still, so I can see you a moment longer,
good monks.
You are alive!
These words are alive.
Let it be said: he always left room to turn around.
A sky of scrolls pulling me now toward the shore
and moon that I am,
these endless rivers and mountains.
Just as we, in our passing, the sea lingers in a syllable, a bell,
a drum, a call.
A diamond lightning bolt.

I am here beside you, and within you, always.
Is it this you have been seeking since first wandering in these scrolls?
Perhaps you have never lost it.
Study this.
We are always meeting in...
just this.

The Temple Sweeper and Enduring Sound

There is a hummingbird outside the café window. Various butterflies flutter in the grass by the bookstore.

Winter passing. Spring arising.

You and I together have drunk three glasses of the finest wine. Shall we meet at the café in the city with the Poet and all of our dear friends from the scrolls?

At the Temple Gates

When we pilgrims finally made it to the temple named after the one called Enduring Sound, we knocked on the huge wooden doors of the monastery. There were stone pavilions, a long road of bells, walls made of statues and engraved with words unknown to us, older than the ancient language we had studied so many years in order to find our way here. We had traveled first by plane, then by train, later by horse and mule, and finally on a small boat to the island shrouded in clouds. We walked the last three days up a mountain, not visible from the mainland. On the boat, we had been blindfolded by the ones our former guides called the Seekers. These Seekers had agreed to take us on their boat when we showed them the pages of our translations from the ancient scrolls. After arriving, we sat outside the gates of the temple for seven days and seven nights. When we knocked, we somehow sensed it was now time. No one had traversed in or out of the gates, yet we sensed we were seen, and often I felt a wave of trepidation, or excitement, at how far we had come.

A monk cracked the latch of the monastery gate, just a little at first, peeked out, maybe surprised to see our worn and tired, yet curious faces. There were six of us in total. The so-called Seekers had left us at the gates without saying a word. We stood in the rain, waiting as the monk studied us. Finally, he said, slowly, as if it were difficult for him to speak—

Do you have an appointment?

Our Abbot is resting.

We cannot disturb him.

Yes, the poet in our group immediately replied—but we made our appointment several lifetimes ago.

The monk paused, then stepped out into the rain with us, more closely scrutinizing our faces, which seemed to appear both strange, but somewhat familiar to him.

In that case, you better come in, he said.

The monk proceeded to lead us through the lush grounds of flowering papaya, banana, coconut, even an udumbara blossom, and deeper on through the mazed and winding corridors going further up into the mountain so engulfed in clouds that on occasion we had to place our hands on the walls to follow along. At some point, we passed through a tunnel of small doorways through which we had to crawl on all fours. Toward the end of the tunnel, we suddenly realized the monk was nowhere to be seen, but that a young girl and boy had joined us as we stood up in what appeared to be a courtyard. The girl couldn't have been much older than nine or ten, the boy himself not much older. When we saw them take one another's hands passing through the archway, leading into the domed entryway, some of us glanced at one another, and began to wonder. Yet as neither of them spoke, it seemed appropriate for us to remain silent. Sometime during our walking, the poet did utter something or another about the surroundings. The girl quickly turned and put her finger to her lips to hush him.

We walked in this way for hours. Sometime around dawn, we found ourselves entering into a great pavilion, a pavilion filled with skylights through which streamed a brilliant array of various contours of light, and at the center, an opening through which a magnificent telescope jetted out of the floor, anchored by stone, above which we saw what seemed to be a blood moon.

After seating us in the Meditation Hall, the boy and girl approached us, and it was then in the radiance of this room that we noticed the boy had only one eye. He promised us tea and food to welcome us after our long journey. The girl laughed, quickly covering his mouth as if embarrassed by the boy's speaking, or the speaking of so many words. She was still smiling as we saw them shuffle off, leaving us there alone.

For the next few days and nights we sat, slept, and ate in this place. We saw no one other than the boy and girl, who quietly attended to us, serving tea and meals at just those moments when we ourselves began to feel hungry, though there was no accounting for time really. After a while, we settled into working on our translations from the ancient texts. The Poet had told us long ago that these scrolls had been bequeathed to him—left in an official will by someone he had never met, nor known.

It was a mystery we had lived with for many years, and we had come to accept it, though it may have been one of the reasons we eventually decided to go on this pilgrimage together. In our long friendships we had deciphered all we could from the hand-drawn maps, the ensōs, poems, stories, and letters of the manuscripts. Those of us who had simply met, seemingly quite randomly, at a café during a poetry reading when we were quite young had grown close over the years.

In the monastery we were free to wander through the rooms, endless hallways, surrounding grounds, and libraries. There was a series of smaller temples filled with altars and shrines. Further up the mountain there was what appeared to be a graveyard with massive stone engravings. The boy and girl furtively followed us around. Still, other than these two children, there was no one to whom we could ask our questions. We looked for, but never saw, the monk who had greeted us at the gate.

The conversations that ensued between us in those days of waiting for the Abbot went so deeply into our bodies that the words themselves seemed to us as those of the dream dialogues we had read from Enduring Sound's *Scrolls of a Temple Sweeper*. As if we old friends were traveling beyond and inside the flow of another time or history and actually hearing the sound of our own minds reaching back through the pages we had studied and translated for so many years now. We were, each of us, I think I can report this without hesitation, yes—each of us were truly thrown back into a deep sense of not knowing. Back into what some historians had labeled the Era of The Dream Masters. Our hearts, bodies, even our innermost thoughts resting and at ease for the first time any of us could recall as we spoke of our feelings. Such stillness and intimacy as we waited for the Abbot, often wondering if we ourselves had fallen into some kind of vision. As if our own pasts, present, and futures were converging as we met day after day, our conversations carrying on, often with laughter, other times with tears or silence throughout those quiet nights. Who were we? Who was the one who held the name of Enduring Sound? Temple Sweeper? Hempis? Ghostwoman? Was it all made up, a fiction we had dedicated so much of our lives to: an imaginary journey-text we were experiencing while actually being at home, asleep in our own beds? Had we slipped into the same dream somehow and any moment we would wake up and say, what a dream! And who were this boy and girl attending to us now? Were these children, or we ourselves, the same as the ones we had studied for much of our adult lives? The Lost Children that Enduring Sound had written about and brought home to this monastery isle of refuge?

When the Abbot at last arrived, he rather humbly bowed as he entered to greet us. He was a small monk with warm, piercing eyes, and with a strong countenance, a sturdy frame, like a peasant whose life is working the fields. For a moment, I thought he was the father of the monk who opened the gate and greeted us, though I have never been certain in the years that have since passed.

> You say you made your appointment several lifetimes ago? he asked. Who were we then? Do you know?

> He grinned, and awaited our response.

> The poet spoke: You were the one called the Temple Sweeper. Perhaps we are the ones we've translated from your scrolls, though we claim to know nothing ourselves. We are pilgrims, and we have

come to find you once more, to find out, in fact, who we ourselves actually are.

Ah, he sighed, pausing and looking deeply into our faces, one by one.

Each of you, each of you are my old friends! Of course!

And you, you are Enduring Sound then, he said, bowing three times to the poet, and gesturing for him to sit in the Abbot's seat.

You have finally come home.

It was only when we glanced out the windows that we saw all these children playing in the courtyard.

P.S. A Few Words—

By Way of an Unwritten Dialogue
Between the Poet & Prophet on an Empty Boat

Take care the gardens,
take care the trees & leaves,
take care the boat returning to sea...

I

I think of all the violence of their wars, the Poet begins. How many lifetimes before the fires end— before we see this violence begins within?

The mystery is that we seem to exist on our own, says the Prophet. Though the story itself is ineffable. If it were only a story of violence, we would have no home, the Prophet sighs, her voice carrying the wind on this open sea.

True, the children and small birds on the horizon move us most—the Poet agrees, circling his aging hands in the shape of a sphere.

And the circles rise like loaves of bread in the boy and the girl's hands, Old Story says, appearing like the stones the Temple Sweeper once carried, like the words never spoken, yet always here. And yet, it has always been down the same road we meet as such. I, Old Story, have been wandering with you for many lifetimes, Poet.

The Poet folds the sheaths of paper in the bone-engraved notebook and leaves it for you, Dear Reader. Just as the Abbot left it for Enduring Sound, and he left it for me.

These voices not yet written, but waiting for you to tell. Perhaps you will now take them and add your own?

The Prophet waves her scarf, her daring eyes mischievous, almost human tonight as we who remain among you listen in for your stories, Dear Reader.

II

The Poet touches the sentence.

Takes it into his mouth.

Tastes the words floating between our worlds.

In the end, you know, everything is like this.

The Prophet sips the wine from her empty cup, nodding.

Things have a kind of reality in their being named, as do we, as do these dreams, the Prophet says.

But not to understand that the dreaming is only a kind of naming is to mistake the vastness of who we are.

> A cypress tree
> Standing on its own
> Growing from the hull of an empty boat
> A whistling child
> Searches its own waves
> Going on

III

The Poet looks over his shoulder, imagining this is a boat he himself is sailing.

When you look closely,
all we can really see are connections? he asks.

The Prophet hums through the bell-weathered
sails.

These small birds rising against the horizon, you
can see them, Poet? See within and around them,
there are no things without connection. They're
like you and me, Poet.

Everything both the same, and different.

A voice in a nameless choir.

The Poet nods, eats another sentence.

IV

Maybe it wasn't the Temple Sweeper,

but we ourselves

wandering in and out of these stories?

V

And yet all these years only seeing each other
in glimpses, Prophet.

Like starlight on the hull of our boat tonight.

The Prophet picks up a fallen bird

from a gust of wind

on the hull of the boat,

lifts her, lightly, back into the sky.

Whose mouth has spoken? the Poet asks, touching
the stern, watching the bird of paradise fly off once
more.

And if I answer, would you still not know who I
am? Old Story asks you.

VI

We exist as an image in the world, the Prophet
goes on, laughing with the fish swimming around
the boat.

The Poet steps forward, stumbles toward the sails.

No one knows our true identity here, he says,
looking starboard.

Better to see the face than to know the name.
What identity do you need? Old Story asks.

There is nothing lacking.
We are never alone
We are friends meeting on continuous seas.

VII

The Poet leans against the mast now, calls out:
you, bird of paradise—you once fluttered into my
face one afternoon as I sat drinking tea in the café.
I saw two shadows by the shade of an apple tree,
the boy and girl strolling along the path. The sun,

a face of awe. Did I imagine them?

What day dawns bliss in a cypress tree growing in
a garden, the Prophet calls back.

VIII

Old age sweetens a hermit's life, she then says.

Just as you pick up

and eat each word,

and find it breathing inside you, Poet.

Humility to accept anything that comes
makes sense.

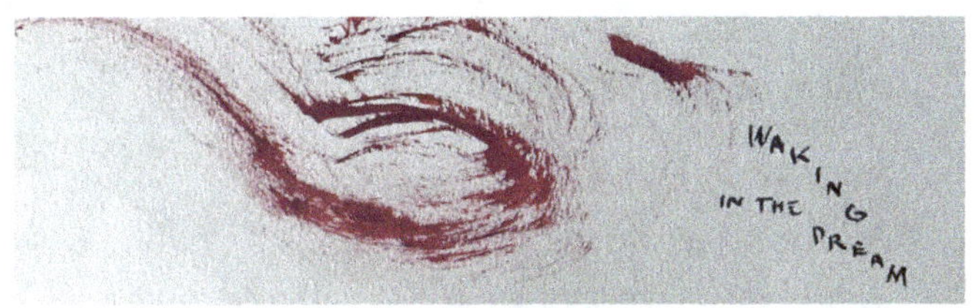

IX

Pps

(I love you.)

White trees line the horizon.
Red cardinals cluster in the rocks of the shore.
You once pulled a leaf from a cypress tree.

Now it is raining in the sea,
and your boat is floating on this rain.
Shadows falling across the sands.
The cliffs steady against the waves,
steady against the hills and forests.

X

What if I falter on this night after traveling so long?
What if I fail to meet you on the shore? the Poet asks.

To leave the dream, Poet,
a sky vanishes into itself
as these children return home.

But I fear we may, too, vanish in this sea, Prophet.

And yet this sea is us, Poet.
This is more true than we can know.

XI

White gulls at our feet,
our boat floating on the sea,
translucent fish swimming around the hull.

Neither you nor I exist in language.
All the same, we sail into the rain.
Who knows who, or what, we will find?
Once you were riding a bicycle down a road.
And we ourselves do not know
if we are coming or going
in this continuous moment
of coming and going.

XII

Our home is nowhere and everywhere.
Yet without one another we wander alone,
Old Story whispers through the voice
of the girl.

When a poet hears the music, she follows the sound.
She is not startled
hearing her own unique voice.

The boy leavens the bread.
The girl fills the bucket.
The boat sails, aimlessly.

XIII

Old Story picks up your notebook, Dear Reader,
begins to read:

I saw you in a dream,
you were standing on a white cliff.
A group of children walked past
playing with you yourself as a wondrous child.

XIV

As a child you once walked across the mountains
of an unknown country. Tonight we have paused
to sit in a wooden boat with an Old Story.

XV

Looking out at the sea inside us,
The boy says: I, too, am this very one,

this very eye.

XVI

We are washing our bowls tonight
on an empty boat drifting freely on an open sea.

Where should we go, Poet?

This very sea, Prophet—

why this very sea is a fine place for a hermitage.

ACKNOWLEDGMENTS

I would like to express my gratitude to the editors at Wet Cement Press: Barbara Roether and Michelle Murphy for their generous support and time in bringing forth this book, and a special thanks and deep bow to editor Thoreau Lovell for his profound dedication, editorial suggestions, and pure artistry in the design and crafting of the pages into such a beautiful object. His care in layout, font choice, and configuration of the ensōs is integral to this work. I am honored to be a part of a small, independent press dedicated to hybrid and experimental work.

I would also like to give a big shout-out to Edward Foster at Talisman House for publishing the tetralogy to which the *Scrolls* are intimately connected: *here, a book of unknowing, you are everything you are not*, and *vanishing acts* (2006-2017). Without his undaunting support of publications of innovative and avant-garde work over the decades since he founded Talisman, this world would be greatly impoverished.

My sincere gratitude to Patricia Pruitt for the two poems: "Tangible and Intangible" in Scroll XV on page 284 and "The way ahead charted" in Scroll XIX on page 339. A scattering of Patricia's other lines also appear in the voices that arise here.

And to Flo & Paulie for all their encouragement, inspiration, and passion for the arts in these worlds of creative transformation over the years—and, indeed, to all of the Libin family.

Finally, I would be remiss not to acknowledge all of you friends, comrades, and writers throughout space and time whose words, literal and imagined, have entered into the voices of *Scrolls of a Temple Sweeper*. And with that said, any and all of the mistakes are of this humbled scribe's own making.

—Ninso

About the Author

Poet and Zen monk, (Ninso) John High, is the recipient of four Fulbright fellowships, two National Endowment for the Arts fellowships (fiction and translation), and a National Endowment for the Humanities fellowship for a co-translation project (with Matvei Yankelevich) of Osip Mandelstam's *Voronezh Notebooks*. Their recent translations have appeared in *The New Yorker, Harper's, Circumference*, and other magazines. He is the author of over a dozen books of poetry, fiction, and translation, including his novel *The Desire Notebooks* (named one of the top twenty-five books of its year by *The Village Voice Literary Supplement*), and most recently, *Without Dragons Even the Emperor Would Be Lonely* (Wet Cement Press, 2020), as well as a tetralogy: *here, a book of unknowing, you are everything you are not, and vanishing acts* (Talisman House, 2006-2017). His work has appeared in numerous literary journals and has been translated into French and Russian. A co-founder (with Lewis Warsh) and former director of the Long Island University, Brooklyn, MFA Program, where he is now Professor Emeritus, he has also taught at universities in Istanbul, Moscow, Hangzhou, and San Francisco. Before the COVID-19 pandemic, he facilitated workshops in creative transformation with children, teachers, social workers, incarcerated youth, and writers in Cambodia, China, Portugal, and the U.S., and plans to continue this work as soon as possible.